Big praise for
BIG GUNS OUT OF UNIFORM

Acclaim for *New York Times* bestselling author Sherrilyn Kenyon's steamy stories about the sexy agents of *BAD*. . . .

Acclaim for Nicole Camden's sexy debut

"...take a well-deserved bow to the standing ovation, Ms. Camden—you've earned it."

—Mrs. Giggles, mrsgiggles.com

"'The Nekkid Truth' is Ms. Camden's first book and I have to tell you it is marvelous. The sex, heck the entire story, has a wonderfully gritty, almost raw and uncut, feel to it. I'm definitely placing Nicole Camden on my list of new authors to keep an eye on and look forward to plenty of books from her."

—Just Erotic Romance Reviews

"To say that 'The Nekkid Truth' is the best erotic romantic novella I've read this year seems like faint praise. The fact is, it's far and away the best contemporary romance I've read this year. I wished it were longer, not because its short length was a shortcoming, but because I wanted more of the same. Who is this woman, and when is her next book coming out?"

—All About Romance

Big Guns
OUT OF
UNIFORM

SHERRILYN KENYON
LIZ CARLYLE   NICOLE CAMDEN

POCKET **STAR** BOOKS

New York   London   Toronto   Sydney

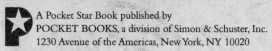 A Pocket Star Book published by
POCKET BOOKS, a division of Simon & Schuster, Inc.
1230 Avenue of the Americas, New York, NY 10020

This book is a work of fiction. Names, characters, places and incidents are products of the authors' imaginations or are used fictitiously. Any resemblance to actual events or locales or persons, living or dead, is entirely coincidental.

ISBN-13: 978-1-4165-0967-7
ISBN-10:   1-4165-0967-4

This Pocket Star Books paperback edition November 2005

10 9 8 7 6 5 4 3 2 1

POCKET STAR BOOKS and colophon are registered trademarks of Simon & Schuster, Inc.

Cover design by Min Choi
Cover photograph by Franco Accornero

Manufactured in the United States of America

For information regarding special discounts for bulk purchases, please contact Simon & Schuster Special Sales at 1-800-456-6798 or business@simonandschuster.com.

Contents

BAD *to the* BONE

Sherrilyn Kenyon

For my mother,
who has given me my overactive imagination,
my husband,
who doesn't mind it,
and my friends and family,
who support me.
God bless all of you!

PROLOGUE

*M*arianne Webernec was completely average at age thirty, but what she desperately wanted to be was extraordinary.

Exceptional. Spectacular.

For once in her life she wanted to be the heroine in one of the Rachel Fire novels that she gobbled up as soon as they were published. To be tall, thin, and devastatingly beautiful. The kind of woman that men everywhere lusted for. The kind of woman who walked into a room and men fought each other just for her smile.

But what she was, even after her makeover, was a mere five-feet-four-inch size-ten woman with medium brown hair that was pinned back from her round face to fall just below her shoulders. She had eyes that were flat brown, not amber, not flecked with anything unusual or worth noticing. Her breasts were too small, her hips were too wide, and her feet were pinched by the narrow tips of her high-heeled shoes.

She was . . .

Average.

Painfully, woefully average.

"I think you're stunning."

Only if she had a stun gun in her hand.

Marianne looked over her shoulder to see Aislinn Zimmerman staring at her. Aislinn was what she wanted to be. Rich, model thin, with long, curly red hair, perfectly manicured nails, and big bright green eyes that seemed to glow. Aislinn was every bit as beautiful as her namesake from Aislinn's mother's favorite romance novel, *The Wolf and the Dove.*

Marianne had spent her entire life hating women who looked like Aislinn. They were everywhere. On television, in magazines, and on the pages of the books that Marianne loved to read. Books where the gorgeous, drop-dead heroine nailed the gorgeous, drop-dead hero.

They were ever an unnecessary reminder that at the end of the day, Marianne Webernec would never be one of them.

She would always be average. White noise in the background of a world that went on oblivious to her presence no matter how much she longed for it to be otherwise.

"Thanks," Marianne said to her lamely, knowing the truth in her heart. But that was okay.

Because in the next few minutes she was going to walk through the door behind Aislinn and become the one thing she'd always wanted to be . . .

A covert CIA agent pursued by the evil archvillain who would turn out to be a good guy trying to uncover the man who had killed his brother.

Okay, the plot was a bit clichéd, even a little trite. But Marianne loved Rachel Fire's book *Danger in the Night*. She had read it so many times that her copy at home was in pieces barely held together by tape.

For the last four years that book and its hero, Brad Ramsey, had lived in her heart and in her mind. He was the man she dreamed of seducing every night when she closed her eyes.

She had licked every inch of his divinely masculine body from head to foot, and had made him beg her for mercy. They had made love everywhere from Caribbean beaches to the snowdrifts of Moscow.

In her mind she had ridden him hard and furiously, and made him hers.

Oh, to really be the book's heroine, Ren Winterbourne. The sultry, sophisticated agent, woman of the world, who knew every way possible to make a man beg for her touch. Ren never doubted herself. She always knew exactly what she wanted and how to get it.

Marianne was still searching for her place in the world. And when it came to men, she would never understand them. They were completely alien beasties.

She sighed wistfully. Her entire life was a study in what could have been. If only she'd been smarter, taller, prettier . . .

But she wasn't.

Her mother had once told her that life was about acceptance. That she needed to be content with what was dealt her and be grateful it wasn't worse.

Starting this instant, Marianne was going to take her mother's advice.

Mostly.

She was going to walk out that door and . . .

Stumble, knowing her.

"Do I have to wear the heels?" she asked Aislinn, holding her foot out toward the beautiful redhead as she flexed her ankle.

Some things were best done with level feet. Especially when the last thing Marianne wanted was to be embarrassed. "I'm really not a high-heel kind of person. I'm more the I'll-stumble-and-twist-my-ankle kind of woman."

Aislinn laughed. "Sure. What would you like?"

"Got anything flat and black?"

Aislinn flipped open her stylish silver cell phone and pressed a button. "Hi, Gwen, Ms. Webernec would like a selection of flat black shoes to go with her rust-colored miniskirt dress. She's a size eight medium. . . . Thanks." Aislinn closed the phone. "Give her ten minutes and she'll bring us a new boxload of them."

It was good to be queen.

At least for the day, or in this case, a whole month. Marianne smiled at the thought.

One full month of being catered to and pampered. Having her every want met without complaint.

Oh, yeah, forget Julia Roberts in *Pretty Woman*. This reality was *so* much better.

After all, Marianne Webernec, average Jane high school teacher, was about to head off to Sex Camp.

CHAPTER ONE

*K*yle Foster lay behind a short clump of bushes, scoping out the large compound that lay sheltered in the sand—his latest target.

It was fifteen hundred hours and all the explosives were rigged. Their timers set. The beach was silent, with a mild northwesterly wind that would carry the shrapnel and debris a minimal distance, toward the empty lagoon.

He was watching the countdown on his watch, waiting for something that would alleviate his extreme boredom.

He'd thought it would be the well-placed, perfectly executed explosion.

It wasn't.

At fifteen seconds and counting, disaster struck as an unknown, unexpected civilian popped out of the small wooded area near the compound.

Kyle cursed. There was no way to stop the explosives, and he didn't dare shout at her.

Damn civilians never took orders well. Instead of doing as they were told, they invariably assumed the position of a deer in the headlights and asked, "What?" Which would be followed by the ever aggravating, "Why?"

By then it would be too late.

If he said "bomb," she'd scream and probably run straight for the explosion. Murphy's Law.

He was out of time.

Combat trained and ever ready to fight, Kyle launched himself from his covert position to intercept her before she drew any closer.

He mentally continued the countdown in his head as he ran full speed toward her. . . .

Marianne saw nothing but a blur from the corner of her eye. One second she was heading toward the small sand castle that looked as if someone had constructed it with careful, minute detail. The next some large something had scooped her up into its arms and run off with her.

Breathless from shock and the feel of two extremely strong arms carrying her while the man ran across the beach, she didn't even have time to protest as the two of them flew in the opposite direction from the castle.

Just as they reached the pathway she'd been following, she heard a sharp *click*.

The man holding her threw the two of them to the ground and rolled them under some bushes as a massive explosion rent the air. The earth beneath them shook.

Her breath was knocked out of her from their fall, and panic welled inside her.

A sleek wall of muscle covered her body again as something began to rain down on the sand around them. She was overwhelmed by the combined scent of Brut, warm masculine skin, and Finesse shampoo.

Marianne instinctively covered her face until the "rain" stopped.

"What in the world just happened?" she asked, her heart pounding as she dared peek from between her fingers.

The man lying on top of her lifted himself up to look down at her.

Marianne gaped.

In all her life she'd never seen anything like him. His eyes were bright and blue. Electrifying and filled with mirthful mischief. They reminded her of the boys in her classes whenever they were planning some youthful prank.

Only there was nothing boyish about the man on top of her. He was obviously in his mid-thirties, his face ruggedly handsome, with sharp cheekbones and at least a full day's worth of stubble on his cheeks and chin.

He was even more handsome than the actor they had playing Brad Ramsey.

And the feel of his long, hard body covering hers . . .

It was heaven. Pure heaven.

He swept a heated gaze over her face and body before giving her a devilish grin that should belong to the worst sort of Regency rake. Not to mention the fact that his waist was lying between her legs, and she felt a sudden swell pressing against her intimately. One that let her know this was no small man. Nor was he completely uninterested in her.

It was all she could do not to moan in pleasure.

"Hi." The deepness of his voice was as startling as their meeting.

"Hi," she answered back rather lamely.

Kyle tried to remember what the woman had asked him a second ago, but all he could really think of was the peekaboo dimple she had in her left cheek. It flashed at him as she frowned.

Not to mention the fact that she felt damn good underneath him.

Her white tank top had fallen off one shoulder, leaving it bare where it beckoned him to touch and kiss the smooth skin it revealed.

Her dark brown eyes were warm and friendly, with a healthy dose of suspicion in them. She had sleek brown hair that fell around her head, onto the sand. It was the kind of hair a man dreamed of running his hands through. The kind of hair a man liked to feel whipping his chest while the woman who had it sat on top of him, grinding her body against his until they both came.

It took every ounce of control he possessed not to rub his swollen, aching groin against her and dream of sinking himself deep inside her hot, wet body.

Oh, yeah, he so wanted a piece of this woman. One small taste of her lush, soft, feminine curves.

"You . . . uh . . . you want to get off me now?" she asked, her voice sounding a bit peeved.

"Not really," he answered honestly. "I kind of like it here." More than he dared admit even to himself.

And he found himself suddenly fixated by the bared skin of her shoulder, which didn't seem to betray a bra strap.

Was she naked under there?

His cock tightened even more at the thought of her naked, unrestrained breasts being only a tiny push of fabric away. Of taking one of them into his mouth and suckling its tip while she buried her long, graceful fingers into his hair.

Marianne arched a brow at the man's unexpected response and tilted her head as she watched him. She wasn't sure if this was part of her whole fantasy package or not. What with the explosion and all, it was possible he was one of the actors who had been playing out her novel.

But Rachel Fire hadn't written a scene about a sand castle being blown up.

Then again, there was a scene in a few more days where they blew up a cabin, so maybe the man had been practicing.

At any rate, he was a cutie-pie. Gorgeous, in fact. His darkly tanned body held the muscular definition of an athlete. One that begged a woman to run her hands over it.

"You always sweep a woman off her feet like this and throw her on the ground?"

He laughed at that, a warm, rich sound that made her actually tingle. "No, I have to say this is a first. But given how it seems to be turning out, I might make it a habit." He winked at her, then pulled back from her slowly and held his hand out to her as if to shake hers.

"Kyle Foster," he said.

Hmm, not one of the names in the book. Maybe he was one of the extras they had hired to play commando with.

"Marianne Webernec," she said automatically as she shook his large, callused hand and did her best not to think about what it would feel like to have it cup her breast or have those long, masculine fingers sunk deep inside her body.

He had beautiful hands. Powerful hands. Strong and manly, they appealed to her in the best sort of way.

"Oh, wait," she said, trying to distract herself from those thoughts. "I'm supposed to be Ren Winterbourne. Sorry, I keep forgetting."

He scowled at her words. "What are you? A federal agent or something?"

"Something, definitely something." She started to push herself to her feet.

Kyle helped her up with an effortlessness that overcharged her hormones and made her yearn to lean into the strength of his body until she swooned from delight.

What was it about this man that made her want to do him right here on the beach? She'd never been sexually flagrant before, but something about Kyle Foster made her long desperately to rip that tight white T-shirt off and have her way with him whether he wanted it or not.

"You must be from the other side of the island," he said in that innately masculine voice.

He released her all too soon, and she ached from the

loss of his body heat being so close. It had warmed her more than the overhead sun.

"Uh-oh. Did I really come all that way? They told me I wasn't supposed to go too far away. Did I end up on the private side of things?"

"Yeah, but it's okay. I'm the only one staying here right now." He glanced around the vacant beach. "It's been boring as hell up until now."

"Tell me about it. For a fantasy vacation, it's been rather meek compared to what I was expecting."

Interest sparked deep in those electric blue eyes. "What were you expecting?"

Marianne squelched a smile. She'd been expecting something along the lines of studly fine Kyle Foster to come into her life and ravish her day and night until she couldn't move, never mind walk.

Marianne bit her bottom lip at the thought and lowered her gaze to the snowy sand to keep him from seeing just how embarrassed she was.

"I don't know," she said with a small shrug. "Some handsome man to throw me down on the ground and save me from an unexpected explosion?"

Kyle laughed again. He didn't know why. Normally, he was about as serious as they came. His sometimes partner, Retter, had often commented on the fact that Kyle's face would freeze if he ever cracked more than a half grin.

But something about this woman made him feel . . . Well . . .

Kind of giddy. There was no other word for it. And he really hated that girly-sounding word. *Giddy* and

Kyle Foster went together about like a cobra and a mongoose.

He must have been even more bored than he suspected. She wasn't ravishing or even beautiful. She reminded him of the woman next door.

A woman who shouldn't draw his notice at all, and yet he found himself staring at her and the way her tiny, light freckles kissed the skin across the bridge of her nose.

Even more startling was the desire he had to taste every one of those freckles with his tongue. To kiss and tease each one and see how many more she might have in other, more provocative areas of her body.

Like those creamy thighs that were virtually hidden by her drab tan walking shorts. Thighs that would look much better naked and wrapped around his neck ...

Marianne felt suddenly awkward as she realized the T-shirt Kyle wore displayed more of his muscled chest than it concealed. Of course, built the way he was, it would take several layers of sweaters and a heavy overcoat to disguise that body.

He reminded her of a linebacker. One with a very tight end.

He was gorgeous all over. From the top of his sun-kissed dark brown hair to the toes of his scuffed black leather biker boots.

She frowned as she noticed that.

"Who wears boots on the beach?" she asked unexpectedly.

He glanced down at his feet. "I didn't even think about it. Guess it's not normal, huh?"

She smiled up at him. "Says to me you don't spend a lot of time on the beach."

"Not really. I'm here under extreme protest. What about you?"

"I'm this month's winner."

He frowned as if he had no idea what she was talking about.

"You know," she said, "the Hideaway Heroine Sweepstakes winner? I'm the one they chose this time."

"Ah," he said, nodding. "So how's it going?"

Twirling a small section of her hair, she shrugged. "It's going, I guess. South more than north, but I suppose nothing's perfect."

"Now, why would you say that?" He indicated the vibrant blue sky with his thumb. "Just look at that sky. It's perfect. Great day. You got the beach to run around on, the surf sliding up. Hell, you can even hear birds chirping."

"Which is why you were blowing up a sand castle?"

He gave her a guilty smile that made her knees weak. "Well, okay, nothing's perfect."

Marianne licked her lips as she watched him hitch his thumbs into the front pockets of his jeans. He had such a manly stance. One of power, like some sinuous beast just prowling the beach waiting for a morsel to gobble.

How she wished she were that morsel.

"So," she said, stretching the word out, "do you do that a lot? Blow up sand castles?"

"Only if they deserve it." He glanced back to the hole in the beach where his sand castle had been. "That one, unfortunately, had gone bad. Real bad."

She covered her face as she laughed again. "I guess

I better stay on the straight and narrow then, huh?"

"Marianne?"

She cringed as she heard the voice of "Brad" coming through the trees from the opposite direction of her uncovered pathway. The actor was extremely handsome, but he was pale and rather feminine compared to the man in front of her.

"I guess I need to be going," she said reluctantly.

She started away from Kyle, but he caught her hand in his. The feel of that steely grip on her skin made her entire body burn.

Before she realized what he was doing, he'd pulled her against the hard, lean strength of his body and lowered his mouth onto hers.

Marianne sighed at the taste of his lips as his tongue explored her mouth, flicking masterfully in and out. It made her breathless and weak. She held on to those broad, muscled shoulders as she felt the heat pounding between her legs. Heat that made her wet and desperate for this man.

His muscles flexed beneath her hand, whetting her appetite all the more. How she wished she were touching his tanned skin, sinking her teeth into all that lush, fabulous maleness.

Kyle growled at how good she tasted. But then he'd known instinctively that she would.

His cock hardened to the point of pain as he imagined what it would feel like to lay her down on the beach and spend the next few hours watching her come for him over and over again while he slid himself in and out of her sleek wet heat.

There were few things in life he liked more than the sight of a woman caught in the middle of an orgasm. The sound of her delighted cries as he nibbled and teased the last tremor from her body.

And this was a woman he could savor from now until the end of time. . . .

"Marianne!"

He didn't want to let her go, but then, he'd never been the kind of guy to perform before an audience, nor did she strike him as the kind of woman who would appreciate him trying to broaden their horizons in that respect.

Reluctantly he released her.

Damn. Kyle didn't say anything as he watched the klutz—who tripped over the sand castle's crater as he crossed the sand—take off with his woman.

He glanced at the blackened hole on the beach.

Target number one had been destroyed.

Target number two . . .

She would have to be conquered.

For the first time in a month he felt the familiar adrenaline rush surging.

At last he had a mission.

Marianne Webernec and her sweet little mouth that had tasted like honey.

One taste and he'd been hooked. And he wasn't the kind of man to leave well enough alone once his curiosity was aroused.

Curiosity, hell, his whole body was aroused, and he wouldn't be sated until he'd tasted a whole lot more than her lips.

No way. Before he was through with her, he would know every minute part of her body and every way to make her scream out in pleasure.

Kyle smiled at the lecherous thought.

This was one challenge he was going to savor well.

CHAPTER TWO

"Hey, Sam," Kyle said to the surly man behind the concierge desk as he entered the lobby of the small luxury hotel where he'd been staying literally against his will.

Since Kyle had been shot in the line of duty (about six times, they assumed—five bullets had been dug out, and there was some debate on what had caused the sixth wound), his boss had decided Kyle needed a vacation at the hotel his agency owned on a remote, private island out in the middle of the Atlantic.

Kyle thought the six-week "vacation" was completely unnecessary, but Joe had insisted, and anyone who had ever tried to argue with Joe Q. Public soon found out they would have a better time moving a mountain than budging Joe even an inch.

So here he was, a highly trained special ops agent, bored, healed, and raring to go, only to find Joe laughing at him every time he called and begged for a plane ride off this godforsaken island.

At least until twenty minutes ago, when fate had finally shone on him again.

Suddenly the thought of the next week looked promising.

Kyle stopped at the desk where Sam sat holding a longneck beer propped on his knee while watching a Lakers game on ESPN. In his mid-fifties, Sam looked like the picture-perfect image of a stout Scotsman. He had a ruddy complexion and a wide, serious face that was topped by a thick unruly mane of stark white hair. He wore black-rimmed glasses that continually slid down his broad nose and that he constantly pushed back up.

But the most interesting thing about him was his companion, Roscoe. An old basset hound, Roscoe had about as much attitude as any dog Kyle had ever met. And in a strange way, Kyle liked that old dog as much as he liked Sam.

Kyle paused at the counter and respectfully waited for a commercial before he interrupted the hotel's manager. "Tell me something, Sam. What's on the other side of this island, and why am I not supposed to go over there?"

Sam shrugged as he looked up from the small television. He took a quick swig of beer before he answered. "That's them weirdos from that publisher, Rose Books. You'd have to ask Joe for more details. He's the one who rents this part of the island from them so we can do some covert training, or in your case emergency R and R. I think he knows the owner of the publishing house or something."

"Do you know what goes on over there?"

"Yeah, and it's spooky as all get-out."

"Spooky how?"

"It's Sex Camp."

Kyle choked at the unexpected answer. "What?"

"Sex Camp," Sam repeated simply, as if there were nothing unusual about the title. "They have these women what read those romance books, and every few months or so one of them wins a trip out here to live out their fantasy novel, and they put on this whole grand show with the winner."

Sam pushed his glasses up. "Makes you want to know what's in them romance novels women read. I've been reading Tom Clancy for years, and all I get is submarines and war stories." He snorted. "I ain't never had the itch to run into the woods with a bunch of sailors and try to throw them on the ground. You know what I mean?"

Not really. Sam had a bad habit of not always making sense. "Beg pardon?" Kyle asked.

"Listen," Sam continued as he idly stroked Roscoe's head. "A word to the wise, son, you got to be real careful walking around after dark whenever one of them fantasies is going on. They don't call it Sex Camp for nothing. I've seen them do things on the beach that'll make you go blind. Hell, some of it I didn't even know was humanly possible."

Kyle couldn't keep his mouth from hanging open as he thought about Marianne being the latest winner. There was no way his sweet little visitor would do something like that.

Was there?

And if there was, then she'd better damn well be doing it with *him*.

"Are you yanking my chain?" he asked Sam.

"Nah, why would I?" Sam gave him an intense stare over the top rims of his glasses. "You think they're normal women when they come off the plane, but they're really raving nymphomaniacs cleverly disguised."

"Bullshit."

"Nah, boy, it's true. They come off the plane looking all nice and normal, and within twenty-four hours they turn into Debbie Does Dallas or Richard or whoever she can find. It's horrifying what happens to these women." He pointed to his dog. "See Roscoe here? He's only two years old. He went into the woods one night and now look at him. Their antics done aged him twenty years overnight. And don't get me started on them men they got. I don't know where they find them. But something about them ain't right, neither. So I stay on my side of the island as far away from all of them loons as I can get."

"I don't believe you."

Sam shrugged and turned back toward the television as the game resumed. "You don't got to believe it. Truth is truth. You should be here whenever they're doing one of those historical reenactments. They make us run around in costume in case we accidentally bump into one of their winners. It's a big pain. We have to say things like 'my lady' and shit. I feel like a blooming idiot. Can you just imagine my fat ass in a tutu or tights or whatever those godawful things are called?" He blew out a disgusted breath. "I got too-too much for those things, and their director, Aislinn Zimmerman, once tried to borrow Roscoe for scenery."

Roscoe whined at that.

"That's right, boy. Don't worry. Old Sam would never let them abuse you." He glanced back at Kyle. "That's why I keep Roscoe hidden. The last thing I need is my poor dog going blind, too."

Kyle stood there stunned by Sam's disclosures. He just couldn't see the woman he'd met doing something like that. She'd seemed so pure. Innocent.

No, he didn't believe it. But this whole scenario would require more research.

Heading for the elevators, he decided it was time to get down to business and do what he did best.

Research, infiltrate, and take whatever action necessary to achieve his objective.

THREE HOURS LATER Kyle sat back in his office chair, reviewing his reconnaissance data.

Marianne Webernec was a high school teacher from a small town outside Peoria, Illinois, whose only claim to fame was once winning the statewide spelling bee in junior high school. She hadn't even been homecoming queen.

She'd graduated with good grades, not exceptional ones. Done college in five years, then went back to her hometown to teach German and French at the local high school.

She'd never even had a speeding or parking ticket. Not even in college.

There wasn't much here to say she was anything out of the ordinary.

Nothing except for the way his body had reacted the moment he had held her in his arms. The way her hard, puckered nipples had looked underneath the cotton of her tank top.

The way her warm, welcoming mouth had tasted . . .

Someone knocked on his door.

Instinctively Kyle reached for his weapon, only to roll his eyes at the reflex. Some habits died hard. It was why Joe had sent him here to the island. There was no chance in hell any of his enemies would ever find him. In all the world, this was the only "safe" place any of the BAD agents had.

He pulled his hand back from the holster.

"Come in."

The door opened to show Sam with Roscoe at his feet. "Hey, you busy?"

Kyle swiveled his desk chair around. "Not really. What'cha need?"

"Well, after you left, Roscoe got me to thinking. . . ."

Kyle arched a brow at that. The older man had a strange relationship with his pooch.

Sam came in and handed him a small paperback. "I sent Lee over to the other side of the island to find out what was going on over there for you, and he came back with that book. It's what they're reenacting at the moment, so I thought you might want to read it for a good laugh or something. I know you're not used to inaction, so I thought it might give you something to do."

Kyle inclined his head to him. "Obliged."

Sam nodded, then turned and left with Roscoe in tow.

Alone again, Kyle stared at the white cover with the title *Danger in the Night* and the author's name, Rachel Fire, emblazoned over it. On the spine was a single red rose logo from Rose Books. He turned the book over and scanned the back. The first thing that caught his attention was the name of the heroine, Ren Winterbourne, which was what Marianne had called herself.

The next one was the plot synopsis.

Undercover agents.

Kyle laughed out loud. This was perfect. His little schoolteacher was dreaming of . . .

Well, him.

Oh, yeah, this was the best. Leaning back in his chair, Kyle began to read the first page of the book, which was a small form and an invitation to the readers:

WHAT'S YOUR FANTASY?

Do you ever dream of getting away from it all? Just for a week or two?

Have you ever read a romance novel and thought . . . What if?

Have you ever, just once, wanted to be the heroine in a book and to have the man of your dreams come in and rock your world?

Your dreams could come true. Enter the Hideaway Heroine Sweepstakes, and you, too, could be headed off to be the heroine in your favorite romance novel. Just send in your name, address, and phone number, the title and

*author of your favorite book, and the reason(s) why you
need a break from your everyday life.*

> *One lucky winner will be selected every two months.
> No purchase necessary. Enter as many times as you like.
> For more information, please visit RachelFire.com.
> Good luck!*

Kyle turned the page, and the hot sex scene on the
first page was enough to shock him to his core and
make his cock so stiff, he couldn't even sit comfortably.

Holy shit, this was what Marianne read for pleasure?

Just what else did his simple little teacher do for fun?

MARIANNE SIGHED AS "Brad" pulled his gun out
from under his coat. Of course, it got tangled in the
hem and he almost dropped it, but once he finally
wrestled it free, he pointed it at the others.

"Back off," he snarled, and yet it sounded somehow
less than convincing even to her.

The other men around them made snarling noises
and animal-like gestures that reminded her of an old
campy *Batman* episode from TV. She half expected Olga
and her Cossacks to come barreling out at any moment,
followed by Vincent Price playing Egghead.

It was all she could do not to laugh.

Strange how the idea of this hadn't seemed ludicrous
when she'd told Aislinn Zimmerman that she wanted
to be Ren Winterbourne, but for some reason the reality of it left her feeling like a fool.

"Come on, Ren," Brad said, taking her by the arm.
"I'll get you out of this."

How she wished he could.

Unfortunately all of this would continue for at least another week until her fantasy life was over and she could return back home to Illinois.

Who would have ever thought *that* would be appealing?

Someone please save her from Brad, the bad actor, and the poor souls who were being paid to act like clean-cut criminals.

She half ran out of the building with Brad towing her along by her hand. This was the part where Brad in the book was supposed to pin Ren up against the wall and kiss her senseless.

Instead, Brad ran with her down the beach toward the hotel where they were staying.

"Are they behind us?" he asked.

"No," she said without looking. In her fantasy vacation package, unlike the book, the bad guys never really came after them. It was as if they were afraid of hurting her, even though she had signed a legal waiver promising not to hold the Zimmermans or Rose Books liable should she be hurt.

Brad stopped and took a minute to catch his breath. Marianne idly found herself wondering if Kyle would be as winded as Brad after so short a run.

How ridiculous was that? But then, she hadn't been able to get that man out of her thoughts since Brad had "rescued" her from him. Especially Kyle's wonderfully tight rump, which had been begging her for a covert fondling.

Too bad she had lacked the courage even to try and grope him.

Well, at least she'd gotten one really good kiss out of this experience.

Hmmm . . . Maybe she should plead a headache and venture to the other side of the island again in search of the only man who'd turned her head since she'd stepped off the plane three weeks ago.

Not that Brad wasn't gorgeous. He was. In fact, he was almost pretty. But his looks didn't make her weak the way Kyle's rugged handsomeness had.

Just as she was about to lament the lack of fireworks, a large unidentified object went whizzing over her head. The next thing she knew, something exploded to her right.

A tree crashed down.

"What the . . . ?" Brad whirled around to face a man in green camouflage.

His features obscured by the paint, the unknown man swung at Brad and knocked him back, then he turned on her, and before she could see much more than a blur, he tossed her over his shoulder and ran for the trees.

Draped over him, she caught sight of an exceptionally nice ass.

Kyle?

The hope hung in her heart as they raced away from the others.

Marianne couldn't form another coherent thought as he sped with her through the dense brush. His shoulder wasn't exactly comfortable as it slammed repeatedly into her middle.

She was about to tell him to put her down when more explosions sounded.

He turned sharply, narrowly missing another bomb.

"What's happening?" she asked in a broken voice that reminded her of Katharine Hepburn as her first real wave of fear went over her.

This wasn't part of the book.

"It's the Big Bad, love. Keep your head down or lose it."

She would have recognized that deep, husky voice anywhere. "Kyle? Is it really you?"

He stopped and slid her down his body, which made her instantly wet and needy. Oh, but he had a body and build made for sinning. But she hated the fact his face was completely obscured by the green and black paint.

"Shh," he said, placing a finger over her lips.

He cocked his head as if listening for something.

She heard the faint sound of firecrackers.

"They're coming for us," he said. Taking her hand, he pulled her deeper into the woods.

"Who?"

"Tyson Purdue."

Her scowl deepened at the unknown name. "Who's that?"

"A nasty arms dealer. He's been looking for me for a long time now."

She looked at him skeptically. "Tyson Purdue? Why do I have a feeling that's a name you made up while at the grocery store?"

Kyle ground his teeth. Damn, she was a little too intelligent. Coming up with cover stories had never been his forte. He left that up to operatives such as Retter and Hunter. They were slick and fast with a lie.

His forte was explosives and muscle.

Still, the other agents had taught him one thing. People would believe anything provided you said it with enough conviction.

He gave her a sincere stare. "Well, we call him the Chicken Man. He kind of looks like a chicken. It's why he has such an inferiority complex. Imagine being tagged with such a name. You'd be psychotic, too. What can I say? The man wants me dead."

"So why am *I* running?"

Kyle froze at her question. The only thing he could come up with was a lame excuse he'd seen once in a bad spy movie.

"You kissed me," he answered partially. What the hell, it made about as much sense as anything else. "One of his minions saw it and now he's after you. I had to go back for you to save you before he used you to get to me."

By the look in her brown eyes, he could tell she wasn't buying it. "Yeah, right. I don't—"

He pressed the trigger for another remote explosive. Marianne took the bait. She cringed in his arms. "Are you serious?"

"Baby, I never lie about minions out to get me." At least not unless it was helpful, and not unless it would keep her in his arms.

"Is this for real?"

He triggered another explosion. "We have to get moving," he said, letting just a hint of an edge into his voice. "It's going to get ugly if we don't."

Marianne swallowed at that. Part of her still doubted

that this could be real, but the look on Brad's face had been sincere. The man wasn't that good an actor. He'd had no idea that Kyle was going to show up.

Any more than she'd known.

"Where are we going?" she asked.

"Don't worry. I have a safe place."

Not sure if she should trust him, but having no other choice, she followed him through the woods until they came to a sheer drop-off near the crashing waves.

Kyle gave her a heated stare. "Feeling adventurous?"

"I can't go down there."

"Sure you can, love. I won't let you fall."

I must be insane.

She hated heights. She hated the thought of falling into the ocean below, and yet something inside her trusted Kyle implicitly. Not to mention the fact he seemed to know what he was doing, while she had no clue whatsoever.

With him helping her, they carefully slid down the steep side of the cliff and moved across the beach until they came to a small cave.

Marianne looked at it skeptically. "You know, I have a really nice room back at—"

His peeved look interrupted her. "And it's just as likely to be riddled with bullet holes. Trust me, being shot hurts." He gave her a devilish grin. "Don't tell me my little teacher has lost her sense of adventure."

"No, but . . ." She paused as his words sank in. "How do you know I'm a teacher?"

"Aren't you?"

"Yes, but how did you know that?"

He hesitated before he answered. "The way you dress."

Marianne looked down at her khaki shorts and white button-down shirt. There wasn't anything to mark her as a teacher. She looked just like anyone else out for a stroll on the beach. "My clothes don't say anything."

"Sure they do," he said, moving closer to her.

Closer and closer until his large muscular body overwhelmed her with desire.

He unbuttoned the top button at her throat, making her entire body instantly hot with sexual anticipation. When he spoke, there was a deep, erotic timbre in his voice. "Only a teacher would have her collar buttoned all the way up to her chin. What? You afraid of driving your students wild?"

"Hardly!"

He smiled down at her as he unbuttoned the next one. "I'll bet the guys you teach spend hours in your classroom staring at your ass while you're at the chalkboard, trying to imagine what you're wearing underneath all this conservative dressing—"

Marianne cut his words off with an outraged squeak. "Stop that. You're skeeving me."

"Skeeving?" he asked with a laugh. "What kind of word is that?"

"A perfectly good one that means I don't want to even think about what you're describing." She narrowed her gaze on him. "You're trying to get me off the topic, aren't you?"

Yes, he was. Damn, she was good. If he didn't

know better, Kyle would think she really was a special agent. "Why would I do that?"

"I don't know."

Kyle couldn't keep himself from touching her lips with his thumb. She had a mouth that had been made for long, hot kisses, and the memory of her taste was still fresh in his mind. Under his skin.

Simmering in his blood.

"You are beautiful," he breathed.

She actually snorted at him.

"What was that?" he asked with a light smile.

"Disagreement. They must be paying you a lot to do this."

"No one's paying me for anything where you're concerned," he said, lacing his hand through her hair. "I've done a lot of bad things in my life, Marianne, but I would never toy with someone's emotions. I'm not that cruel."

He lowered his mouth to hers.

Marianne sighed as his arms tightened around her. This man had more magic in his touch than every member of Harry Potter's school. She'd never seen anything like Jungle Jim.

He was incredible, and the woman in her was completely captivated by him and his powerful touch. His sensuous taste. His warm, male scent.

His mouth blistered a trail from her lips to her neck, where his breath scorched her. She buried her face in the soft locks of his dark brown hair and inhaled the warm, manly scent of his shampoo and skin.

Goodness, but this man set her on fire.

He pulled back to stare down at her with those captivatingly blue eyes. He rubbed gently at her face, letting her know he must have gotten some of his camouflage paint on her skin. "Have you ever made love to a stranger before, Marianne?"

"No," she said, her voice weak. In truth, she'd never before wanted to.

But she did now, and the depths to which she wanted him scared her.

He was truly irresistible.

Kyle took her hand into his and led it to the swollen bulge in his pants. She could feel the whole outline of his cock in her palm. Feel it straining toward her hand as if as eager for her touch as she was to touch him.

She should be offended by his actions.

She wasn't.

"Would you like to take a walk on the wild side with me, little teacher?"

This was insane. The very thought of it was . . .

Heavenly.

Decadent and frightening.

Dare she?

He trailed her hand up to the top button of his pants, where he lifted his shirt ever so slightly so that she could touch the hard, warm skin of his lower abdomen. He curled her fingertips into his waistband, then released her hand so that he could cup her face with his large hands.

She swallowed at the sensation of the short, crisp hairs that led from his navel downward.

"It's entirely up to you, Marianne," he whispered. "Do you have the courage to live out your fantasy?"

Did she?

How many nights had she lain awake dreaming of this? Dreaming of some hot man saving her from something bad and then taking her madly into his arms and making love to her in some wildly erotic location?

More times than she could count.

Seize it or leave it.

Woman or weasel?

I'm a weasel. I'm a weasel. I'm a weasel.

No, her days of weaseldom were over.

Taking a deep breath, she undid his pants.

Her heart stopped beating as she saw the size of the swell of him underneath the thin white boxer briefs. He was huge!

His smile was tender, warm, and if she didn't know better, she'd swear she saw relief in his gaze.

This time when he took possession of her mouth, his kiss was demanding. Bold.

His kiss literally made her dizzy. He pulled back long enough to jerk his olive green T-shirt over his head. He took a moment to wipe the paint off her mouth and then his, but ended up only smearing it more across his face.

Marianne laughed as she took the shirt from him and carefully removed the paint from his skin. "I suspected there might be a human somewhere underneath all of this." She'd meant the words to be light and funny.

He didn't take them that way.

Instead, he made an odd noise in the back of his throat. "Not really. Once I don the garb and assume the mission, the human in me is trained to be shoved deep into the background."

With his chin in her hand, she paused while wiping a particularly stubborn bit of camouflage from his temple. The sincerity of those deep blue eyes scorched her. "You were trained?"

"What they didn't kick out of me from birth, the military finished."

His words tugged at her heart, and she felt strangely close to him, as if he had just shared something with her that he didn't normally share with others.

As gently as she could, she wiped his tawny skin clean.

He watched her with a hint of suspicion behind his eyes, as if it were more habitual than anything she'd done or might do to him, and at the same time she felt his trust. It was a heady contradiction.

And as she toweled the last of the color from his face, she let her gaze roam his hard body.

Her breath caught at the sight of his wide chest and broad shoulders that tapered down into a narrow waist and lean hips. He was built like a professional athlete.

Every single muscle in his chest was discernible.

But what caught her attention most was the sight of several scars over his ribs and the two in his chest, which looked vaguely like healing bullet wounds. Or at least what she thought healing bullet wounds might look like.

Having never seen a real bullet wound, she didn't

have a basis for comparison. Still, those scars looked authentic, not like makeup or window dressing.

Before she could ask him about them, he picked her up, cradled her against his chest, and took her deeper into the cave. He laid her down on a pallet that was made up of several military blankets and an air mattress.

He turned on a small battery-operated lamp.

"What is all this?"

"Boy Scout motto. Always be prepared."

She trembled as he slowly unbuttoned her shirt. Her heart hammered in anticipation as she felt trapped between her common sense, which told her to run, and her lust, which told her to rip the pants off him and have her wicked way with all that lean, masculine strength.

"Are you always prepared for a tryst in a cave?"

"No, ma'am. But I was hoping you'd take me up on my offer."

"Because you were bored?"

He paused with his hand at the last button and gave her a hot, intense stare. "No, because I happen to think you're sexier than hell."

She had a hard time believing that, but there was no doubt *he* was sexier than hell. He had a body that had been torn from her dreams.

He undid the last button.

Marianne gulped for air.

Kyle slid his large, callused hand through the opening of her shirt to cup her breast through her white lace bra. She moaned at the feel of his palm against her swollen nipple. Even with the fabric of her bra between them, his hand was scorching.

It had been way too long since she'd last made love to a man.

For that matter, it had been a long time since she'd really wanted to make love to a man. Now all that repressed sexuality thrummed through her, wanting him desperately.

But with that desire came the fear that he might think her lacking in her inexperience. She wasn't the kind of woman who played the field, and in spite of what she'd done with Kyle, she'd never fallen into bed with strangers.

What was he expecting from this?

He pulled back from his kiss to smile down at her. His eyes were blazing and hot.

"Say the word, Marianne, and I'm out of here."

She answered him with a demanding kiss of her own.

Kyle closed his eyes as he inhaled the scent of her hair combined with the sweet scent of some kind of womanly perfume. But it was the earthy smell of woman that made his heart race even faster. Made his mouth water for more.

He'd never been with a woman like her before, and for the first time in his life he was nervous.

As a teenager, he'd run with the worst sort of New York gang. At fifteen he'd lost his virginity in the back room of a run-down slum in the Bronx to a woman in her mid-twenties who was on the make and looking to nail any handy dick she could find.

He'd fought his way out of the streets to enlist in the

navy. At age eighteen he had done his best to turn his life around and not become another statistic of urban poverty and bad parenting. Even so, he'd never dared dream a woman like this would want to be with him.

Someone soft and gentle. A teacher. Not a woman on the make. Not an operative out to blow his cover or a criminal wanting a fast lay before she blew his brains out.

Marianne was just a nice, average lady from a small town in the Midwest.

She was safe. That word alone was so alien to him that it made him ache even to think of it.

He'd never known safety. Never known unconditional acceptance.

He could vaguely remember his mother once telling him that sometimes the best dreams were simple ones. He'd never understood that.

Not until this moment.

He didn't crave the excitement that was his life. He craved the slice of normality Marianne offered. The simple taste of wholesome woman.

The simple taste of Marianne Webernec.

Marianne was breathless as Kyle moved down her body to unlace her shoes and pull them from her feet. She couldn't believe she was doing this with a complete stranger.

It was so out of character for her.

And yet she couldn't stop herself.

"Tell me something about you, Kyle." She needed to know something so that she wouldn't feel so self-conscious.

He pulled her other shoe off and massaged her sensitive arch with his thumb. Oh, but it felt sinfully wonderful as it made her stomach tight. She felt a rush of moisture between her legs.

"What do you want to know?" he asked, his deep voice intoxicating.

Everything. There was nothing about him she didn't want to know.

"What do you do for a living?"

He tossed her socks by her shoes and gave her an impish stare as he nibbled the arch of her foot.

She moaned in ecstasy.

He blew a stream of warm air over her skin before he spoke again. "Honestly?"

She nodded, breathless from the pleasure that rippled through her.

"I'm a federal agent."

For a second she couldn't move as his words sank in. Then she laughed at the absurdity. "Can you break out of character for one minute and be serious?"

"I am serious," he said earnestly.

But she didn't believe it. It was too perfect to be real, and what were the chances of a federal agent being here with her right now, when that was her fantasy?

He was just one of the men playing on the island. She didn't want that. She wanted to know about *him*. The truth. "Who do you work for?" she asked skeptically. "The CIA?"

"The Certified Idiots Association?" he asked, as if offended by her question. "Hardly. We eat those wannabes for breakfast. I'm with BAD, the Bureau of American Defense."

She scoffed. "There's no such agency."

"Yes, there is."

Part of her wanted to believe him, but the rational part of her knew better. She'd never even heard of such a thing. "And what part of D.C. are you located in? The White House?"

"We're not. Our offices are in Nashville."

She laughed even harder at that. "Oh, please. What kind of agency would have their headquarters there?"

His look was devilish. "The smart one. If D.C. gets wiped out or bombed, we're still able to function. No one's ever going to take out Nashville. It's barely on the terrorist map. Besides, we don't do anything by the book. Hell, our director is so whacked, he put us on the ground floor of the bat tower just for shits and giggles."

She arched her brow at that. "Ahh, the bat tower. Let me guess? Your director is Commissioner Gordon."

She groaned as he sucked her toe into his mouth and used his tongue to gently massage it. He nipped her large toe, then pulled back. "Trust me, BAD would make mincemeat out of Commissioner Gordon, Sergeant O'Hara, and Batman combined."

"BAD, huh?"

"Mad, bad, and dangerous to know."

"Have much luck with that line?"

He laughed gently as he crawled up her body like a languid panther and pressed his lips to her belly. His breath tickled her stomach as he parted her shirt more. "So far it's working."

Yes, it was. Much better than it should be. Who

would have ever thought that she could be seduced by some cheesy little line?

No, she realized. She wasn't seduced by a cheesy line, but rather by his stunningly blue eyes. His tender lips.

Oh, who was she fooling? It was that sinful body that she wanted.

All of it.

She'd never made love to a man who looked like this. One who was so handsome he should be on the cover of a book or in a movie.

One who set her blood on fire just by being with her.

She stared down at him while his hot mouth skimmed the flesh of her stomach. He lay between her spread legs with his chest pressing against the center of her body.

Oh, how she ached for him. Marianne ran her hands through his dark hair, letting the swirls of his tongue sweep her far away from what they were doing.

She arched her back as he sat up slightly and pulled her shirt off. Then he reached behind her and unfastened her bra.

"Mmm," he breathed as he bared her. "What have we here?"

"Breasts," she said simply as she fought the urge to cover herself. "Two of them."

He laughed at that. "Good, 'cause I was afraid you might have three."

"Nope, no Anne Boleyn here. Just two, like any other normal woman."

Kyle smiled at her teasing and her intelligence. He

couldn't recall ever being so at ease with a lover. It didn't feel as if they were strangers.

There was an odd sense of belonging with her. It didn't make any sense.

"Tell me something, Marianne," he whispered in her ear. "Tell me what schoolteachers dream about when they're all alone at night. Tell me what fantasies keep you awake while you lie in bed, wanting to feel someone inside you."

Her face flushed.

"Don't be embarrassed," he said, teasing the corner of her mouth with his lips.

He'd always wondered what "good" girls dreamt of. The scenes in the romance novel he'd read had shocked him more than the first time he'd read a *Penthouse* letter. He still had a hard time believing Marianne read such things.

"I don't know," she said with a small shrug. "I think of someone dangerous. Deadly. A larger-than-life officer or agent who can come in like Rambo and yet still be tender to me." Her brown eyes seared him with a heartfelt longing. "Someone who sees me."

He frowned at her words. Who in their right mind couldn't see her? "I see you, Marianne," he whispered, kissing her, tasting the warmth of her mouth.

Her tongue was heaven. He loved the sensation of it stroking his while her breasts were flattened against his chest.

Marianne sighed as he left her lips and trailed scorching kisses over her. His lightly whiskered cheek scraped her while he moved down to her shorts.

She lifted her hips as he slowly, sensuously slid them down her legs and left her completely bare to him.

She'd never felt more vulnerable.

Kyle's gaze locked and held hers as he rose to his feet and kicked his boots off.

She held her breath as he reached to the waist of his unbuttoned pants and then slid them and his briefs down his long, hairy legs.

If she lived to the end of time, she wouldn't ever forget the way he looked standing there in the dim light of the lamp, his cock erect, his body perfect. He was pure male beauty. Completely unadorned and completely stunning.

With a charming smile he moved to a small backpack and pulled out a box of condoms and an army green bandanna.

"What are you doing?" she asked as he started folding up the olive green cotton fabric.

"Remember the scene with Ren in the cavern?"

Her face heated up instantly. "What about it?"

His smile turned ravenous. "I couldn't find the chocolate sauce, but . . ."

She stiffened as he put the bandanna over her eyes. "I don't know about this."

"Trust me, little teacher. I promise you, you won't regret it."

"I'd better not."

He knotted the blindfold over her eyes. Marianne swallowed as she tried to see through the fabric.

It was useless.

She had no idea where Kyle was. Not until she

heard the sound of foil tearing. Then Kyle was back, his warm hands urging her toward the back of the cave.

"What are you doing?"

It felt as if he was seating her on a large rock that he had covered with one of the blankets. "I'm going to take my time savoring you, little teacher."

He rested her hips against the rock, then nudged her legs open. Marianne leaned back, unsure why she was allowing him to do this, and yet it was so wildly erotic that she couldn't bear the thought of stopping him.

Her entire body sizzled and throbbed with anticipation. With demanding hunger that longed to feel him deep inside her.

He trailed his hands from her knees, up the insides of her thighs. She shivered in expectation of him touching her where she ached for him.

He didn't, and she almost whimpered in disappointment.

Instead his hands skimmed up her ribs, massaging and tormenting her more.

"Touch me, Kyle," she whispered.

She felt his lips touch her breast. Marianne groaned as he swirled his tongue around her nipple, drawing it deep into his mouth while his hand skimmed down the outside of her thigh until he finally trailed it to the center of her.

His long, hard fingers parted her nether lips before they stroked her swollen cleft. She shivered as he massaged her clitoris.

She hissed as he finally gave her a modicum of relief.

Kyle growled at how good she tasted and at how well she responded to his caresses. He liked a fiery woman, and this one had more fire than her share.

Wanting more of her, he left her breast and kissed his way down to the part of her he wanted most.

She actually yelped the first time he licked her cleft. Laughing at her reaction, he spread her nether lips wide and ran his tongue over the hard edge of her clit, sucking and teasing her until she was on the brink of climax.

Marianne struggled to breathe. She leaned back on her arms, giving him as much of her as she could. Never in her life had she felt anything more incredible than him tasting her.

Wanting to see him, she started to remove the blindfold, only to find his hands stopping her.

"I thought you wanted to be Ren," he said.

She hesitated. Ren was the kind of woman who would be in this cave with a stranger, not Marianne Webernec. Marianne always played by the rules. She always played it safe.

Today she didn't want to be a Goody Two-shoes.

"Okay."

Kyle kissed her shoulder, then turned her over so that she was leaning on her arms and stomach against the rock. Her back was completely exposed to him.

"Mmm," he breathed, running his hand over her hips as his nails gently scraped her skin and made her tingle all over. "You have the nicest ass I've ever seen."

He licked his way down her backbone until he reached the sensitive spot at the base of her spine. His hands massaged her thighs, sending ribbons of pleasure through her while his tongue delivered stroke after ecstatic stroke to her flesh.

He slid one finger down her cleft, making her shiver again. "Do you want me inside you, Marianne?"

"Yes."

He slid two fingers deep inside. She moaned at the ecstasy of his touch as he teased her unmercifully while she slowly rode his fingers.

He leaned his body against her so that she could feel his erection against her lower back as he rained kisses on her neck and shoulders.

She was breathless and weak from the pleasure of his touch. No one had ever been more attentive to her. With Kyle, she actually felt beautiful. Desirable.

And that made her melt.

He moved his hand and then shifted behind her.

Marianne moaned as he slid himself slowly, inch by lush, incredible inch, inside her until he filled her to capacity.

Kyle growled at the feeling of her body welcoming his, of the way she felt as she lowered herself from her tiptoes down until he was even deeper inside her. It took every piece of control he had to make love to her slowly, gently, when what he really wanted to do was ravish her.

Since the moment he'd met her, he'd wanted nothing more than to have her.

And she was so worth it.

He held himself perfectly still as she rode him with soft, long strokes. Grinding his teeth to hold off his orgasm, he cupped her breasts with his hands and let her take her satisfaction first.

Every woman had a rhythm to her, and Marianne's was sweeping and sweet. Slow and sensuous like a gentle breeze.

He savored the sensation of her hips grinding against him, of her sweet low moans of pleasure.

He leaned forward, over her back, and braced one hand beside hers on the rock so that he could use his other hand to stroke her clit in time with their movements.

Marianne groaned aloud as he touched her again. She reveled in the feeling of him behind her and in her while his hand teased her, and when she came, it was so intense that she screamed out.

"That's it, baby," Kyle whispered in her ear. "Don't hold back on me."

She didn't. Nor did he. He continued to stroke and tease her until the very last tremor had been gleaned from her body.

Weak, she fell forward.

Kyle picked her up, carried her back to the air mattress on the floor, and removed her blindfold. His smile was dazzling as he covered her with his body and entered her again.

Marianne arched her back, groaning as his hard shaft slid back into her sensitive sheath.

Kyle's heart hammered as he thrust against her, wanting his own satisfaction. Her legs and arms were wrapped about him, cocooning him in her softness.

It was all he'd ever wanted.

Her body was paradise.

And when he found his own release, his head reeled from it. Growling, he buried his face in the fragrant sweetness of her neck and let the pleasure rip through him until he could barely breathe.

Every spasm, every wave, shattered some part of him until he couldn't do anything more than whisper her name.

Now, that had been the best sex of his life.

Weak and spent, he gathered her into his arms and held her against his chest.

Neither spoke for the longest time as they lay there, sheltered together, completely relaxed.

Kyle didn't care if he ever moved again. Nothing could top what he'd just experienced.

"Do you think Tyson will be back after us?"

It took him a second to remember who Tyson was.

"No," he said. "I secured the perimeter. I'd know if he was anywhere nearby."

"You sure?"

"Absolutely. I made certain this place was safe from any intruders."

Marianne sighed as she lay in the shelter of his arms.

Kyle ran his hand over her soft skin as he savored the feel of her breath on his naked skin. He'd always loved the sensation of feminine flesh against his, but never more than he did at this moment.

How strange that he'd been honest with her, when he'd never told any woman before what he really did for a living. BAD had been set up as a covert, ghost agency. The government, even those who had commissioned their bureau, denied all knowledge of its existence.

The BAD agents answered directly to Joe, who only answered to the president, and not even the president would acknowledge their mandate. Each and every member of BAD was an orphan who had been recruited to lie, steal, cheat, and/or die or kill for their country. Whatever it took to secure their objective, they would do without anything as cumbersome as morals or ethics getting in their way.

They were the modern-day Spartans who either returned with their shield or upon it.

There was no such thing as family for them. The agency was the family.

In this world they only had each other, and up until now that had been fine with Kyle. But his last bout with terrorists that had almost cost him his life had got him to thinking. . . .

He had been trained zealously to guard his country. But what was he really fighting for?

It wasn't until Marianne smiled up at him that he'd remembered.

He fought for those who couldn't fight for themselves.

"Kyle?" Marianne paused as she traced one of the smaller scars along his ribs. "What is this from?"

He glanced at it and the two similar ones below it. "A bullet."

Marianne frowned at his words. From the sincerity of his eyes, she could tell he was being truthful. "It looks recent."

"About a month ago."

Her jaw went slack. "And these?"

"Same."

She leaned up to study his chest. Now that she was closer, she saw even more of them, and no, they weren't makeup. The scars were real. "How many times have you been shot?"

"What are you asking? How many *total* bullet wounds or how many times has someone shot me up?"

There was a difference? She was aghast at his nonchalance. "Both."

He actually had to pause to think. "I've had a total of twenty-two bullet holes. Though we're still debating one of them. The doc said she thought it was a bullet that passed clean through, but I think the wound was caused by some shrapnel that hit me when the grenade went off. As for assholes who've taken shots at me, I'm at the unlucky thirteen mark."

Marianne's jaw opened even more. "Are you serious?"

He nodded, then turned his head and showed her a scar behind his ear.

"That was the first one," he said, placing his finger over the small round scar. "I was only seventeen and it was a drive-by from a rival gang. They took out my best friend Angelo as we came out of his house, headed for a movie. I got caught in the cross fire." He shook his head. "It's what got me out of the gang and made me want to do something with my life other than be target practice. Little did I know it would lead me into a field where drive-bys are even more likely than they were in New York."

She didn't know what to say. Part of her believed him and part of her found it hard to swallow. It was too close to what she would expect from a Rachel Fire hero and too alien to the sheltered world she'd known growing up.

She couldn't imagine being shot.

"You really, truly—swear to the Lord above—are a federal agent?"

He made an X over the center of his chest. "Cross my heart. And hope not to die on my next mission."

She sat back on her heels. "How long have you been an agent?"

"The last two years."

"Before that?"

"I was a navy SEAL."

Yeah, right. "You almost had me going. But for the record, the SEAL thing blew it."

"I swear," he said, as if offended by her doubt. "I really was a SEAL. I'd still be one if I hadn't been recruited for BAD."

She looked at him suspiciously. "What does BAD do?"

"That I can't tell you. Well, I could, but then I'd have to kill you, and no offense, I'm rather attached to you." He ran his hand down her backside and over her rump. "Especially this part here."

She squeaked as he clenched a handful of her buttocks.

He pulled her on top of him. Marianne straddled his waist and watched as he closed his eyes and sighed contentedly. She felt him stiffen against her hip bone.

Opening his eyes, he stared up at her and cupped her

face in his hands. "You have no idea how beautiful you are, do you?"

"I've never had anyone call me beautiful before. Heck, I had a guy in high school run screaming from the room when he lost a bet and was told he'd have to take me to the prom."

"He was an idiot."

She smiled at his words, amazed by them. "Who did you go to the prom with?"

"I didn't."

"Why?"

He shrugged. "My junior year I spent prom night in jail, waiting for my dad to sober up long enough to bail me out, and I didn't have the money to go senior year."

"Jail?" she asked. "What did you do to go to jail?"

"Nothing too bad. I was in for fighting."

"Over what?"

"Bella Marino. She broke up with her boyfriend and then threw herself at me. He got pissed and we got into it at the mall. He pulled a knife, I pulled a knife, and they called the cops on us."

"Kyle!" she said, stunned by his confession. "You're not making up any of this, are you?"

"No."

She let her breath out slowly as she stared into his blue eyes.

He laced his fingers through her hair. "I'm not proud of my past, Marianne. I've spent most of my life trying to forget it. I just . . ."

She waited a few minutes until it became apparent

he wasn't going to finish his sentence. "You what?" she prompted.

"I don't know. I feel like I can tell you things and I don't know why. It's not something I normally do. Hell, I barely talk to anyone. And then I meet you on the beach and I can't seem to shut my mouth or resist you."

She leaned forward and kissed him. "I can't resist you, either."

His cock hardened to full size at her words. He pulled back with a wicked grin.

Marianne melted at the look. He was better than anything she'd ever read in one of her books.

A real-life hero. One with a very sad past. How she wished she could make it up to him.

She moaned as he lifted her up and set her down on top of him. He was so hard and full inside her, and the tip of his shaft went straight into her G-spot from this position.

"Ooo," she moaned. "You keep doing that and I might not ever let you leave this cave."

He guided her hips with his hands as he watched her. "You keep doing that and I won't even try."

Marianne covered his hands with hers and felt the strength of him in his grip. She trailed her gaze over his tawny skin, pausing at the multiple scars. He was her fantasy come to life. Only he was real. His scars were deep, and she suspected he carried a lot more inside than those she saw on his body.

How many more did he carry in his heart?

"Have you ever killed anyone?"

"That's a strange question to ask while I'm making love to you."

"I'm sorry. I guess it was rather nosy."

He trailed his hand up her body and sank it deep in her hair. "Yes, I have," he said softly. "And no, I'm not proud of it. My life has been very ugly."

She held his hand against her cheek and kissed the scars over his knuckles. "I wish I could make it better."

"Trust me, love. You are."

She smiled at that.

Kyle raised his hips, tossing her forward, onto his chest. He wrapped his arms around her and rolled over with her until she was pinned under him.

How he loved the way she felt beneath him. The feel of her breath falling gently on his shoulder. The warm, sleek wetness of her around him.

How he wished he could make love to her without a condom. To feel the whole of her wetness surrounding him.

She was magnificent and he didn't want to leave her body. Not even when they came together in one swirling moment of blissful orgasm.

He still held on to her while she ran her hands over his bare back and shook under him. He was worn out and sated to a level he wouldn't have thought possible.

He laid his head down against her hard nipple so that he could feel the puckered areola against his cheek. It was the tenderest moment of his life.

But he knew it wouldn't last. Good things never did.

CHAPTER THREE

arianne woke up mid-morning to find Kyle already awake and dressed. Or at least partially dressed. He wore a pair of faded jeans and those biker boots again, but the rest of him was gloriously bare and glistening in the bright sunshine.

Yum!

Resting on his knees, he had his back to her while he cooked over a small Coleman camping stove.

Wow, the man really was prepared for anything.

She felt a tiny shiver as she stared at him and remembered the night they had shared. They'd made love so many times and in so many different ways that she was sure she wouldn't be able to walk straight today. Not to mention, they would definitely need another box of condoms—which might be her only saving grace from all that glorious temptation he offered.

The smell of coffee and bacon made her empty stomach growl.

"How long have you been up?" she asked.

He looked at her over his shoulder and grinned as he came out of that deadly crouch like some lethal, languid panther who had been tamed only by her. "Morning, little teacher."

"Good morning."

He made her a paper plate of eggs and bacon and brought it to her, then went to the small cooler to fetch some butter for her toast and a small carton of orange juice.

"Wow, full service in bed. I like that," she said as she sat up on the air mattress, which had been surprisingly comfortable while she slept. Marianne made sure to keep the sheet wrapped around her.

His eyes turned dark, seductive. "I have to say that servicing you in bed gives me a great deal of pleasure."

She blushed even more.

"Not to mention you gave me quite an appetite after last night."

She smiled at the depth in his voice, knowing exactly what it heralded, and one quick glance at his groin confirmed it. Kyle Foster was a sex machine.

"So, what's on the agenda for today?" she asked before she took a bite of her bacon.

Kyle drew a deep breath as he thought it over. In the book they were supposed to be outrunning the drug dealers who were enemies to the arms dealer, or some shit like that. For all he knew, it could have been a car dealer chasing them.

He'd spilled coffee on the book earlier that morning and hadn't been able to finish the chapter. Not that it mattered. With just the two of them, there wasn't really a way to fabricate a group of people pursuing them.

He was good, but that was beyond even his abilities.

So he'd have to think up something else for them to do.

"Well, I think we're safe here on our private beach. I say we enjoy the day. What about you?"

Her smile dazzled him. "It sounds like a plan to me."

Marianne finished her breakfast and dressed while Kyle cleaned up and shut down the stove. As soon as he had it cleared, he got up and pulled a gun out from under his folded shirt. Ejecting the clip, he checked his ammunition, then returned it to the hilt. He put the gun back in the concealed holster and then fastened it around his waist before he put his shirt on to cover it.

His movements appeared reflexive, as if he wasn't even aware of what he'd done.

"You always do that?" she asked as she tied her shoes.

"Do what?"

"Check your gun."

He frowned. "My gun?"

"The one you just put behind your back."

"Oh," he said, his face lighting. "My weapon. Yeah, I guess I do. I never thought about it."

She sucked her breath in between her teeth. "You're a scary man, Kyle Foster."

"So they tell me. But how about I put Scary Kyle away for the day?"

"I think I would like that." She pulled his shirt up. "Want to leave *that* behind?"

He cringed at her suggestion. "I don't think I can. That's like asking me to leave my arm behind."

"Yeah, but I don't want either one of us to get shot in the event I get a little frisky with you later."

One corner of his mouth twisted up at that as he pulled her into his arms. "Frisky, huh?"

She nodded.

He dipped his head down and kissed her while reaching behind his back to unfasten the gun. "All right, teacher. For you, but only for today."

He moved away to unload the ammo and then placed the gun and clip in a small box near the stove.

Marianne sighed in relief. She might like to read about cops and robbers, but real guns made her very nervous.

Kyle grabbed a hand shovel and bucket, took her by the hand, and led her down to the beach.

"You like clams?" he asked.

"Yes, why?"

"Want some for dinner?"

"Sure."

She frowned as he walked around the beach, studying the sand. After a second he bent over, presenting her with an exceptionally nice view of his butt.

He started digging.

It was awfully hard not to walk over to that butt and cup it. Or better yet, to cup the nice-sized bulge that she had become more than just a little acquainted with the night before.

"What are you doing?" she asked, moving closer to him. She had to fist her hand to keep from stroking him while he worked.

He glanced up from his task. "Digging up dinner. Want to help?"

She was astonished when he produced a clam from the beach. "I've heard of doing this, but I've never seen anyone do it before."

He examined the clam, then put it in the bucket. "Want to try it?"

"Sure. What do I do?"

He took her hand and pulled her along the sand. "We're looking for airholes," he explained. He paused by a small dimpled circle in the sand and indicated it with the toe of his foot. "That one's called a keyhole. Clams make it so they can breathe. All you have to do is put the shovel a few inches away and then you can dig it up."

Marianne was a bit timid at first. "How is it a New York City boy knows about digging up clams?"

"Travis Lamb, one of the guys I was in the navy with, showed me how to do it when we were on leave in Charleston years ago. His mother took the whole house full of guests out at dawn, and we dug up enough clams for her to make a shitload of chowder for an Independence Day party that night."

"You really were in the navy, weren't you?"

"Hell, I can even fax you the discharge papers if you want. They have the official seal on them and everything." Kyle smiled warmly, then helped her dig.

Marianne closed her eyes for an instant as she felt his

warmth surround her. She'd never done anything like this or enjoyed anything more than just feeling him behind her as the sun shone down on them.

This was peaceful. Comfortable.

She laughed in triumph as she uncovered a clam of her own. Kyle reached for the bucket. His hips brushed against hers, letting her know he was hard again.

She felt heat sting her cheeks.

"Why are you always blushing?" Kyle asked.

"I . . . uh . . ." She cleared her throat, not sure what to answer. The truth was, her sexuality had always embarrassed her, and Kyle was so at ease with it.

Then again, she'd never been more sexually aware of anyone else. Every time she looked at Kyle, she wanted to take a bite out of him. Pull him into her arms, throw him down on his back, rip his clothes off, climb on top of him, and then ride him madly until they were both sweaty and spent.

Of course, she'd done a lot of that last night, and it still wasn't enough to satiate her.

She wanted more of him.

He stared at her intently as he took her hand into his. He laid a gentle kiss into her palm, all the while staring into her eyes.

"What's the matter, Marianne?" he whispered. "Are you scared of how much you make me want you?"

"A little."

He brushed a light, tender kiss across her lips. She moaned at the taste of him as he moved her hand so that her palm was pressed against his swollen erection. "Have you ever made love on the beach?"

She cringed at the thought. "Someone might see us."

His look turned mischievous. "Afraid? I thought you were Ren Winterbourne. Woman of adventure."

She bit her lip to keep from laughing. "Ren doesn't have to live with herself or the embarrassment of being caught in flagrante delicto by a stranger."

He pulled his shirt over his head and tsked at her. "So much for fantasy, huh?"

Marianne stared at his tanned, muscular chest. He really was scrumptious. Irresistible.

And this time when he kissed her it was fierce, demanding. Every part of her thrilled at the taste of his tongue dancing with hers. At the way his hand felt cupping her face.

He laid her back on the beach.

The sane part of herself told her to push him away, but the repressed part of her refused. She'd lived sheltered and safe the whole of her life.

Kyle hadn't. A man who was riddled with bullet scars knew nothing of fear. Nothing of trepidation.

He only knew how to live in the moment.

How she envied him that.

He pulled back and reached for the buttons of her shirt. "Well?"

Marianne swallowed. "If *anyone* catches us, you're a dead man."

He laughed at that. "I'll even loan you my weapon to shoot me."

"Promise?"

"Absolutely."

Taking a deep breath, she slowly unbuttoned her shirt.

Kyle watched breathlessly as she opened her top for him. It was the most erotic thing he'd ever seen. Strange. He'd had much better looking women striptease for him. Watched them peel their clothes off like a pro.

None of that had ever turned him on the way Marianne's timid movements did.

Her quiet hesitancy was a breath of fresh air. She wouldn't do this for someone else. He wasn't just another lay to her.

He liked the feeling of being special.

In his life, that was something that had always been sorely missing. The type of women he'd dated had always known the score. Always known their way around a man's body.

Not Marianne. She was just an unassuming woman from Middle America, living a life that was nothing special.

Nothing special to anyone but him.

He found her remarkable.

She moved her hands away from her shirt and ran them down his back. Kyle dipped his head down so that he could taste her bared flesh.

"Hmmm," he breathed as he flicked his tongue around her navel. "I think I'm addicted to your taste."

Marianne closed her eyes while his hot breath scorched her. This was the most unbelievable moment of a life she had spent playing it safe. A life made up of daydream fantasies of something like this happening to her.

To her surprise, she found herself laughing.

Kyle lifted himself up to stare at her with a stern

frown. "You know, it's not a good thing to laugh at a guy when he's trying to seduce you."

She brushed his hair back from his face and smiled up at him. "I'm sorry. I was just thinking of how you swept me off my feet yesterday. Literally."

His frown faded as his face relaxed into a heated, intense stare. "Anytime you need a hero, baby, you just call me."

She moaned as he dipped his head down and kissed her fiercely. Mmm, how she loved the taste of his mouth. The way his muscles rippled around her.

Marianne wrapped her body around his and reveled in the sensation of his bare chest against the part of hers that was bared by the opening of her shirt. She felt him from her lips all the way to her toes.

Her heart thundering, she ran her hands down his back, feeling the dips and welts of old scars there. Her heart wrenched at the thought of how much pain he must have lived through.

"I don't know," she whispered against his lips. "I think you need a keeper a lot more than I need a hero."

Kyle froze at her words. "Would you care to volunteer for the job?"

"Would you let me?"

Her question hung in the air between them.

"I've never had anyone interested in it."

"Never?"

He shook his head as the truth of that sank in. "No, it's why I joined the navy. All those sappy, stupid commercials about teamwork got to me, and I thought it might be nice to be part of some kind of family."

She toyed with his hair as she watched him quietly. "Did you find it?"

"I did with the SEALs. I knew with them I had a kindred bond."

"Then why did you leave?"

"Joe came in and selected three of us from my unit. Tony and Doug had been like brothers to me and I didn't want to let them down. When they signed up for BAD, I followed suit."

"Do you regret it?"

"Not until they dumped me on this damned island and told me to rest here for a few weeks."

She gave him a peeved stare.

He offered her a wicked grin. "Now I'm thinking I should thank them for it."

"You'd better be thinking that."

He rubbed himself against her, letting his body caress hers. "Believe me, Marianne, I am."

Marianne sighed as his kiss swept her into heaven. She didn't even protest when he removed her shirt and laid her back against the scratchy sand. Strange, this didn't look uncomfortable in movies and such, but in reality ...

She groaned as Kyle unzipped her shorts with his teeth, then pulled them down her legs. And when he did the same with her panties, she almost came just from the sheer eroticism of the act. He was like a wild predator set loose on her.

One who wanted only to devour her.

What was it about him that made her burn like this? That made her forget the fact that they could be discovered at any moment?

"You do like to live dangerously, don't you?" she asked as he crawled sinuously up her body, nibbling every inch of the way.

"There's no other way to live." His hot breath teased her taut nipple before he opened his mouth and claimed it.

Marianne sighed in satisfaction as she cradled his head to her. His hair teased her skin while his tongue encircled her areola, teasing it to a hard, bitterly sweet nub that made her stomach contract every time he licked it.

The waves ran up the beach, lapping gently against her bare feet, while the hot sun heated her almost as much as Kyle's touch did.

Kyle pulled away only long enough to remove his jeans.

Marianne couldn't fathom why a man like this was interested in her. "Are you sure you're not one of the actors they hired for this?"

"Positive. Why do you ask?"

"I don't know. You just seem too good to be real."

He snorted at that, then turned over with her so that she was on top of him. He reached for his discarded jeans and pulled out a condom, which he opened with his teeth, then reached around her so that he could put it on.

"I think you're the only person in my life to ever say such a thing to me. Most people I know curse the day they met me."

"I don't believe that."

She gasped as he lifted her up and set her down on

his hard shaft. Marianne moaned at the feel of him inside her. The tip of his cock tickled her deep, making her entire body throb from the feel of him there.

Bracing her hands on his shoulders, she rode him slow and easy, savoring every lush stroke of his body with hers.

"I can't believe I just met you," she said. It felt as if she'd known him much longer.

Kyle watched her as she milked his body with hers. Her hair fell around her lightly freckled shoulders, which had just a hint of red to them from their exposure to the sun. She was so beautiful there. Like some ancient goddess who had been washed up on the shore to seduce him.

He took her hand into his and suckled the pads of her fingers. He let the salty taste of her skin whet his appetite for her even more.

She was unlike any woman he'd ever met. She was cut from the same cloth as the pure, innocent homecoming queens he had dreamed about in his youth. The women he'd passed countless times on public streets and elevators. Decent women who knew nothing about espionage or lies. Deceit.

She was the kind of woman who would turn in the wallet that contained a thousand dollars without stealing a single bill.

His head reeled as she quickened her strokes. He reached up for her and pulled her lips to his so that he could feel closer to her.

Let some of her decency creep inside him.

He wanted to crawl inside her body. To find a safe, warm spot where such a thing as goodness lived.

Maybe if he stayed with her just a little longer some of her decency would rub off on him.

She came calling out his name.

Kyle didn't move as he watched the ecstasy on her face. When the last tremor had shuddered through her, she collapsed against him.

He rolled over with her again so that he could take control.

Marianne held him close, brushing the sand from his back as he slid himself in and out of her, thrusting against her in a demanding rhythm.

He was incredible. Powerful. Every stroke went through her, exciting her, and when his orgasm came, he cried out, then lay down on top of her.

She held him there, letting his breath stir her hair as his heart pounded against her breasts.

She closed her eyes and sighed contentedly. "Wow," she said quietly. "I think I felt the earth move."

He chuckled, but didn't make any move to leave her. "More likely it's just the waves moving the sand out from under us."

She blew him a raspberry. "You're such a spoilsport."

He kissed her lightly on the lips, then pulled her into the surf so that they could bathe in the crystal clear water where little tropical fish swam around their feet.

It was a perfect, surreal day.

"I feel strangely like Jane in some Tarzan movie."

Kyle beat his arms against his chest in imitation of an ape and made a Tarzan cry.

Before she could draw the breath to laugh at him, he

bent at the waist and rushed toward her, lifting her up and tossing her over his shoulder.

Marianne shrieked and laughed at his antics. Until she saw the sight of the pink wounds in his back. She had felt them while they made love, but this was the first time she had really seen them up close in the light of day.

Her heart thudding, she touched one long, ragged scar that ran just under his shoulder blade. "What is this from?"

"I think that one's from the razor-wire fence I slid under in Beirut about a year ago. Thank God I had my leather jacket on, or it would have done some serious damage."

"From here, it looks like it did."

"Nah," he said, setting her back on her feet. "It's a flesh wound."

She rolled her eyes. "You're like that psycho knight in *Monty Python and the Holy Grail,* aren't you? The one who has his arm lopped off at the shoulder who looks at it and goes, 'Ah, it's just a scratch.' "

"Hey, in the neighborhood where I grew up, any sign of weakness was an invitation to a serious ass-whipping."

"And where I grew up, we went to the hospital and got ice cream afterward."

Kyle frowned at her words and the idyllic world she described. "I don't think such a place as that really exists."

"Didn't you ever have anyone kiss your boo-boos?"

He thought about it a minute. "No. My mom was

killed in a car wreck when I was five. There wasn't anyone around to kiss much of anything after that."

She shook her head at him, then pressed her lips to
the scar on his chest, the one just an inch to the side of
his heart that was fresh and pink.

Closing his eyes, Kyle enjoyed the feel of her lips on
his flesh. The strange warmth that rushed through him
from her actions.

So this was tenderness . . .

He liked it a lot more than he should.

"Marianne!"

They both jumped at the sound of someone calling
from somewhere in the trees.

Kyle moved away from her long enough to scoop up
their clothes and hand her hers.

"Wait here," he said, pulling his jeans on.

Barefoot and shirtless, he reached for his weapon,
only to remember he didn't have it with him.

Damn. His military training snapped, making him
creep toward the sound of the intruder. . . .

Marianne dressed quickly as she wondered what
Kyle was going to do.

As soon as she was dressed, she headed off after him.
No sooner had she reached the trees than she heard
something snap.

A man yelped, then Kyle came running toward her,
laughing.

He sobered instantly.

"What was that?"

"Nothing," he said, clearing his throat. "It was just
one of Tyson's men."

"Let me down!" the unknown man's voice rang out through the trees.

She looked at him suspiciously. "What did you do?"

"I put him someplace where he can't follow us or tell Tyson where we are."

Unsure if she should believe him, she frowned. "Are you sure about this Tyson?"

"The Chicken Man is deadly, love. I promise. Come on, we need to go quickly before he sends more guys after us."

Still skeptical, she followed after him as he gathered their clams and shovel and headed off down the beach, far away from where he'd left "Tyson's" man.

They walked down the surf for quite some time before Kyle judged it safe again to dig clams. Once they had the bucket full, Kyle led her carefully up the rocky slope that led back to the wooded area of the island.

"Boo!" she said at one point, making him jump.

"Don't do that," he said in a hushed, peeved tone.

"I couldn't help myself. You look so serious."

"This is serious. One of those bastards could get his hands on you and take you away from me. That's the last thing I want." The sincere anger in his voice set her back.

"Really?" she asked.

"Really."

Marianne bit her lip as warmth gushed through her. She laced her fingers with his and let him sneak her back to their isolated cave, where they made steamed clams and made love until the very wee hours of the morning.

They made love until she was weak and breathless, but so well sated that she just wanted to sleep in the shelter of Kyle's arms for eternity.

For the next few days they hid in their cave, running during the daylight from Tyson's men and spending their nights getting to know each other and every detail of their lives.

There was nothing she hadn't shared with Kyle, and as she fell asleep snuggled against him on the fifth day, she knew all of this would end soon. She only had a few more days on the island, and then her fantasy was over.

Would Kyle still want her then, or would he put her on a plane and make ready for the next contest winner?

The anger and fear that question evoked startled her.

But what stunned her most was how much it hurt to think of letting Kyle go.

CHAPTER FOUR

*K*yle and Marianne sat on a blanket on the beach long after dark with a small fire crackling before them. He was leaning back against a large piece of driftwood with Marianne sitting between his raised legs, cradled against his bare chest while she wore his T-shirt.

He adored the sight of her in his clothes, which she had been wearing every day since he'd "kidnapped" her. There was no way he was going to let her return to her hotel room, where one of the others might be able to keep her from him.

Not that they could. He just didn't want to have to hurt someone unnecessarily. But he would hurt anyone who tried to pry her away from him even a minute earlier than he had to let her go.

She was braless underneath his shirt, and the thin material reminded him constantly of the fact that she was ready for him at any time. Her nipples were puckered nicely against the thin white cotton fabric, begging him to reach out and touch her while she had her head resting back against his shoulder. Her hips were nested firmly against his groin, and every time she moved, his cock jerked with awareness of her warm softness so close to him.

With the awareness of just how much he enjoyed her company and her body.

It was quiet now, with only the sound of the surf and fire to intrude on their peace.

But Kyle was concerned. The men from her side of the island were getting more resourceful and insistent that Marianne return to her "fantasy."

He'd be damned if he was going to let her go. Not until she asked him to, and so far she seemed utterly content to stay with him.

But those pesky vermin kept running after them, and today they'd gotten a little smarter.

One of the buggers had almost caught up to them on the cliffs. But a few well-tossed grenades had sent the man running back the way he'd come.

Tomorrow Kyle would have to move them to a new location farther down the beach.

Marianne continued to play along with the idea of their pursuers being Tyson's henchmen out to get them, but by the light in her brown eyes whenever he spoke of it, he could tell she didn't believe him.

It was just as well. Tyson had been a stupid idea, but it had brought him the best moments of his life, and if she didn't call his bluff, he wasn't going to confess the truth to her.

He just wanted to enjoy what little time they had left.

Marianne snatched her stick up as her marshmallow caught fire. She quickly blew it out. Her long hair tickled his skin as she moved, stirring the air between them so that he could smell the fragrance of his shampoo in her hair.

He loved the smell of his scent on her. It touched him on a level that was profound and frightening.

Entranced, Kyle watched as she pulled the gooey mess from the tip of the stick and carefully took a bite.

The sight of her tongue flicking back and forth over her lips undid him.

His body burning, he pulled her close to taste the sugar on her lips. She moaned the instant he swept his tongue against hers.

"Are you burning your marshmallow, Kyle?"

He rubbed noses with her and inhaled her womanly scent before pulling away to see his stick and marshmallow buried deep in the fire. "It would seem so."

She tsked at him. "And that was the last one, too. Shame on you."

Shaking his head at her, he tossed his stick into the fire. They were running low on supplies. He'd snuck over to his hotel to get a few more essentials such as soap and shampoo while she'd slept last night, but the truth was they would have to go back to the real world all too soon.

Their time was so limited.

"If I have to die for my country, Joe, then I'd like to know what the hell I was living for."

Those angry words haunted him now as he remembered saying them to Joe right after he and Retter had blown their way out of the Middle East.

Marianne was the answer, but he couldn't stay with her. His duties were elsewhere. Men like him didn't have liabilities, and Marianne Webernec was a huge liability. He didn't need to have the stress of worrying about the widow he would leave behind if he died.

Such things guaranteed death with cold-blooded certainty. In the field the best soldiers were the ones who had nothing to focus on or worry about except the job.

The job was everything.

But at least now he understood what it meant to be alive. To feel deeply for a woman and to know, while he was getting the crap shot out of him, why his job was so important.

It kept people like Marianne safe. She was no longer some faceless stranger. An abstract ideal.

He had something real to hold on to.

Closing his eyes, he leaned his cheek against hers and just held her in the quiet solitude, wishing that time could stand still and that he could make this moment last for eternity.

He never wanted to leave her.

He never wanted to leave this island.

Marianne sighed as she absorbed the sensation of Kyle's whiskers lightly scraping her skin. His strong arms were wrapped around her chest as if he were afraid to let her go.

She loved that feeling, but more than that, she suspected that she might actually love *him*.

These last few days they had shared so much of themselves with each other. She had told him of her fears of dying alone without ever having one spectacular moment to say Marianne Webernec had lived. That she was important to someone other than her rogue tomcat.

Kyle had listened and he, too, had shared his sad past with her. And with every nugget he had entrusted her with, she had fallen for him more.

No one had ever been closer to her. Never meant more to her. Kyle was wonderful.

She didn't know how much of what he'd told her was truth and how much was made up, but she didn't think he was lying about the important things, such as his best friend and mother dying. The pain in his eyes when he spoke of them was too real to be faked.

No, he had opened himself up to her, too.

Her heart thrilled at the thought. Warmed by him and his concern, she turned around to face him. The firelight played in his hair and across his face, making shadows along the sharp, handsome planes.

"You are so delectable," she said.

He arched a brow at that.

Smiling wickedly, she reached for the button of his jeans.

"What are you doing?" he asked.

She unzipped his fly. "Why, I'm having my wicked way with you, sir."

His swollen cock, nestled by his short, dark hairs, jutted out, arching back toward his stomach. Luckily his underwear was still drying from where they had washed their clothes earlier, so now he was all naked and exposed to her.

Mmm, how she loved the sight of him like that. Hard and ready for her. She ran her hand down the length of him and delighted in the way his cock followed the motion of her caress. The way it lifted and arched in reaction to her touch.

She brushed her hand along the sensitive tip, letting his wetness coat her fingers.

Kyle watched her with hooded eyes as his breathing changed to sharp, intense breaths.

Marianne licked her lips and lowered her head so that she could draw the tip of him into her mouth. She closed her eyes as she tasted the salty sweetness of him. How she loved the taste that was Kyle.

He hissed in reaction.

She growled deep in her throat as she took more of him into her mouth, while running her tongue around the large vein, and allowed the vibration of her voice box to add to his pleasure.

He cupped her face in his hands and ran his hands through her hair while she cupped the soft sac of him in her hand to massage him in time with her long licks.

Kyle's head swam as he leaned back to allow her more access to his body. There was nothing better than the sensation of her sweet little mouth teasing him. Her timidity was gone now after the days they had been together. She was bold with him.

And he liked that most of all.

She no longer hesitated to touch him. She'd learned he couldn't deny her anything. Whatever she wanted was fine by him, and in truth, he liked being her chew-toy.

She sucked him gently, then licked her way from the base to his tip. His pleasure was so intense, he swore he could see stars.

And when she reversed direction, it was all he could do to not cry out in ecstasy. Oh, the feel of her mouth on him, especially when she kept going and drew one of his balls into her mouth to suck and nibble.

He dug his heel into the blanket as he carefully balled his hand into a fist in her hair without hurting her.

She didn't take an ounce of mercy on him. Instead, she continued her bittersweet assault. Breathless, he ran his hand down her jaw while she returned to his cock and took him all the way into her mouth again.

The sight of her there was enough to finish him off. Unable to stand it, he let his orgasm tear through him. His entire body shuddered and convulsed.

Weak and spent, he collapsed back against the drift-wood. Marianne kissed her way up his body slowly, as if savoring every inch of his skin as much as he savored hers.

He groaned when she paused at his nipple to draw it deep into her mouth and flick her tongue back and forth over it. "I love the way you taste," she said, her breath scorching him.

"I love being tasted."

Her smile made his heart pound even more.

Then she dug into the pocket of his jeans and pulled out a quarter.

"What are you doing?" he asked suspiciously.

"Turn over."

He laughed nervously. "I'm not sure about this."

"C'mon," she said, wrinkling her nose at him. "It's something I've been wanting to do."

When he hesitated, she shook her head. "Don't be a baby, Kyle. Trust me."

Reluctantly he moved so that he could lie down on his stomach. "Okay," he said slowly. "But I want to be able to use that quarter later. You know what I mean?"

Laughing, Marianne pulled his pants down to his buttocks. "You are such a worrywart. Relax."

Suddenly very nervous, he lifted himself up on his forearms so that he could stare at her over his shoulder.

She stared at his butt, then took the quarter and bounced it off his left cheek.

"I knew it!" she said triumphantly. "Your butt is so tight the quarter actually bounces."

"What?"

She smiled even wider at him. "You have the tightest ass in the world, you know that?"

"Yeah, okay," he said again. This had to be the strangest moment of his life, and when you considered the fact he spent a great deal of time with drug dealers and terrorists, that was saying something. "You do this a lot?"

"Nope," she said, putting the quarter into her pocket. "I just wanted to test my theory."

"And now that you have?"

Her look turned wicked. "I have plans for that tight butt cheek."

She placed her hands on his cheeks and gave a hard, pleasurable squeeze before she leaned forward and took a nip in the same spot where she'd bounced the quarter.

Kyle laid himself down, content to let her have her way with his body.

Marianne never ceased to surprise him. He found the challenge of her the best part about all of this.

And as the night sped by, he realized something.

For the first time in his life, he was in love with someone.

Someone who had come to mean everything to him.

Someone he was going to have to leave behind forever.

KYLE WOKE UP inside the cave the next morning so sated that he was sure he must have died and gone to heaven. This last week with Marianne had been unlike anything he'd ever known.

The more he got to know her, the more he liked her.

No, it was more than like. She made him feel things he'd never felt for anyone.

And he adored the scent of her on his skin. The feel of her hands on his body. He loved waking up with her lying next to him.

Dreamy and warm, he rolled over to pull her close for some serious snuggling, only to find himself alone on the air mattress.

Frowning, Kyle opened his eyes to see the strangest sight of his life.

Someone had placed a toy rubber chicken on Marianne's pillow.

"Marianne?" he called, laughing at what he assumed was a prank. She had an odd sense of humor at times.

No one answered.

And now that he thought about it, where would she have gotten a toy chicken?

Extremely concerned, he sat up instantly. His gaze fell to the handwriting on it, and his blood ran cold.

If you want to see Marianne alive again, call Tyson Purdue, 212-555-6209.

What the hell?

His heart pounding, Kyle shot out of bed and dug his cell phone out of the small backpack he'd brought along days ago. For the first time in a week, he turned it on and dialed the number.

"Kyle?" The voice was electronically distorted.

"Who is this?" he demanded.

"It's Tyson Purdue, and you have been a bad boy. Literally. I'm sick of you interfering with my business, and it's time I taught you a lesson."

"What are you talking about?"

A sharp click sounded. It was followed by Marianne's terrified voice. "Kyle? What's going on? Who are these people who have me?"

He saw red at the fear he heard from her. He'd kill whoever had scared her like this. "It's okay, baby. Don't worry. I won't let them hurt you. Can you stay calm for me?"

Marianne didn't answer. Another sharp click sounded and then the electronic voice responded.

"Don't worry, Foster. She's okay so long as you do what we say."

"What do you want?"

"I want *you*, Kyle Foster. I want you dead for what you've done."

"Who the hell are you?"

"You know who I am. Don't be stupid. And at the risk of being cliché, if you want Marianne to remain healthy and living, meet me at dusk on the south beach. Oh, and you'd better be unarmed."

The phone went dead.

MARIANNE WAS SO scared she couldn't breathe. Couldn't move. All she knew was that one minute she'd been sleeping happily wrapped around Kyle, and the next minute someone had pressed a pungent-smelling rag against her face.

Then everything went black again.

She'd awakened a short time ago with a ferocious headache to find herself blindfolded, with her hands tied behind her back and her feet tied to the wooden chair she sat on.

From what she could tell, there were three men with her. The one who had awakened her to talk on the phone seemed to be an American. His voice was extremely deep and seemed to have a very light hint of an unknown foreign accent to it.

The man on her right spoke with a heavy Spanish accent while another man's voice was definitely German.

"Why did you tell him to wait until sunset?" the

man with the Spanish accent asked. "I'm ready to get this done and go home."

"Reno, you were born impatient, *mi'jo*. The beauty of dealing with your opponent is playing with his head. Let's make him sweat a little. By nightfall he'll be so rattled, he won't even be able to think straight."

Marianne heard something click that sounded like a gun being cocked or maybe loaded.

Reno laughed. "You are an evil bastard."

"Yes, I am, and if you were wise, you'd be taking notes. Learn from the master, boys, and learn well."

Marianne was so afraid that her teeth chattered. She was freezing cold, shaking even though her hands were tied behind her back.

She wanted to be brave for Kyle, but she wasn't a secret agent. The character in her novel would be able to get out of this. A small-town high school teacher couldn't.

What was she going to do now? This wasn't supposed to happen to her. She was . . .

Marianne paused as the men started talking about blowing up the cabin she was in.

Wait, this was familiar to her. She knew this part. Being tied to the chair, the phone call.

The cabin explosion.

Chapter 9!

Her mind raced as relief coursed through her. *That's right. Halfway through the book Ren ends up captured by the villain and Brad has to come to the rescue, only Ren ends up being the one who rescues him.*

It was the book!

These men must be more actors, and they had finally recaptured her from Kyle.

Well, it was about time. They'd been woefully inadequate up until now.

She relaxed at the discovery. This wasn't real. It was only part of her fantasy.

Oh, thank God no one was going to kill her or Kyle. She let out a long breath as she tried to wiggle out of the ropes.

"Okay, guys," she said, her voice surprisingly steady. "You can untie me now."

"Untie you?" the American repeated, his tone filled with disbelief. "Why should I?"

"Because I asked you to?" She waited expectantly for them to untie her.

They didn't. Nor did they say anything, and she had a sneaking suspicion they were staring at her.

"Look," she tried again, "I realize that you guys finally managed to get me away from Kyle. Bully for you, you did good for once. But now we're back to the book, and since I'm the heroine and I'm supposed to escape, I need some help. This chair is really uncomfortable and my hands hurt."

She waited for them to obey her, and again they didn't make a move to undo her.

Time stretched out interminably.

"C'mon," she said, hopping in the chair. "I can't undo these knots. See, I know Ren Winterbourne, Secret Agent, is supposed to be able to get out of the chair, but Marianne Webernec from Peoria can't, and until I get loose, we can't move on to the next scene, so would you guys help?"

"What is she talking about?" the Spanish man asked.

"Who is Ren Winterbourne?" the German asked.

The American laughed.

Another ripple of fear went through her.

They're just playing with you. You heard them, they like to play with people's heads.

Play with Kyle's head.

Marianne paused as she realized this wasn't about her. They might really be after Kyle after all. Otherwise, why use the name Tyson Purdue?

Dear Lord, what if Tyson Purdue was a real man?

Stay calm, Marianne.

"C'mon," Marianne said again, hoping she was wrong and they were just being mean for all the times Kyle had scared them off. "I know this isn't real. Just let me go and I won't tell Mr. Zimmerman how bad you scared me."

"Do you guys know a Zimmerman?" the German man asked.

Marianne felt someone move closer to her.

"Not real?" The American stood so close that his voice was nothing more than a growl in her right ear. "Lady, do you know what BAD is?"

"Bureau of American Defense. It's the agency Kyle made up."

She heard the American move away from her then. It sounded as if he might have huddled with the others.

The men began speaking to each other in German. Little did they know, German was one of the languages she taught at her school, and she understood them perfectly.

"If she doesn't believe him, then we can let her go, right?" the German man asked.

"How much did Foster tell her?" the Spanish man asked. "You were the one who had him bugged."

The American answered, "A lot more than he should have. I don't know. . . ."

There were a few seconds of silence, and again she heard something that definitely sounded like a gun being cocked this time.

"I'm thinking she's a liability, and you know what I think of liabilities."

"Put your weapon down. You can't just kill her," the German man said. "I'm tired of cleaning up body parts after you get through."

Oh, God, it's real!

These weren't actors from the island.

Someone pulled the hair back from her neck, and then something sharp and cold was pressed against her throat.

"Are you scared, teacher?" the American whispered in her ear. "You said you wanted to be an agent. Were you really prepared for it?"

I don't want to die! The words tore through her mind. No, she didn't want this any more than she wanted Kyle to die.

Against her will, she started sobbing uncontrollably.

"Hey, hey, hey!" the American said as he moved whatever was against her throat away from her. "What is this?"

She couldn't speak past her wrenching cries.

"Ay caramba! What have you done? Look at her."

The blindfold came off instantly, and she realized she was inside a very small cabin that had next to no furniture. Her chair and a table appeared to be it.

Well, that and a whole lot of ammunition and guns. There were boxes all around her bearing the words *Fragile, Danger, Explosives, Ammunition, Grenades,* etc.

Marianne saw the three men through her blurry eyes. The one in front of her was gorgeous for a psycho. He had shoulder-length black hair that fell around a face that belonged to some Calvin Klein model. His dark skin was perfectly tanned, his eyes so pale a blue they didn't look real.

He reached out and wiped the tears from her face. "Don't cry," he said, letting her know he was the American. "C'mon, I can't stand to see a woman cry."

Reno cut the ropes on her feet.

Angry and scared, she reacted without thinking. She kicked the American in the leg.

"Ow!" he snapped, moving away from her.

Reno untied her hands, flipped closed his knife, then slapped a hand against the American's shoulder. *"Pendejo!"* he snarled. "I told you not to tie her up like this."

The American hissed and took a fearsome step toward Reno, who stepped back instantly. "Don't come at me, *maricón,* unless you come bearing a weapon."

"I've got your weapon, right here," Reno said, flipping open the large black butterfly knife he'd used to free her with.

The tall, blond German stepped between them. His hair was cut short, and he wore a pair of black aviator-style sunglasses. His white T-shirt was tight over a body that was huge and well built like a major bodybuilder. A colorful tattoo spiraled down his right arm.

"Enough!" the German said, keeping them at arm's length with his body between them.

Marianne decided to take advantage of their fight to run for the door.

She'd barely reached it before the American caught her. He swung her up in his arms.

She kicked with everything she had and screamed while trying to claw his eyes out.

The other two men laughed.

The American sat her down hard in the chair and held her there with an ease of strength that was truly terrifying.

He turned his icy gaze back to hers. "Look, no one's going to hurt you, okay?"

"You're going to kill Kyle."

A lopsided grin broke across the man's face, showing her a set of perfectly white teeth. "Not today, I'm not. I just want to teach him a lesson."

She launched herself at him.

He actually laughed as he held her easily away from him. "Well, the little teacher has spunk." He set her back in the chair. Again. "Listen to me, Marianne. You had a fantasy to be a damsel in distress, right?"

She swallowed her tears as she looked back and forth between the men. "You don't look like actors."

"Yeah, well," the American said. "That's because we're not."

"Then what are you?"

"We're friends of Kyle's."

The German snorted at that. "Since when?"

Marianne glared at the American. "I knew you were lying."

"Look, I swear, I'm not lying about this." He looked at the German. "Dieter, really, don't help me here, okay?"

"Fine, Retter. Don't call me the next time you need some *Scheiflekopf* to help you."

That diabolical half smile played across the American's face. "Your words, not mine."

Marianne froze as the man's name registered in her mind.

Retter . . .

The name went through her like glass. She knew who this man was. Kyle had told her much about his pseudo-partner who didn't listen to anyone except himself. Kyle's exact words had been, "Retter is a dickhead, but he gets the job done with scary reliability. The man strikes like lightning."

Retter turned back toward her. "I'm just playing a joke on Kyle for making me have to come out here to retrieve him. Since you wanted to be a damsel in distress, I was going to give you what you wanted while I jerked his chain. I'm sorry I scared you so badly. I'm used to dealing with agents who would sooner have their hearts cut out than cry."

She narrowed her eyes on the man before her. Still skeptical, Marianne wasn't sure what to believe. "How do I know you're who you say you are?"

"You'll just have to take my word for it."

"If I don't?"

Reno laughed. "I really like this woman, Retter. She thinks you're an asshole, too."

He gave Reno a cold, brutal look before those piercingly blue eyes moved back to her. "You'd be wise never to accept my word on anything, but if I kill Kyle, I'd have to explain it to Joe, and then he'd get bent and then I'd have to kill him, too, and that would make his woman go wild on me. And it's all just more trouble than even I want to deal with at the moment. So, see, he's safe."

There was a light in his eyes that said he would enjoy the challenge of the fight in spite of what he said, but there was also something charming and oddly warm about this man.

Marianne nodded quietly at him. "He'd better be safe," she warned him. "I don't know who Joe or his woman is, but if you do anything to Kyle, I swear Joe's woman going wild on you will seem like a walk in paradise compared to what I'll do to you."

KYLE STALKED BACK and forth in anger as he tried to figure out who could have taken Marianne while he slept.

He discounted the morons on the other side of the island. He'd been hanging them from trees and escaping them with barely more than a fierce growl. They could never have perpetrated anything like this.

It would have to be someone stealthy. Someone who knew how lightly he slept and how to move about without waking him . . .

He cursed as one name resonated in his head.

Retter.

There was no one else it could be.

Kyle's sight clouded at the thought. It had to be. Retter was the only man Kyle had ever known who could maneuver around him while he slept and not wake him. The man was part ghost.

But how did Retter know about Tyson Purdue?

He'd made the name up and . . .

He paused as he glanced back at the chicken and the crisp handwriting.

There must be a bug on him somewhere. There had to be. Joe was ever paranoid about losing agents and bugged almost every piece of equipment they had. The only reason Kyle hadn't thought of it sooner was the fact that every time he called Joe demanding a ride out of this place, Joe had laughed at him and told him to get lost.

It had never occurred to him that Joe would have the stuff on the island tagged, but since he'd raided the BAD supply closet for supplies, he should have known.

"Damn it."

Pissed and wanting blood, he called the number again.

No one answered.

So he dialed Joe's office, where Joe's assistant director, Tee, picked it up on the third ring.

"Tee, this is Kyle. Is Joe in?"

Tee Ho was the extremely attractive assistant director of the agency. She was a Vietnamese immigrant, and her intelligence was off the scale. So was her memory and her need to exact revenge on anyone dumb enough to mock her name. It was a mistake Kyle had made only once, and he was lucky he didn't have a permanent limp from the experience.

She was a top-notch agent and Joe's right hand, and she never let anyone forget those two facts.

"Well, well, Mr. Foster," she said in her crisp, flawless English—Tee could speak somewhere in the neighborhood of fifteen languages fluently—"how nice of you to finally check in. Blown up any busboys lately?"

"I beg your pardon?"

"Please, don't beg, it's not becoming of you, Mr. Let-Me-Kidnap-a-Woman-and-Drag-Her-Back-to-My-Cave. Joe is so hot about you right now, you're lucky you're still living. He's on the phone with Wulfgar Zimmerman from Rose Books trying to assure him you haven't hurt Marianne and that she will be returned to him shortly."

"I'm not the one who hurt her. Retter kidnapped her from me this morning."

Silence answered him for a few heartbeats until Tee started laughing.

"It's not funny, Tee."

"Sure it is. You're just mad he got away with it. At least he didn't punch you in the nose before he grabbed her. The actor playing Brad Ramsey, in case you're wondering, is fine, but bruised. He also quit his job and was threatening to sue us until I introduced him to Tessa and convinced him that a lawsuit would be extremely hazardous to his health."

Tessa was Tee's prized Glock 33. Which was only

slightly more deadly than Tee's other lethal weapon, Petey the killer Pomeranian.

"I swear, I'm going to kill Retter for this."

"Uh, no, you won't, hon. He's vital to national security and falls under extreme protection."

Kyle growled into the phone. "Then tell me how to get ahold of Retter and call him down."

"Ooo," she breathed. "I don't think that's possible. See, he was off in Rio having a grand old time on the beach when Joe had to call him in to come get you away from Wulfgar's tourist. You were bad, Kyle, not BAD. So sorry. If you want to talk to Retter, then call him. There's nothing I can do."

She actually hung up the phone.

"Fine," he said loudly, hoping that whatever mic was hidden, it picked up his voice. "You'd better hide, Retter, because tonight I am going to kick your rotten ass all over the beach."

THREE HOURS LATER Kyle came across the beach, loaded for bear, or in this case, loaded for Retter.

He'd fought beside the bastard enough to know what he needed to beat him. And beat him he was going to do.

For the last three hours Kyle had done total recon on the island. There was only one place where Marianne could be.

One place Retter would deem "secret."

He already had the small cabin in his sights. It sat alone at the base of a small mountain. It was used for supplies that Joe didn't want near the hotel in the event of a fire or something else that might make it explode.

Kyle didn't break stride or hesitate as he headed for it. He was less than three yards from the door of it when he heard a sharp click.

Cursing, he dived away from it an instant before the shack blew apart.

Debris rained all around him.

Kyle couldn't breathe as terror overwhelmed him. Marianne!

"It's not sundown, Kyle."

Kyle saw a two-way radio in the sand a few feet from him. He got up and grabbed it. "Where the hell are you, Retter?" He looked around, scanning everything.

"Look up."

He did and found Retter, Reno, and Dieter standing on the cliff. Marianne was nowhere in sight. "What kind of game are you playing?"

"Hide-and-seek. If you can find Marianne, I'll let you keep her."

"And if I don't?"

"Your loss. Literally." He saw Retter motion for Reno and Dieter to leave. Once they were out of hearing range, Retter spoke again. "Do you feel her loss, Kyle? Tell me the truth."

Yes, he did. He'd been feeling the emptiness of it since he'd awakened and found himself alone again.

Every minute he'd been away from her, he hurt. The desolation inside him was unlike anything he'd ever known.

He didn't want to live without Marianne.

But Lucifer would freeze solid before he ever admitted that to Retter. "Go to hell."

"I most likely will, but in the meantime the clock is ticking for you. If you don't find her by nightfall, it's over, and you, my friend, are on a plane out of here."

It was all Kyle had wanted. But that was before he'd met Marianne and had learned to have fun without explosives. Fun without someone taking potshots at him.

What would he do without her?

He didn't want to find out. Tossing the radio down, he backtracked through the woods and tried his best to focus on where Retter would have hidden her now.

MARIANNE SAT IN the lobby of Kyle's hotel, wrapped in Kyle's jacket. The scent of his body clung to it, making her want to bury her face in the sleeve and just inhale it until she was drunk from the scent.

Sam sat behind the concierge counter, staring at her. His old basset hound lay beside him on its back with all four of its paws up in the air.

"Are you sure that dog's not dead?"

Sam glanced at him. "Nah, ole Roscoe always sleeps like that."

She nodded, then frowned. Sam was a strange bird. "How long before Kyle gets here?"

"I dunno. Depends on what Retter does to him for taking you."

"Do you think they'll be really harsh on him?"

"Well, back when I worked for the CIA, we'd have

killed him for being such a pain, and Retter might yet. He's got a lot of the old school in him."

Marianne felt the color drain from her face.

"But his boss, Joe, is a bit more understanding about such things, so it's hard to say. I figure the worst thing that could happen to Kyle is nothing."

"What do you mean?"

"Well, he must have thought a lot of you to keep them actors and all on their toes. He had to have known that sooner or later Mr. Zimmerman would call in Joe to come get him. So to my way of thinking, he must have thought you were worth the trouble that's now coming his way."

Before Marianne could speak, Aislinn Zimmerman came running into the lobby. She was followed by an extremely tall, devastatingly handsome man. There was an air of refined elegance to the man, who wore an expensive tailor-made suit.

"Oh, Marianne!" Aislinn exclaimed. "Thank goodness they found you. We have been worried sick."

The man with her rubbed his brow as if Aislinn's dramatics were giving him a headache.

He held his hand out to Marianne. "Hi, Ms. Webernec. I'm Wulfgar Zimmerman, and I just wanted to tell you personally how sorry I am for your ordeal."

So this was the mysterious owner of Rose Books. He was devastating and rumored to be one of the richest men in the world. Marianne shook his hand. "There really is nothing to apologize for. I've had the time of my life."

Aislinn snorted. "Yes, but that was before that lunatic Kyle Foster ruined it."

"You're the one who put her here, Ais," Wulfgar said calmly.

Aislinn turned on her brother with a snarl. "Well, the next time the island is occupied by *them*, I wish you would put something down on paper."

He arched an elegant brow. "Forgive me, but I thought the word *occupied* on the schedule was self-explanatory."

"I thought you meant it was occupied by *our* people, not *theirs*. You're supposed to put *training* down when they're training here."

"Excuse me," Sam said, interrupting them. "But I take exception to that. Me and Roscoe are always here, and we definitely fall under the *them* category."

"You're you, Sam," Aislinn explained. "You don't count."

Sam looked extremely offended by that.

Wulfgar shook his head. "You'd better stop while you're behind, Ais. You're just getting in deeper at the moment."

Aislinn ignored the men and took Marianne's arm. "Don't worry, hon. I'll take care of this mess. We'll extend your stay another week and get back to your fantasy."

"It's okay, really," Marianne said. "I've had a great time with Kyle." She stared up at Wulfgar, hoping to make him understand. "Look, I don't want Kyle to get into trouble. Had he not shown up, I was ready to call you and ask for the fantasy to be canceled."

"Really?" Wulfgar asked.

She nodded.

He looked at his sister, who appeared horrified. "Well, how was I to know Brad was having an affair with Spencer?"

"I don't want to go into that again, Ais, but this is the last time I leave a fantasy package up to you."

"Fine," Aislinn snapped. "I don't want to do another one anyway. You get entirely too cranky when the guest goes AWOL. So I leave it up to you from now on. I'm through." Aislinn stalked out of the hotel and left Marianne alone with Wulfgar.

Wulfgar gave her a patient stare. "Tell me something, Marianne. What could possibly make this story turn out to be a happily-ever-after for you after everything that's happened?"

Marianne opened her mouth to say having Kyle as her own, but the minute the thought occurred to her, she realized something.

Mr. Zimmerman might be a billionaire magnate. But he couldn't give her the one thing she needed.

Only Kyle could do that.

And right now she had no idea if he even wanted to.

CHAPTER FIVE

*K*yle searched all the likely places Retter might have stashed Marianne.

He was out of options.

Disgusted and angry, he leaned back against a palm tree at the edge of the beach and raked his hands through his hair. If he closed his eyes, he could feel Marianne with him. Feel the touch of her hand on his skin. The warmth of her body under him.

He just wanted to see her one more time.

"C'mon, Kyle," he said to himself. "Think through this. You've never given up on anything in your life. You can do it."

Nothing had ever been more important to him.

He had to find her.

The best hiding place is always the most obvious. No one will ever think you're dumb enough to put something there. Kyle froze as Joe's words from training went through his mind.

Most obvious . . .

Surely Retter wouldn't have done that. He was never obvious. The bastard loved being complicated and vague.

But the more he thought about it, the more sure he was that Retter had chosen someplace easy. After all, Retter wouldn't think he'd think to look there.

Running as fast as he could, Kyle headed back to his hotel. Time seemed to slow down as he ran. He couldn't remember anything ever taking longer.

Please let me be right. . . .

If he was wrong, then he was totally screwed.

As soon as he reached his hotel, he went crashing through the door, only to find Sam sitting at his desk, watching TV.

There was no one else in the place.

No one.

Damn it to hell!

It had been a stupid thought.

His heart heavy, Kyle actually wanted to cry in frustration. What would he do now?

"Welcome back, Mr. Excitement," Sam said, looking up from the TV. "Heard you've had a high time with them weirdos from the other side of the island. I told you not to go over there, didn't I? Told you they'd do strange things to you." He paused as he adjusted his glasses and frowned. "You okay, boy? You don't look right."

Kyle couldn't speak. All he could do was struggle to breathe past the pain in his chest. One that had nothing to do with his mad sprint and everything to do with what he'd lost.

"Where's Marianne, Sam? Have you seen her?"

Please tell me she's here. . . .

Sam scratched his cheek. "Well, she was here a while ago, but that Mr. Zimmerman from the publisher came and took her away."

Kyle's heart leaped with hope. "Where did he take her?"

He shrugged. "Marianne said she wanted to finish out her fantasy. I'm not sure what that means."

She must be on the other side of the island again, which meant he could find her.

Sam opened up the small red Igloo cooler at his feet and pulled out a cold beer. "Here," he said, twisting the cap off. "You look like you could use a drink."

"No, thanks. I've got to find her."

Sam nodded as if he understood. "You know, I had a woman I loved once. Long time ago." He sighed dreamily. "Her name was Ethel Burrows. Oh, she was beautiful. Smart. Quick as a whip. She made me feel like I could fly."

Kyle frowned at his words, wondering why Sam was sharing this with him when Sam usually shared very few personal things. "What happened to her?"

A sad, faraway look covered Sam's face. "Me, mostly. I didn't ever tell her how I felt about her. I was about your age and working for the CIA all the time. I was afraid to take a wife. Afraid I'd get killed, or she might be in danger. Either way, I knew I wouldn't be home much to be with her. I didn't think it would be fair to her to be married and have to go off on missions while she stayed behind with my kids." He pierced Kyle with a dark, meaningful look. "I never stopped to think about what would happen if I *didn't* die."

"What do you mean?"

"Well, at the time I had fourteen more years of active service before they sent me to the desk or retired me. Fourteen years seemed like forever when I was twenty-eight. It didn't dawn on me that I'd be spending more years than that alone, wondering what would have happened to me if I'd just asked her to marry me." Sam reached over to scratch Roscoe's ears. "But that's okay. I've got Roscoe here to keep me company in my old age."

Kyle stared at the man and his dog, and in that instant he saw a very sobering future for himself. One he didn't want to even contemplate.

"Thanks, Sam."

Sam nodded at him and started drinking the beer he'd offered him. "Don't make my mistakes, Kyle. Go find your woman and tell her what she means to you."

Kyle tore out of the hotel and headed for the other side of the island.

He had a destiny waiting for him, and come hell or high water, he was going to find it.

AT LEAST THAT was what he thought. By five o'clock Kyle knew it was hopeless.

Marianne was nowhere on the island. Nowhere.

He'd searched every place he could think. Every corner, every cranny.

It was as if she'd vanished off the face of the earth. Of course, none of the busboys or actors from the other side would help him. Hell, they barely spoke to him after the trouble he'd given them while they had tried to find her and he'd scared them off.

It seemed they thought turnabout was fair play.

One of the little bastards had even laughed at him when he'd asked if the man had seen her.

That was okay. He'd stopped laughing the minute Kyle shot out his tires.

At four-thirty he'd finally found Aislinn Zimmerman in Marianne's hotel, debriefing the staff for their next guest, who would be arriving within the next few weeks. The redhead had promptly read him the riot act for screwing up the one and only fantasy her brother had entrusted her to run entirely on her own.

"You want Marianne?" she'd snapped at him. "Then find my brother. Last I checked, she was flying off on his private plane back to civilization."

Kyle had gone immediately to their airstrip, only to find out Wulfgar Zimmerman was long gone.

Which meant so was Marianne.

Damn it!

Defeated and tired, Kyle walked the long distance back to his side of the island. He didn't stop to say good-bye to Sam, though he should have. He just couldn't face the old man right now.

So he bypassed the hotel and went straight to the private airstrip they used, which wasn't all that far from where he'd been hiding with Marianne. His throat tightened at the thought.

Retter was standing by the small luxury jet, waiting for him.

"You're right on time."

"Stay away from me, Retter. In the mood I'm in, I just might kill you."

"No luck, huh?"

"Shut up."

Retter stepped aside so that Kyle could reach the stairs to the plane.

Kyle snarled at him as he paused by his side. "I really hate you for this. Couldn't you have given me twenty-four hours before you came crashing in?"

"Would that have been enough?"

No, it wouldn't have. It wouldn't have made any of this a bit easier to swallow. Shoving Retter aside, Kyle ascended the stairs and bent his head down to enter the plane.

Retter was only a few steps behind him.

He saw Reno in the cockpit, wearing the pilot's headgear, waiting for them.

"So what did you do with her?" he asked as he took a seat up front, not far away from Reno.

Retter shrugged as he sat down in the row across from him. "Talked to her for a while. I found her fascinating."

Kyle saw red at his words. "Don't talk about her like that. She's too good for you."

"She's too good for *you*," Retter shot back.

Kyle didn't say anything. It was true.

It still didn't lessen the pain he felt.

Reno started making their flight plan.

In that moment Kyle knew what he needed to do.

He stood up again. "Reno," he said as he neared the cockpit. "I want you to fly us to Peoria."

Reno's jaw went slack. "Excuse me?"

"You heard me."

"I can't do that, *mi hermano*. Joe wants you home."

"Fuck Joe and what he wants."

"Whoa," Retter said, moving to stand behind him. "I think you need to take a more civil tone, bud. Have you any idea how much your little 'date' has cost us already? There are countries with a smaller GNP than the tab you've spent on Marianne. Now you want us to fly your ass to Peoria?"

"Fine," Kyle said angrily. "I'll just book the flight when we land in Nashville and head out then."

Retter shook his head. "Are you insane? Joe will fire you for this."

"Then let him."

Retter's face hardened. "Think about this for a minute, Kyle. You'll lose everything. Is she worth it?"

He didn't even have to hesitate. "She's worth everything in the world to me."

To his surprise, Retter stepped back and smiled.

Three seconds later the rear emergency door was ripped off the airplane and a smoking canister was thrown into the aisle.

Before Kyle could reach for his weapon, a small commando dressed all in black tripped through the doorway, carrying an M-16.

She paused at the opening and stared agape at the plane. "Wow, this is really nice."

Kyle smiled the instant he recognized that less-than-fierce voice. Not to mention he'd know that body anywhere, even when it was decked out in ill-fitting fatigues and her face was covered in black paint.

It was Marianne.

And she was joined by another commando he recognized as Dieter, also dressed in full commando gear. "Terrorists," Dieter whispered to her loudly, "hostage, remember?"

"Oh, yeah," she said, gripping her weapon and looking fierce, or at least as fierce as a high school teacher could look. "Don't anyone . . ." She started coughing from the smoke as she moved through it.

Dieter pounded her lightly on the back and nudged her out of it. "It's okay. Breathe deeply."

Marianne coughed a few more times and nodded. "Don't . . ." She coughed more.

"She says don't move," Dieter finished for her.

She started toward Kyle, only to be stopped the instant her gun got wedged between the two seats on opposite ends of the row. She *whoofed* as it caught against her middle.

"That thing's not loaded, is it?" Kyle asked Retter.

"Hell, no. I told you I spent the day with her. Last thing I want is to be shot dead by friendly fire."

Dieter helped her get unhooked.

Retter held his hands up.

"You!" Marianne said, waving Retter aside with her gun. "Stay out of my way or I'll blow your head off."

"Yes, ma'am." Retter moved toward Reno.

Marianne took another step forward with her gun a little higher this time. "I'm Ren Winterbourne, Secret Agent, and . . . um . . . um . . . um . . ." She paused, thinking. "Wait a second . . . I'm Ren Winterbourne, Secret Agent, and . . ."

"And I'm here for the hostage!" Reno shouted out.

Kyle turned to see Reno in the cockpit with a copy of the book for Marianne's fantasy.

Marianne took a step toward him, but Dieter caught her and showed her how to walk down the aisle without catching the gun on the seats.

"Move, you scum," Reno prompted again.

Kyle stared at Marianne as she came even with him. He couldn't take his eyes off her.

"Hey," Reno said, raising his voice. "Move, you scum. This is the part where you make the terrorists get down on the ground and tie them up."

"Bullshit," Retter said. "This is the part where she shoots the pilot."

"Nein," Dieter joined in, moving past them toward the other two. He pulled a copy of the book out of his back pocket and opened it up to a bookmarked page. "She makes you get down, Retter, and eat the floor. It says so right here. You must get down."

"Yeah and this is the part where you get sent back to Pakistan, Adolph. I'm not kissing dirt for nobody."

"I am not Adolph, I am Dieter."

Kyle was only vaguely aware of the others arguing about the book. His attention was solely on the woman before him.

"Were you really going to fly to Peoria?" she asked him.

"Well, yeah. I thought that's where you were. Aislinn told me you were on Wulfgar's plane."

She smiled. "I am, kind of. We both are."

Kyle glanced around the luxurious jet. He hadn't noticed just how nice it was earlier. It should have dawned on him the minute he entered it.

But then Marianne always had a way of distracting him.

"You know," she said quietly, "I always wanted to be the heroine in the book."

"Funny, I only want the woman who is reading the book."

She smiled up at him and his groin jerked.

"So how does the story end?" he asked her.

"You kiss her, sheez!" the guys said in unison.

"Didn't he read the book?" Dieter asked. "It says right here—"

"Shut up, Dieter," Retter snapped. "I think we should leave them alone."

Laughing, Marianne stepped into his arms and held him tight. "It ends like all good romances do. We live happily ever after."

LET'S TALK
ABOUT SEX

Liz Carlyle

CHAPTER ONE

"Hi, this is *Let's Talk About Sex!*" The polished, professional voice oozed out over the airwaves. "Our next caller is Brian from Murfreesboro, Tennessee. Brian, you're on the air with Dr. Delia Sydney."

Inside the glass-walled sound booth, Delia listened through her headphones to Brian's loud, ragged breathing. "Um, yeah," he finally said, huffing the words into his telephone. "Um, is this Dr. Delia?"

"Good afternoon, Brian," said Delia smoothly. "You're our next caller. Did you have a question or a comment?"

"Uh, well, yeah." Brian from Murfreesboro was definitely struggling. "I, like, had this question. I w-wanted to ask, um, about guys. When they, you know, are j-jerking—"

"Ah, I see," Delia gently interjected. "A question about masturbation?"

"Yeah, that." Brian exhaled too loudly into his telephone again. "Well, uh, anyways, my, um, my uncle told me something one time. About—er, about it. He said if you did it, you know, a lot, that it could make you go, like, blind or something."

"Well, that's a common old wives' tale," said Delia, speaking calmly into her microphone. "But there's no truth to it, Brian. I expect your uncle was just teasing."

"Um . . . Dr. Delia, are you sure?"

Delia paused for a split second. "Is masturbation a problem for you, Brian?" she asked coolly. "What I mean is, do you feel guilty about doing it? Because you shouldn't, you know. It is a perfectly natural thing for a healthy young man to do in private. And it isn't anyone else's business."

"Oh, no, *I* don't do it," said Brian, his voice leaping an octave. "I was, like, you know, just wondering if my uncle was lying. That's all."

"I see." Delia's patience slipped a notch. "Brian, has your uncle gone blind?"

"Um . . . nope."

"Then he's lying."

"Oh."

Through the glass wall, she watched Frank grin and jerk a finger across his throat. Time to wrap. Delia pushed her chair back and signaled her sound engineer to disconnect Brian. "And that's all the time we have today for *Let's Talk About Sex,*" she purred into her microphone. "This is Dr. Delia Sydney inviting you to join us on Friday, when my special guest will be sex therapist Dr. Jeffrey Bozner, discussing his newest book, *Healthy Sex, Healthy Marriage.* Thanks for tuning in."

Through the glass Delia watched her engineer punch a button and toss his headphones. The theme song for *All Things Considered* trumpeted in her ear. Delia yanked off her headset and shook the kinks out of her hair just as Frank came around the glass partition, making an obscene jerk-off gesture. "Jeez, what a bunch of losers!" His cultivated announcer's voice had vanished. "Where're those sexually frustrated housewives when I need a little thrill, Doc?"

"Frank, you're pathetic." Delia stood and shoved her chair under the desk. "Where's Becky Jo?"

Just then, Delia's assistant came streaking into the sound booth, her wild red hair flying out behind her. "Jeff Bozner's secretary just canceled," said Becky Jo breathlessly. "He's on his way to the hospital. Looks like those triplets are going to put in an early appearance."

"Dang," said Delia.

"And Dr. Despiza called this morning. The department chair says one of you has to take on another Deviance and Development class for spring semester." Becky Jo paused to laugh. "He says he tossed a coin, and you lost."

Delia resorted to cussing. "Well, shit."

"Yeah, well, keep shitting, honey, 'cause it gets worse."

Delia groaned. "Like how?"

Becky Jo snapped her gum. "Perkins just arrived from New York to see you. It's about your contract, and Delia darlin', he's got that tight, poker-assed look on his face again."

Frank shoved his face between them. "Aw, my heart

bleeds for you, Doc," he said, far too cheerfully. "Well, gotta jet, girls. I'm late for a scorching hot lunch date."

"Where?" shot Becky Jo. "Down at the Fuzzy Beaver Club?"

"Yeah, you're a laugh a minute, Becky Jo," said Frank, slipping out the door.

"But what about my syndication?" wailed Delia, oblivious. "We're in eight of the top markets now. My God, today we had a caller from Kalamazoo!"

Becky Jo pursed her lips. "Perkins doesn't give a rat's ass, Delia, I'm telling you. You won't get another nickel out of that cheapskate until your listener numbers firm up—and then only if you pitch a fit."

"But how much longer will that take?"

"You'll have to ask Perkins." Becky Jo laid a cool hand on her shoulder. "Sorry, hon."

Shit. Shit. Shit. Delia closed her eyes and watched her new S80 sedan disappear into the dreamland whence it had come. Black. It was going to have been black. With a turbocharged engine, dynamic stability control, and seventeen-inch aluminum alloy wheels. A symbol of her thrilling new non-station-wagon lifestyle.

Oh, hell, who was she kidding? Her new lifestyle was a fantasy. She barely had time for what was left of her old one. But she needed a new car badly. In the last three months she'd been stranded on the I-40 median about a dozen times, and her old station wagon was belching smoke like a Blackhawk with its tail shot off.

Somehow the image of war steeled her. For once in her life, Delia wasn't giving up without a fight. Today she would fire her first salvo in what was doubtless destined to be a long and tiresome battle. But Perkins was up against a desperate woman.

"Becky Jo," she said, jerking up her briefcase and heading for the door. "I am woman, hear me roar. And this woman has *got* to have a new car."

Fleetingly, Becky Jo hesitated. "Well, alrighty, then!" she finally said. "You go, girl."

OF COURSE, her meeting with the weasely Perkins was less than satisfactory. The show was too new, he'd whined. They were still building listeners and assessing programming options. More money was out of the question just now. Perhaps they'd talk further in a couple of months?

Under her breath Delia said *screw it,* and left early. So it was not quite five in the afternoon when she coaxed her antique Volvo station wagon down Westwind Drive, the street that skirted the edge of exclusive Hidden Lakes Estates. Through the canopy of trees blazing red and gold, the Carolina sun dappled and shifted across her dashboard. In Durham the weather was still glorious, though the calendar said October. At the security gate she turned right, waved to the uniformed guard, and eased forward to let the scanner read the bar code on her back window. The gate buzzed up, the guard saluted, and Delia rolled through.

The first half-mile of Greenway Circle snaked between a row of five-bedroom architectural monstrosities and the subdivision's golf course. Delia shoved the wagon into second and chugged along at the mandatory fifteen miles per hour. Here in exclusive Hidden Lakes, it was considered a gross act of ill breeding to speed near the greens, thereby endangering the lives of the club's well-heeled, well-insured members. A humiliating letter from the Hidden Lakes Homeowners' Association was reportedly the penalty, but Delia had always harbored the sneaking suspicion that the association probably just burnt a cross made of old three-woods on your lawn.

Near the twelfth hole a trio of thin blondes lingered around a sand trap, their cute, clubby clothes simply screaming Talbot's. At the sound of Delia's old car rumbling past, the trio turned and gave her one of those long, old-Carolina-money looks, as if doubting she belonged. Or was she just imagining it? The women had already turned back to their sand trap.

But she didn't belong, did she? Fate, in the maddening form of her ex-husband Neville, had dropped her into the middle of Hidden Lakes, then abandoned her, leaving her to feel like an alien whose spaceship had crashed into some foreign landscape. Delia lifted her chin and drove on, swearing for about the twelfth time that *next* month she would put the damned house up for sale. She *would* get the carpets cleaned, the windows washed, the closets emptied; all those chores she hadn't been able to find time for this past year were now essential to make the house look pristine and virginal for its next happy mortgage holder. And oh, what a mortgage it was. Neville might have been a brilliant plastic surgeon, but he'd apparently flunked Math 101.

At the foot of her steep driveway, Delia noticed a

Southern Power and Light truck parked a few yards up the street. Ignoring it, she jerked open the mailbox, fished out another pile of bills, and tried not to cry. Then she shoved the gearshift into first, tapped the gas, and prayed the station wagon wouldn't stall out. It didn't. She nosed gently over the hill, hit the garage remote, and . . . nothing. Delia cranked down her window, leaned out to listen, and punched it again. Nothing. Well, just an awful, impotent grinding noise. Damn. First the car, now the garage?

Delia jerked the remote off her visor and started to hurl it into the rhododendron. Just then, deep in the backyard, something caught her eye. A big, bright orange Husqvarna chain saw. Her elderly neighbor, Bud Basham, stood on the rock outcropping above her flower beds, brandishing the thing like a lunatic. Two SP&L utility workers, one male, one female, stood in Delia's backyard, their hands on their hips, shouting up at Bud.

The first worker held a ten-foot pole pruner, the second a clipboard. Behind them stood a broad-shouldered man in a blue blazer, his feet spread wide, his expression of exasperation plain even fifty yards away. He was waving his hands and telling them to calm down and shut the hell up. Bud, who'd never been the passive type, responded by raising his arms high above his head and revving the chain saw for all she was worth. The Husqvarna roared and popped like a nest of angry hornets.

Curious, Delia cut the ignition. Unfortunately, the old Volvo chose that moment to backfire. The explosion ricocheted off the garage door like a shotgun blast, and all hell erupted. The woman from SP&L screamed and hit the deck. As if acting on instinct, Mr. Blue Blazer hurled his body protectively over hers. Bud dropped the chain saw, sending it clattering and sputtering down the rocks. The second utility worker chucked his pruner and bolted for cover. Then realization hit, and everyone froze, as if some sitcom director had just yelled "Cut!"

Wincing, Delia shoved open her car door with a rusty creak and crawled halfway out. By the time she opened her eyes, Mr. Blue Blazer was already up and helping the utility worker to her feet. "Sorry!" shouted Delia into the backyard. "Bad timing."

The running utility worker stopped short, his face flushed with embarrassment. Delia slammed the car door and strode past him. Then she saw it. Her lush row of pine trees was now little more than a line of stumps. Heaps of green foliage lay along the back edge of her property, and the tang of evergreen was sharp in her nostrils. Horrified, Delia just kept walking, right past the indignant Mr. Blue Blazer, all the way to the property line.

Delia pressed her hand to her chest. "My trees!" she cried. "Good Lord, what happened to my trees?"

"I tried to tell 'em, Delia!" crowed Bud Basham, the wattle at his neck quivering with indignation as he clambered down after his saw. "Told 'em you'd be mad as hell! And I told 'em they weren't coming up here! I saw that young whippersnapper there take his pruner to my junipers—and by gum, I put a stop to it!"

The female utility worker stepped forward. "Your trees were in the subdivision's greenspace, ma'am," she said, still dusting grass off her uniform. "SP&L has a right-of-way through there, and we're clearing trees back off the power lines. We have to, ma'am. It's a new company policy."

Delia turned and looked at her incredulously. "Clearing back?" she cried. "But they . . . they've been *murdered!*"

The woman shrugged, but her expression was not unsympathetic. "They've decided it's cheaper to cut them down, ma'am, than to trim them back every year," she said gently. "Folks threw such fits after losing power during the ice storm last year, SP&L has no choice. It's the new policy, just started this week."

Delia had been lecturing on the West Coast during last winter's ice storm, but she still recalled hearing of the horror her neighbors had suffered. Heavy trees had torn down utility lines across the state, and in Durham, many had gone a week without electricity or heat. Candles, propane, and bottled water vanished from store shelves. SP&L had been overwhelmed. People had been outraged.

"I see," murmured Delia, looking at Mr. Blue Blazer, whose expression had gone from exasperated to truly pissed. Boldly she thrust out her hand. "I don't think I've had the pleasure," she said sweetly. "Delia Sydney. Sorry about the car. I think it needs a tune-up."

"Yeah, or euthanasia," he suggested in a slow, Deep South drawl. Lazily he lifted one hand to push a shock of dark hair off his face. It was then that Delia noticed the gun, a big chunk of lethal-looking black steel, poking out of a shoulder holster beneath his coat.

"You planning to shoot it and put me out of my misery?" she asked, lifting one brow. "Or do you carry that just for looks?"

His hard mouth softened, and he took her still-extended hand. "Nick Woodruff," he growled. "Sergeant Nick Woodruff. I live behind you." He jerked his head toward the butchered evergreens. "On Westwind."

Westwind Drive was a pretty street that led past Hidden Lakes' grand entrance, but definitely wasn't part of it. For the first time, Delia actually *looked* at the property that backed onto hers. Nick Woodruff lived in a rambling, rustic house on a huge lot randomly dotted with oak, pine, and mounds of azaleas rather than the perfectly placed, artificially irrigated landscaping of Hidden Lakes.

Now that the thick foliage was gone, Delia could make out the long, narrow lap pool that edged Woodruff's back porch, and the hot tub that sat adjacent. Closer to her property line stood some sort of workshop, part of it open on two sides, where Woodruff appeared to be in the process of gutting a small red sports car. A mountain of firewood sat nearby—the real stuff, too, not those prissy little plastic-wrapped packages from Kroger.

"Look, Mr. Basham," drawled Woodruff, nudging Delia back into the present. "Eventually you're going to have to let these utility people do their job."

Bud was now cradling the battered orange chain saw

as if it were his favorite grandchild. "Not today, Nick," he said in an unrepentant tone.

Woodruff shrugged, as if his big black gun were chafing him. "Well, it's almost quitting time," he said with authority. "You folks go on back to SP&L, and tell 'em somebody's gotta explain this policy. I'm real sorry for what happened today, but they can't just go sending you folks out with no word or warning."

The utility workers shrugged, hefted up a couple of serious-looking power tools, and headed for their truck. The excitement over, Bud Basham trudged back up the hill with his chain saw. Delia shrugged, too. To hell with the dead pines. Like the house itself, the trees had been Neville's idea. He'd demanded the real estate developer install them, to shield them from the "riffraff" he'd been sure resided on Westwind Drive. Now the sight of Neville's evergreens hacked down to oozing little nubs was giving Delia a perverse sort of pleasure.

Beside her, Nick Woodruff cleared his throat, and suddenly Delia realized she was alone with the riffraff in question, a big, surly-looking neighbor whom she'd never bothered to meet. "So, *Dr. Delia*," he drawled. "At last we meet."

So he knew who she was. Delia felt a stab of irritation. People always seized on her radio persona, when in reality, she also worked as an assistant professor of psychology, collaborated on research projects at half the Ivy League, and had co-authored two textbooks. But then, Woodruff didn't look like the academic type.

"Hey, I want to thank you for calming Bud down,"

she said, trying to sound gracious. "He has a bad temper but a good heart."

Woodruff snorted. "He's a crazy old coot, is what he is," he answered. "But I keep an eye out for him."

Delia tried to smile. "Did you begin as an innocent bystander?"

Woodruff nodded. "Just coming home from the office. I could hear Basham bellowing from my mailbox."

"So you're a cop, huh?"

Woodruff seemed to scowl. "SBI. In Raleigh."

State Bureau of Investigation. "Oh," said Delia. "I've done some work for them."

Woodruff's brows went up at that. "Yeah?"

Delia smiled tightly. "A serial rapist case down in Charlotte last year," she said. "They needed some of my research on the behavior of sexual predators in court. And I got my face plastered all over cable TV in the process. It was pretty awful."

Woodruff grunted. "Not much of a topic for a radio talk show, either."

Delia looked up at him. Way up, as it happened, since Woodruff probably stood six-two in his big, bare feet. "No, it certainly isn't."

He looked over his shoulder at his house as if impatient to be gone. "Well, looks like my work here is done, Dr. Delia," he said, backing away. "Sorry I couldn't save your fancy landscaping. I know you folks in Hidden Lakes like your privacy."

Delia caught the hint of sarcasm in his tone, and it inflamed her. "Not a problem," she said sweetly. "I'm moving. But I hope *you* like your new neighbors, Mr. Woodruff, because they'll have one hell of a view of your hot tub."

She watched Woodruff's eyes flash and his jaw clench. Then Delia tossed him a cheerful wave and turned toward her house.

FOR DELIA, Friday's edition of *Let's Talk About Sex* turned out to be a hellish nightmare. At least ten calls came in for the absent Dr. Bozner, whose book had just hit the *New York Times* best-seller list, and who would have been a hot property had he actually shown up. The remaining callers turned out to be cranks, creeps, and perverts. Delia liked her new radio show, she really did. And she thought she could make a difference in people's lives by bringing topics like sexually transmitted disease and healthy physical relationships out of the closet and onto the airwaves. But sometimes Frank did a piss-poor job of weeding out the weirdos before sending the calls through.

After work Delia drove down to the bank to transfer money from her fast-dwindling savings account. She'd added up her growing pile of bills after waving good-bye to the cheerful Mr. Woodruff on Wednesday and realized that, as usual, there was just too much month left at the end of her money. Once parked, Delia shoved in the clutch and stared at the glistening plate-glass door. She hated having to visit the bank again. Hated being twenty-nine years old and still burdened with a staggering student loan, not to mention a big, ugly house she'd never really wanted. Just then, as if to lengthen her list of woes, the Volvo shuddered, belched, and died.

Delia let her head fall forward onto the steering wheel. *Well, it's your own fault!* she could hear her mother carping. *You were a fool to sign that prenuptial agreement. A man should support his wife, Delia, not impoverish her.*

Oh, her parents had been thrilled when she'd married a doctor. Now they thought she was proud, stubborn, and foolish. But Delia had wanted a marriage, not a meal ticket. She had wanted children, a real family, and she had wanted to build her own career. And although Neville had changed his mind about the children, she'd succeeded with her career. Her income was barely a third of her ex-husband's, but it was enough to live well on.

Soon the house would be sold, and they would split the equity. Then Delia's dreams of a new car and a new condo would come true. On that somewhat consoling thought, Delia got out of her car, but at that very instant the bank's shiny glass door swung open, and Neville's new wife walked out, her long blond hair swinging.

Alicia was tall, tan, and totally oblivious to Delia's presence. Lifting her face to the sun, Alicia slid on a pair of cat-eyed Oakley sunglasses which had probably cost more than Delia's car was worth, then beeped open the door to an olive-green Jaguar XK8 convertible. The car roared to life, then swung deftly into the traffic flow, leaving Delia behind, a little heartbroken.

Yes, there was a lot about Alicia to envy. And this

time it was more than just her hair and her car. Delia had been unable to miss the flowing, baby-blue tunic the new Mrs. Sydney had been wearing over her slim spandex slacks. No mistaking the slight swell of her tummy. And this time it wasn't the sort of plumpness old Neville could liposuction off. Well! So much for Neville's old complaint about pregnancy ruining a woman's figure. No wonder he'd rushed to the altar.

Oh, to hell with Neville *and* her banking. Everything would just have to wait until Monday. Weary and discouraged, Delia crawled back in the Volvo, said a prayer, and cranked the engine. It gagged and sputtered, but she made it out of the parking lot. In fact, she made it all the way across town, all the way out I-40, and almost—*almost*—all the way down Westwind. And then, only a quarter-mile shy of the Hidden Lakes entrance, it began wheezing again. Delia let off the gas, wondering if she could coast to the security gate.

Nope. The Volvo went into death throes and spasmed its way only as far as a long, tree-lined driveway on her right, then promptly died. Delia was still trying desperately to start the car when a black Silverado pickup came flying down the drive backward. It was definitely one of life's *Oh, shit* moments. Frantic, she turned the key again as the Silverado's backup lights got bigger and bigger and bigger. *Jesus Christ, isn't he even going to look?*

Then, at the very last instant, the truck's brakes locked up, and the black beast skidded to a halt in a cloud of dust and dead leaves. Embarrassed, Delia got out of the station wagon just as a big, broad-shouldered

man in a pair of baggy Adidas shorts climbed out of the
Silverado. He stood in the dust cloud, his hands lifted
expressively in one of those *What the fuck?* gestures.
Delia's embarrassment quickly shifted to total humilia-
tion when the dust cleared.

Nick Woodruff?

Feeling a little sick, she shifted her gaze past the Silverado. Yep, there it was, her big ugly house, just visible
through Woodruff's tree-filled yard. Funny how she'd
never bothered to look before. And man, oh, man, was
she ever going to pay for that bitchy parting shot two
days ago. His expression made that abundantly clear.

Woodruff stood in front of the Volvo now, hands on
his hips. "Well, Dr. Delia," he snapped, "we meet again."

Delia bit her lip. "I'm sorry," she said. "It just sort of
died here."

Nick made a sweeping gesture at the road. "Well,
kick it out of gear and drift it out of my driveway,
honey," he growled. "Because I'm late for pickup basketball, and believe me, I need the exercise bad."

Delia opened her mouth to tell the big ox to go
screw himself, but nothing came out. Instead, she felt
herself start to crumple inside. What else could possibly
go wrong with her day?

Nick Woodruff wanted to bite back his spiteful
words almost as soon as they left his mouth. Almost,
because it took him a couple of seconds to realize that
those really were tears pooling in Delia Sydney's silvery
blue eyes. Suddenly Nick was halfway glad his mama
was dead. Because if she'd been living, she'd have laid a
hickory switch to his butt, and no maybe about it.

However rich and snooty Delia Sydney might be, she was a lady in distress. And she was also wearing very wicked shoes.

"Hey, look, Doc, I'm sorry," he said, slipping his fingers into the crack beneath the Volvo's hood. "I've had a couple of real bad days at work, and my fuse is short. I'm not usually such a jerk."

"Well, jeez, I'm sorry I broke down!" Her face pale, Delia Sydney circled around the car. "Wh-what are you doing?"

Nick found the latch, popped it, and shoved the hood up. "Let me have a look," he said. "I reckon I can miss a ball game."

"Oh, heaven forbid!" she said stiffly. "Just give me a push, and I'll call the auto club from my cell phone."

In response he shoved his hands in his pockets and rocked back on his heels. "Hey, Doc, it's okay," he said quietly. "I'm a shade-tree mechanic. So what's up with it? Need a tune-up?"

At that, her anger seemed to melt, and she poked absently at a little rock with the sharply pointed toe of her black high heel. "Well, what I *need* is a new car," she said, sighing. "But that's not going to happen until I can get the house sold. So, yes, I need a tune-up. Probably a complete overhaul. I never know whether to believe what the mechanics tell me."

Nick let his eyes run over the filthy engine. "You really selling out?"

Delia exhaled. "I've been meaning to, yes," she admitted. "But the last few months have been hell. I teach and travel a lot. So it seemed easier to just write the mortgage check and hang in, but the truth is, I hate that house. And I can't afford it, either."

Nick tried not to look skeptical. "You're Neville Sydney's wife, right?"

"*Ex*-wife," she answered, a little too quickly.

Nick narrowed his eyes and stared into the afternoon sun. He was trying not to feel sorry for Delia Sydney. But he did, and he couldn't help it. Her guard was down, and despite her snug black suit and perfectly coiffed hair, she was starting to look young and vulnerable. Worse, he was starting to get the uncomfortable feeling that she was neither rich nor uppity. In fact, she seemed real nice. And awfully pretty. Then there were those shoes, shoes that made a man think of kinky, erotically painful things.

Jesus. Nick rolled his shoulders, trying to relax. Trying to stop looking at her shoes. But his shame was deepening over his mean-spirited words. It sure wasn't Delia Sydney's fault that his day had been total shit. The least he could do was help her out of a jam.

"So," he finally said. "Let's see if we can coax this rattletrap 'round back of my house, Dr. Delia. I just started a two-week vacation, so I can tune up your car."

Delia was dumbstruck. "But you . . . you don't know me. Your family—you must have plans?"

Woodruff's eyes raked over her. "No, I don't know you," he admitted in a voice that was just a note lower, but a good deal warmer. "And I don't have any family. Not here, anyway. And my vacation, well, let's just say it was unexpected."

Delia didn't know what to think. The cost of an

engine overhaul would probably be three times what the car was worth—if it was even needed. But this man, this very large, very virile-looking stranger, was offering to work on it as a favor? She looked at him suspiciously. "Now, why would you want to spend part of your vacation working on my car, Mr. Woodruff?"

Finally he laughed, a rich, sexy laugh that came from somewhere deep in his chest. "Because idle hands do the devil's work, Dr. Delia," he said, holding his palms out as if for inspection. "That's what my Granny Woodruff says."

The devil's work. The words were vaguely fascinating, the hands more so. Woodruff's palms were broad, the fingers long and blunt. One thumb had a bruised nail, and on his left index finger, a scar ran from the first knuckle into the callused heel, the suture marks painfully visible. They were a worker's hands. A warrior's hands.

Jesus, she was getting fanciful. Still, there was no denying Woodruff was a fine example of manhood, if you preferred your men . . . well, a bit primitive. Delia swallowed hard, tore her gaze from his hands, and focused—rather imprudently—in the general direction of his hot tub. What do you suppose a man like that looked like with his clothes off?

"So, Dr. Delia, what do you say?" asked Woodruff, his voice suggestively low. "Wanna let me poke around under your hood?"

Delia felt herself turn pink right down to her toes.

Woodruff made a little choking sound in the back of his throat. "Jeez, Doc, you're blushing," he muttered. "Give me a break."

"I'm not blushing," Delia lied. "I'm—it's—hot out here. And frankly, Mr. Woodruff, I've had kind of a crappy week. Look at my pine trees. They're shaved down to bloody nubs. On top of that, my boss is a jerk and my car won't run. I barely avoided a bad remake of *The Texas Chainsaw Massacre*. My ex-husband's new wife almost ran me down in her brand-new Jaguar. And—oh, let's not forget this—half the perverts on the East Coast called me up to chat this afternoon."

Woodruff flashed a sudden, sexy grin. "Oh, yeah, that Doris Jean from St. Augustine was one scary chick," he remarked, shaking his head. "Where do people get that kind of bondage gear, anyway? Sadomasochists-R-Us?"

Delia's blush deepened and she swiftly dropped her gaze. "You . . . you're . . . *a fan?*"

Nick Woodruff was casually tossing his car keys now. "Oh, yeah, Dr. Delia," he answered smoothly. "A big one. A real big one."

It was only then that Delia realized just where her gaze had landed. She was staring straight at Nick Woodruff's crotch.

CHAPTER TWO

Delia rolled out of bed Saturday morning at seven sharp and shrugged into her favorite sweatshirt. Downstairs, she punched the silver button on Neville's four-hundred-dollar German coffeemaker and listened to it chew up a precise measure of mocha-Kona blend. The machine dumped the grounds into its filter, the water began to hiss, and Delia headed down the hill for her newspaper. As she popped back over the rise of her driveway, she could see her station wagon, its big rear end poking out of Nick Woodruff's shed, the hood already up. Looked like Woodruff was an early riser.

After pouring her first cup of coffee, Delia hitched a stool up to the kitchen island and flipped open the *Herald-Sun*. Bush's numbers were down, the market was up, there'd been another shooting on Alston Avenue, and Senator Elizabeth Dole had a new hairdo. *Well, thank God, Liddy,* Delia almost said aloud. *The eighties are finally over.*

But instead of carrying on a full-blown conversation with herself, as she'd been known to do, Delia kept reading. At the bottom of the front page a headline screamed the story of a major drug bust in the I-95 corridor just east of Raleigh. Delia skimmed the topic sentences. A Florida man had been killed, another badly wounded. Three million dollars' worth of uncut, New York-bound cocaine had been seized and two SBI officers placed on administrative leave pending a deadly-force review.

And then the name *Woodruff* leapt off the page, causing Delia to choke on her mocha-Kona blend.

My vacation, he had casually remarked, *was unexpected.*

Wow. It certainly had been. And Delia thought *her* Friday had sucked.

Still shaking her head, Delia finished her coffee, poured the rest of the pot into two thermal travel mugs, then dashed upstairs to dress.

NICK WOODRUFF WATCHED his pretty little neighbor flounce out of her kitchen door, and tried to keep his mouth from going dry. Dreams of Dr. Delia—*strange* dreams—had kept him awake last night. He'd been better off, he realized, when he'd thought she was snooty and rich. This morning she'd exchanged her snug black suit and pointy-toed high heels for some sort of floaty brown skirt that swirled above her ankles in the unseasonable heat. And they were just the kind of ankles you'd expect a rich, sultry-voiced psychologist to have, too. Very, very fine ones.

But on the whole, Dr. Delia Sydney was definitely *not* what he'd expected. Over the airwaves her voice really was a little sultry, but a whole lot suave, too. And right now *Let's Talk About Sex* was the hottest new show on talk radio. With her million-word vocabulary, she dispensed advice in blunt, no-nonsense terms which made that bald-headed drill sergeant Dr. Phil look like a big ole wuss. And no matter how kinky the question, Dr. Delia never, ever lost her cool.

But out of her dark suit, Nick's next-door neighbor was just a slip of a girl, with a wild mane of black curls and a sprinkle of freckles across her nose. Hell, she didn't look old enough to vote. No, worse—she looked like jailbait. And good Lord above, thought Nick, watching as she crossed from her yard into his, Dr. Delia Sydney was just about the prettiest thing he'd seen since crazy old Bud Basham's cat had a litter of kittens in the driver's seat of his Triumph.

Just then, Tiger Lily herself came slinking through the spindles of the porch railing that edged the open end of his shed, her orange fur glistening in the morning sun. Nick bent down to scratch her rump as she twined around his left ankle. But he kept one eye on Dr. Delia.

"Hi," she said, stepping hesitantly around the railing and into the shed. "I thought you might like a cup of coffee. It's black—is that okay?"

"I love black," he said, looking at her hair and searching for something clever to say. "Thanks."

"Oh," she said, noticing the cat. "There's Tiger Lily!"

"Yeah, I have visitation rights," he said, giving the

cat another scratch. "Basham and I fished her out of that culvert across the road. I guess I kinda let him have her."

Sudden knowledge lit Delia's eyes, and Nick noticed yet again how pale and arctic blue they were. "Oh, my God, was that you?" she said, nodding toward the disassembled Triumph. "Is that the car? The one Bud calls the Cat Mobile?"

Nick grinned. "Yeah, but cats are real neat," he said. "There wasn't much to clean up."

Tiger Lily leapt onto the workbench that ran across the back of the shed, curled up on an old newspaper, and began to lick one of her front paws. Nick sipped the coffee again, then plucked a socket wrench from one of the drawers of a tall red tool cabinet. "So," he said, turning around and giving the wrench a neat little spin. "Sleep well? Or did the thought of my performing surgery on your car give you nightmares?"

Delia sat down on a rickety chair by the railing and rolled her eyes. "God, no, going to the garage gives me nightmares. I think my service manager is the Antichrist."

Nick spun the wrench again, and decided to go for it. "Can I ask you something?" he said. "Something personal? I mean, I've looked under your hood and all, so I guess we're already kind of intimate, right?"

She turned faintly pink—for about the fourth time in their very short acquaintance. "Yes, sure," she said. "Ask."

"How old are you, Dr. Delia?"

Delia pursed her lips. "Older than I look."

Nick laid the wrench down and leaned back against the door of the Triumph. "You know, I don't think so."

Delia sighed. "Thirty-one, going on fifty," she said.

"Yeah, that's what I thought," he said, studying her. "How in the hell did you get through school and . . . and accomplish so much?" Nick made an expansive gesture with one hand.

She actually clasped her hands between her knees, a little-girl-lost gesture if ever he'd seen one, and cops *knew* body language. "I was kind of a child prodigy," she said softly.

"A what?" Shit, he'd been afraid of that.

"You know, one of those smart kids—kids so smart they're weird, right?—so they pushed me out of high school and into college when I was, oh, about fifteen."

"Uh-huh," said Nick. "And you finished college at, what, seventeen? Grad school at nineteen?"

"Something like that."

While he tried to think of something else to say— something besides *God, I'd love to see how your knees would look hooked over my shoulders,* which was the first thing that came to mind—Nick loosened the distributor cap on the Volvo. Then methodically he began to extract the spark plugs, only four of which were working. Number five looked like a chestnut roasted by an open fire. Jesus H. Christ, Dr. Delia was either the world's worst skinflint, or she was poor as a church mouse, and Nick was now betting on the latter.

"Is it bad?" came a small voice from the chair.

Nick bent over and rested his head on the radiator cap. "Sugar, I don't even have the heart to tell you how bad," he said. "Let me put it off a bit, okay?"

"Sure." Dr. Delia started to fiddle with her hair. "So, how old are you?" she suddenly blurted.

Nick straightened up and tossed the last bad plug in his trash barrel. "Thirty-six going on seventy, it feels like," he said, just as his lower back tried to spasm. "Ouch."

She saw his hand go to the small of his back. "Are you all right?" she asked, jumping out of her chair. She closed the distance between them, looking anxious enough to offer him a back rub.

Please, please, oh, God, please.

"It's nothing," he lied. "Nothing a good soak in the old hot tub won't fix."

And then, to his amazement, Dr. Delia circled behind him, set her hands on his shoulders, and squeezed. "Gosh, you're tense," she said. "You need to relax. And I can tell just by touching you that you need a good massage."

"Mmm." Nick squeezed his eyes shut and wondered if his dreams were about to come true. "You offering, Dr. Delia?"

Delia didn't seem to take the question amiss. Her thumbs, surprisingly strong, were digging deep into the muscles of his shoulders now. "Well, I guess I *could*," she said uncertainly. "But it would only be Swedish. I'm an amateur. I can't do deep tissue work, and really that's what you need."

"I like it Swedish," he choked, eyes still shut. *Hell, I'd like it Lebanese,* he thought. *Just don't stop.*

"Bend over and let me feel," she commanded, tugging his T-shirt out of his jeans.

"Dr. Delia, I've been just dying for you to ask." He planted his hands on the front of the Volvo and leaned forward.

Delia laughed, but she kept feeling her way down his spine, her touch clinical, her tiny thumbs digging into places he didn't know he had. Lower. And lower. And oh, God, it felt good. Almost orgasmi—

"Shit!" Pain shot down his leg, and Nick jerked like a nervous horse. "Oh, Holy Mother, what'd you hit?"

Delia was quiet for a minute, her strokes lightly soothing. "Well, I'm no orthopedist," she said, her voice no less husky, though it was matter-of-fact. "But you've got a little disk degeneration down here, don't you?"

Nick snorted. "Maybe," he admitted. "But I manage."

Her voice was chiding. "What did you do?"

"Hurt it in the Army," he answered. "But let's keep that our little secret, Doc."

Delia was making soft little circles with the heel of her hand now. Around and around, along the ridge of his hip bone. The pain was gone, his skin was warming, and his every nerve ending was coming to life. Some other things were on the verge of coming to life, too.

As if she'd read his mind, Delia suddenly stopped. "I'm sorry," she said, jerking his shirt back down. "I'm afraid I can't handle you."

"*Try*," he begged, choking out the word.

Dr. Delia seemed to miss his point. She stepped around and shook her head. "I'm just a psychologist," she said. "And a professor at that. We don't have any real skills, you know." She paused and shot him a heart-melting grin. "I'm going to make you an appointment with a neuromuscular therapist I know."

"Well, I'm not sure . . ."

"Did you like what I was doing to you?" she asked in her sultry voice.

"Hell, yes."

"Then you're going to simply adore Hans." Delia patted him on the shoulder. "Trust me, Mr. Woodruff, he's much better than I am."

"*Nick*," he rasped, stabbing his shirt back in. "Women who remove my clothes, even partially, have to call me *Nick*. It's a quirk of mine."

Delia grinned at him again. "Okay, Nick," she said, as if trying out the word for the first time.

Slowly she returned to her chair, the brown cotton skirt swishing about her ankles. It was one of those earthy-looking skirts, and she'd paired it up with a baggy peasant blouse and a pair of clogs, like one of those overweight dowds you'd see shopping over at the Chapel Hill health-food store. But Delia was no dowd, not even in that getup. And she was one of those rare women who could probably load on an extra thirty pounds and still look sexy.

Jesus H. Christ. Didn't he have it bad.

Delia kept watching Nick Woodruff as she returned to her chair. He was flirting with her, she thought. Or teasing, at least? Today, he didn't seem mean at all. And she liked him, Delia realized. Woodruff didn't seem very complex, but nor was he shallow. There was a clean, in-your-face honesty about the man that pleased her. It was a refreshing change from the academic types she was usually surrounded with. And he certainly was more . . . well, more *male*.

Right now he looked like some sort of caged animal prowling around in the narrow shed, as if there was just too much of him to be contained. In his tight white T-shirt, he looked like a dark-haired version of that sexy actor in *Dirty Dancing*—if that guy had been pumped full of steroids. His jaw was hard, his chin square, and to top that off, he had a pair of hooded bedroom eyes to die for.

Woodruff wore jeans that were snug around what looked like a nice, tight butt, the cotton worn soft at the fly and the knees. Yep, the man was definitely packing—and something a little more exciting than a loaded gun, she'd wager.

Shooting his snug butt one last glance, Delia folded her skirt neatly around her legs and sat back down in her chair. "So, Nick," she said very quietly. "I hear you shot somebody yesterday."

Woodruff turned to his tall toolbox, slid open a drawer, then tossed in a wrench with a bang. "Yeah."

Delia waited, but Woodruff said nothing more. "I see," she responded. "That might make a man's shoulders a tad tight, mightn't it?"

"Yeah, I guess."

Delia hesitated. "It must have been an emotionally

difficult experience, too. Do you . . . well, want to talk about it?"

Woodruff turned slowly from the toolbox, wiping his hands on a rag. "Nothing difficult about it, Doc," he said. "The bastard had a blade jabbed against my partner's carotid artery. And no, I don't wanna talk about it."

Delia studied him. "But maybe you should," she suggested. "It can be cathartic."

"Ex-Lax can be cathartic," he said. "That doesn't mean I need a dose. Besides, this isn't that new-age barter shit we've got going here, Doc."

"Barter?" Delia asked. "What do you mean?"

Woodruff smiled, but it didn't reach his eyes. "Oh, you know, I fix your car, you weave me a basket or psychoanalyze me?" he said. "I mean, if you'll reconsider that massage, I'll sure take it. But screw the therapy, Doc. Shooting at people—if it's necessary—is what I get paid to do."

"Oh," she said softly. "I see."

"Good," he said, bending over the engine again. "'Cause I think that's enough chitchat about the office. Now, darlin', when's the last time you had your timing belt replaced?"

Delia wanted to argue, but she sensed it would be unwise. "I don't even know what a timing belt is," she admitted.

Woodruff reached deep into the bowels of the Volvo and gave something a good yank. "Shit," he muttered.

Delia sighed. "How bad?" she demanded. "Come on, I'm a big girl, I can take it."

His arms braced wide on the sides of the engine

compartment, Woodruff turned his head, then winked at her. "Can you now, darlin'?" he asked. "That's good to know."

"Be serious."

"Oh, this is serious," he admitted. "Your mechanic was right. You need an overhaul. And you've got a head gasket that's oozing oil faster than Trent Lott. Plus, all your belts are about to start squealing, fraying, or just plain snapping. It also looks like the water pump's leaking, and you've got two broken motor mounts—probably because the damned thing's been idling so rough it's rattled itself loose. And let's not even talk about that exhaust system."

Delia felt herself wither inside. "Sounds terminal."

"Nah." Woodruff brightened. "Should be just enough work to keep a jackleg mechanic like me out of trouble for . . . oh, about two weeks."

"But you'll need belts and parts and . . . and things," she interjected. "It'll be expensive, won't it?"

Woodruff shook his head. "Labor intensive, but not that expensive—unless you need a new water pump. That'll run you about eighty bucks. The rest of it, all totaled, maybe two-fifty?"

"Oh." Relief flooded her. "Oh, that's good."

With motions that were loose and easy, Woodruff ambled across the shed and propped one hip on a tall stool by the workbench. "Still, you gotta think long-term, here, Doc," he warned, sipping from his coffee. "You need a new car. We can beat and kick another year out of this one, maybe. But that's it."

"Right. I know. I've been looking."

He swilled more coffee, the muscles in his throat

working up and down. "So, how long you been driving this P.O.S.?" he asked.

"P.O.S.?"

Woodruff shook his head disbelievingly. "Never mind. How long?"

Delia shrugged. "I bought it used after graduate school."

Woodruff opened his arms wide. "Then it's time to buy your fantasy car, Dr. Delia," he crooned. "Now dig into the secret recesses of your brain and tell old Saint Nick. What gets your motor running, mechanically speaking?" He winked again.

Delia's face warmed, and not from the coffee. "Oh, I don't know."

"Aw, come on! Everyone's got a dream machine."

Delia closed her eyes. "An S80, then," she whispered, feeling just like a kid on Santa's lap. "A black one— turbocharged—with the fancy wheels."

Woodruff guffawed, and Delia opened her eyes.

"You're shitting me, right?" he said. "Your fantasy car is another *Volvo*? A four-door sedan?"

"But think about the safety!"

Nick eyed her skeptically over his thermal mug. "Now, why is it, Dr. Delia, I get the very distinct impression there's been way too much safety in your life already?"

"I like Volvos," she insisted. "I like being safe. I've made up my mind. Talk about something else."

"Okay, let's start again," he agreed. "So, Dr. Delia . . . no boyfriend?" He watched, a little guiltily, as that pretty pink blush lit her face again.

"Boyfriend?" she said on a laugh. "That sounds . . . quaint. But I don't think I've had a boyfriend since my undergraduate days."

Nick slid off the stool. "Dr. Delia, you are so not what I expected," he said, abruptly deciding to go for it. "How many *boyfriends* did you have in college, anyway? No—let's put it this way—how many *relationships* did you have prior to marrying that asshole husband of yours? And yeah, I know he was an asshole, 'cause Basham already told me."

"Well, I was a grad student!" she protested. "I had other priorities."

Nick stepped a little closer. "How many?"

Delia blinked. "I'm not sure it's any of your business, but four, maybe five?"

A faint smile curled Nick's mouth. "Yeah, maybe, but you didn't sleep with many of 'em, did you?"

Delia was truly indignant. "Well, I was hardly a virgin when I got married, if that's what you're implying."

He laughed. "Sugar, there are all kinds of virgins."

"Well, I had experience!" she said. "Enough, anyway."

Logically, Delia knew she was right, too. But her experience hadn't kept her husband from straying, had it? Sometimes she felt like such a fraud.

She had dropped her gaze and turned away again. Nick slipped his finger under her chin and gently turned her face back to his. "And they were lucky, lucky guys, Dr. Delia," he said, softening his tone. "But something tells me you don't see it that way."

Delia blinked again, feeling suddenly on the verge of

tears. "Well, Sergeant Woodruff, you know what they say," she snapped. "Those that can, do. And those that can't, teach."

In response, Nick Woodruff leaned down and braced his well-muscled arms on the porch railing, imprisoning her shoulders between them. "Then teach me something, Dr. Delia," he whispered, his mouth suddenly hovering over hers.

Delia felt her eyes widen and her breath hitch. And then his lips melted over hers, warm and pliant. He slanted his mouth and nibbled, coaxing her to return the kiss. She did, turning her face fully into his. Lightly he stroked the seam of her lips with his tongue, but went no further. It was a kiss of exquisite tenderness, and it shocked her that so big and brutal a man could be that gentle.

When he broke away, he lifted his mouth just an inch. "Well, Dr. Delia, you sure do kiss just fine," he murmured, brushing his lips beneath her right eye. "You know what I think the problem is?"

"I wasn't conducting a survey," said Delia. "But go ahead, take a crack at it."

Nick laughed softly. "I think your ex was a fool, and probably no damn good in bed," he said. "And before that, I just don't think you'd ever been with a man who had the experience to appreciate and pay proper homage to your many fine assets."

Delia cut her eyes up at him. "Now, there's a theory."

"Could be right, too," said Nick, still leaning over her. "Now, I'm not saying your textbook knowledge isn't first-rate, 'cause I'm a regular listener, Doc, and you know your stuff. But every once in a while, even a pro needs a little hands-on experience, right?"

Delia closed her eyes, rocked back in her chair, and let her head fall back against the porch railing. "Oh, God, you Southern boys are so full of it!" she said. "Why do I get the feeling this car repair is going to cost me a lot more than two hundred and fifty bucks?"

She could almost feel his flash of irritation. "Look, sugar, what I'm offering now has nothing to do with your car," he rasped, shifting his body away. "I'll fix it, and gladly. But what I *want* is to take you to bed."

Delia's breath caught and her stomach bottomed out. "Why?"

"Why?" Exasperation choked his voice. "Because you're damned pretty, that's why. And because that weird tree-hugger getup you're wearing fires every one of my spark plugs, for reasons I can't even begin to explain. And because, quite frankly, Dr. Delia, you look like a troubled, overworked woman who needs her brains fucked out."

Delia leaped to her feet. "Why, I never——"

"Sugar, I'm half afraid that might be true."

Delia placed a finger in the middle of his chest. "Nick Woodruff, you are one arrogant man," she said. "I barely know you."

"Yeah, and there's a certain attraction in that, don't you think?"

"In casual, semi-anonymous sex?" Delia returned. "I don't think so."

"Oh, yeah, you do." Nick set his hands on her shoulders. "I can already see the fire in your eyes. You find the prospect of having wild, mind-blowing, cat-clawing, tie-me-up-and-spank-me sex with a man you hardly know exciting. And darlin', it looks to me like your life could definitely use a little jump-start."

"Will you please stop expressing everything in automotive terms?" Delia demanded. "And while we're on the subject of spanking—"

"Okay," he conceded. "No spanking."

But Delia wasn't finished. "Besides, do you even know what you're talking about? No. No, not when it comes to me, you *don't*. How did we get here, anyway? We just met two days ago! I don't know you. You don't know anything about my lovers. About my sex life. You don't know anything about me, or my marriage, or how good Neville was in bed—"

"Sugar," growled Nick. "He was named *Neville*. That's one big strike against him right from the get-go."

Delia set her hands on her hips and looked at him incredulously. "Who *are* you?" she demanded. "I mean, *really?* And where do you get off with this good ole boy schtick of yours? I'd be a fool to have sex with a man I don't know."

Nick smiled, gave her a courtly bow, tugged two slender leather cases from his front pockets, and thumbed the first open. A silver badge winked in the morning sun. "Robert James Nicholson Woodruff III, at your service, ma'am," he said in his most melting voice.

She looked at his SBI photo, then the wallet. "So?"

"I'm the third of five children, born to a respectable family and raised in genteel, small-town poverty in South Georgia. My mama's dead, but any of my three sisters will give me a glowing reference. Phone numbers are in the wallet, help yourself. I'm a good Baptist boy who got shipped off to LSU. I was ROTC, graduated with honors, and joined the Army, where I stayed put until the SBI begged to make my acquaintance. I'm not married, I'm not divorced, and I don't hit women, dogs, or children. I don't use drugs or tobacco, and rarely get drunk. I don't have AIDS or the clap or even a bad case of the sniffles at the moment. So there, Dr. Delia, you know all there is to know about me. Want to have sex now?"

God help her, she did. It was so ludicrous, Delia burst into laughter. "This is insane!"

"What's insane about it?"

Delia shook her head and stared into the depths of his backyard. "See, yesterday, I was just this mild-mannered, boring college professor with a piece of junk for a car and a nice row of evergreens in my backyard," she said. "And now, I'm trapped in some sort of fifth dimension filled with cats, rickety chairs, old cars, and hunky guys who wear their jeans way, way too tight for my comfort level, and the whole bizarre scenario has this weird Randy Newman song playing in the background."

Nick narrowed his eyes. "Which weird Randy Newman song?" he asked. "And don't say 'Short People,' Delia, or I swear to God, I really *won't* fix your car."

Delia hiccuped. "No, the one about good old boys."

Nick groaned. "Sugar, most all Randy Newman's songs are about good old boys if you listen close enough."

Delia laughed again, almost hysterically, then half-chanted, half-sang:

"College men from LSU,
Went in dumb. Come out dumb, too.
Hustlin' round Atlanta in their alligator shoes,
Getting drunk ev'ry weekend at the bar-be-ques."

Nick was dumbstruck. Delia did a good Newman impression, he'd give her that. But he was still aggravated as hell. "Sugar," he said, looking her straight in the eye, "I'm a lot of things, but dumb I'm not. And I hate to break it to you, but that wallful of degrees you've probably got hanging in an office someplace can't tell you shit about real life—and they can tell you even less about good sex."

"Oh, wait! I get it!" Delia sat back down in her chair and shoved her hands into her hair. "This is, like, some sort of challenge for you, isn't it? You know, a sort of 'I did Dr. Delia' bragging-rights kind of thing?"

Softly Nick cursed, the f-word this time, and headed for his tool chest. "Okay, darlin', that's it," he said, yanking out a drawer to rummage for his filter wrench. "I deeply apologize if I've insulted you. Now, I'm fixing to crawl under that Volvo and drain the crankcase. And it won't be a pretty sight when I finish. So if you'd excuse me, I'd be real grateful."

He heard the cane seat in his old chair squeak as she rose. But he was shocked when he felt her cool hand touch his shoulder. "Nick, I . . ."

Nick decided to make it easy on her. He'd been

insane to hit on her so hard anyway. He turned, forcing her hand to drop. "Look, Delia, I was just teasing," he said. "It was just a flirtation—a hot one—and I was enjoying it, and I let it get out of hand. Which was easy, because you're pretty *and* you're smart—which isn't all that easy to find in the same woman, you know."

Delia's gaze shifted to the old Triumph. "Thanks. I guess."

Nick forced his most neighborly smile. "Now, honest to God, honey, I have got to pull that oil filter off," he said. "So go on home, okay? Thanks for the coffee."

Delia was rubbing her hands up and down her arms as if she were cold, but Nick knew that wasn't it. "You're sure you don't mind?"

Nick laughed, and reached up to lift his old wooden creeper off its wall hook. "I didn't mind yesterday," he said. "And nothing has changed. Sorry I kissed you."

Delia smiled, and started from the shed. "Well, I'm guilty, too," she admitted, pausing to run a hand over Tiger Lily. "So, anyway, you let me know if I need to buy some belts or parts or—or whatever, okay?"

"Yeah, sure," he said. "And, Delia?"

She turned around, her expression expectant. "Yes?"

Nick rolled the creeper toward the Volvo with the toe of his boot. "I could really use the diagram for this fuse box," he said. "I looked through the glove box, and *nada*. Do you have the owner's manual?"

Delia bit her lip. "It used to be in there, but Neville probably filed it," she said. "He filed everything, right down to those little warranty cards that come with toasters. But I'll find it. I'll look this afternoon."

Nick eyed her narrowly for a moment. "That'd be great," he said. "But can I just mention a couple of things before you go, Delia? *Owner's manuals go in glove boxes.* You knew that, right? So don't let a dumb shit like Neville tell you otherwise—about anything."

"Fine advice, but it would've been a lot more helpful five years ago." Delia grinned. "So, what was that other thing?"

It was the grin that got him. Nick swallowed hard. "The other thing is, I quit work at sundown," he said, jerking his head toward his back porch. "Then I'm going to swim laps in that pool up there until it gets pitch dark. And after that, I'm getting in my hot tub. Naked, Delia. So if you somehow manage to change your mind about fooling around with me—or even if you'd just like a nice soak—you'd sure be welcome. Otherwise, I'd appreciate it if you didn't turn your back floodlights on tonight. Being as the pines are gone, and all. Bud Basham might not appreciate the view."

Delia smiled and turned to go. "I'll remember that," she said, then stopped again. "Oh, and Nick? I was just curious . . ."

"Yep?"

Delia tilted her head to one side. "If you don't use tobacco," she said, "what's that big, silvery pouch poking out of the back pocket of your jeans?"

Nick blanked out for a moment, then remembered. "Oh, right," he said, fishing back into his pocket. "That'd be the really huge condom I keep around, just in case I get lucky. Wanna see?"

Delia hesitated. "Seriously, Nick."

Tiger Lily, too, seemed curious. She stood up on the workbench and stared fixedly at Nick's backside.

"Seriously?" Nick extracted the package. "Cat treats. Tartar–control salmon. Want one?"

CHAPTER THREE

From the seclusion of her upstairs bedroom, Delia watched Nick work on her car for the rest of the afternoon. Oh, she didn't *watch* him, exactly. Not like some puppy with its nose pressed to the window. But the window drew her nonetheless. And Nick Woodruff disrupted her thoughts for the rest of the day. His butt sticking out of the front end of her Volvo was particularly unhelpful.

In between watching Nick's hindquarters, however, Delia found time to call Readi-Steam Carpet Cleaners, schedule a crew of professional window washers, and start dumping out closets like a fiend. Her divorce had been final for three months, Neville had been remarried for two, and it was time—dear God, was it time—for Delia to move on. If a blatant offer of casual sex from a near stranger could tempt her past the point of all logic, then she really needed to get a life.

Not that she'd been holding up things on Neville's account. No, the sad truth was, she hadn't missed him.

She'd merely been enraged that after convincing her they *had* to have this house, he'd lived in it less than a year. Then he'd met Alicia, one of his wealthy mammoplasty patients. Apparently, Alicia's new boobs had been a huge—no pun intended—success, because Neville vanished six weeks after the sutures came out, leaving a neatly typed note of apology and most of his high-end shit behind. And leaving Delia with six months of speaking engagements and an incomplete manuscript due on her editor's desk.

But that was then, Delia reminded herself. *And Nick Woodruff—whether I want him or not—is now.*

Thus encouraged, by late afternoon, she'd managed to haul six huge boxes of Neville's junk down to the garage and dump it near his thirty-thousand-dollar speedboat, just one step away from Monday's curb pickup. And that damned boat was headed to the curb next, Delia decided, if he didn't get his ass up here to haul it out of her garage. Feeling empowered, she marched back into the kitchen, dialed his office, and left him a voice mail to just that effect.

That done, Delia dusted off her hands with a certain amount of pride and decided to reward herself with a hot bubble bath. But on her way back upstairs, the window caught her eyes again—and this time they almost popped out of her head.

Nick Woodruff had taken off his shirt.

Gosh. Oh, God. Delia slapped one hand across her eyes and forced herself into the bathroom. Ten minutes later she was up to her chin in English lavender, but still wallowing in Nick. Most specifically, she was wallowing in the memories of his kiss, and pretending her interest was ... well, *analytical*.

Ha! Nick kissed a woman as if she were the only one he'd ever wanted—and as if she were the last one he ever meant to kiss, too. That fine, full mouth of his had been soft and certain, yet far from overpowering. There was no way she could trick herself into believing he'd forced that kiss. And no way she could trick herself into believing she didn't want another one, either. *Dang.*

With her toes, Delia snared her drifting sponge, then blew a clump of bubbles off it. Clinically, she mused, one had to marvel at Nick Woodruff's composure, at his absolute certainty that he was sexually desirable. Yet despite the accusation she'd thrown in his face, there hadn't been one ounce of genuine arrogance in him. Just a matter-of-fact acceptance of his sexuality. And of his interest in her. What gave him such confidence? she wondered. Did women just never say *no* to the man?

That was ridiculous! *She* had said no to him. And right now, with night falling fast and her body being teased by warm bubbles, Delia was beginning to think that had been a really dumb thing to do. Almost worse was the fact that, when she had said *no*, the man had simply smiled and shrugged. His self-confidence had been intact, his neighborly demeanor unchanged. He just seemed, heaven help her, like a *real nice guy*.

But they all did, didn't they? She, of all people, should know how unwise it was to go with your gut in such a situation. Oh, Nick Woodruff was no sexual deviant—Delia trusted her professional instincts that far—but he might well be the world's worst heart-breaker. And there was no educating a gal about *that* little problem, save the school of hard knocks, and Delia had already flunked out once.

Suddenly something was nagging at her brain. School? Flunking? Records? *Filing?* Still musing, Delia pulled the plug and stood up. Then it hit her.

The owner's manual. Oh, no! She had promised Nick she would find it! Swiftly, Delia dried her hair, dressed, and dashed downstairs. It was a simple task to find the owner's manual in the study. Neville had made it its own little manila folder, carefully typed out a label, and tucked it neatly behind *V* in the bottom drawer of the file cabinet.

Eager to tell Nick, Delia grabbed the phone book, then flicked a quick glance out the window.

Dark. It was just getting dark. And Nick had big plans for the evening. *I'm going to swim laps,* he'd said. *And after that, I'm getting in my hot tub. Naked.*

Oh, dear heaven. It was almost showtime.

Delia couldn't help herself. She bolted back upstairs, cut all the lights, and pressed her nose to the window again. Not like a puppy. Nope, more like a bitch in heat. But no lights shone in Nick's big backyard. Delia couldn't see a thing. Still clutching the phone book and her owner's manual, Delia threw herself on the bed, dug around for the remote, and watched a round of CNN.

How long could you stay in a hot tub anyway? About fifteen minutes? Delia thought she'd seen that posted at a hotel spa someplace. And how long to dress?

Eat dinner? Hard to say. So Delia watched another round of CNN—which was strange, considering that all she really needed to do was dial up his number and say, *Hey, Nick, I found that owner's manual.* How big an interruption was that?

To kill time, Delia went back downstairs and uncorked a bottle of cheap Chablis—*real* cheap, on her budget. But she took a little test sip and found it tolerable, so she plucked one of Neville's antique Baccarat goblets out of the breakfront and went back upstairs with the bottle. Delia crawled in bed and grabbed the remote. Surfing through the channels, she caught a rerun of *Leave It to Beaver*—the one where Beaver fakes a school excuse from his mother, her all-time favorite. Oddly enough, it was even funnier when washed down with Chablis.

But soon *Beaver* was over, and impatience got the best of her. At nine sharp Delia rolled over, grabbed the phone, and punched out the number she'd already memorized. He answered in a rough, drowsy voice. "Woodruff."

"Nick?" she said at once. "I found it. The owner's manual, I mean. Can I drop it by tomorrow?"

There was a long pause, then a sleepy chuckle. *"Mmm,* Dr. Delia," he rasped. "My radio fantasy voice. Say something else, sugar."

Delia was taken aback. "Like . . . what?"

Springs squeaked, as if Nick were shifting his weight on a bed or sofa. "Darlin', who cares?" he whispered. "Read me your grocery list. I know it'll sound good."

"Well, I . . . I mostly eat take-out."

He laughed again, wide awake this time. "Honey, do you always take life this seriously?"

He was teasing her, Delia realized. "Did—did you enjoy your swim?" she managed, feeling like a doofus.

"Naw, that part's a workout," he said. "For my bad back, remember? But I had a nice soak afterward."

"Right," she said, cradling the phone to her cheek. "I remember your mentioning it."

"Do you, now?" he whispered. "I don't suppose you would say 'Sorry I missed it,' and make my night, would you?"

Delia fell back into the pillows and exhaled. Damn it, she *had* missed it. "I'll bet it was real nice," she answered.

"Real nice," he echoed a little wistfully. "Hey, Dr. Delia, whatcha wearing?"

Delia sat straight up, almost knocking Neville's five-hundred-dollar wineglass off the night table. "What am I *wearing?* What the hell kind of question is that?"

Nick laughed again, the sound flowing over her like warm whiskey. "Come on, sugar, it's a simple one," he said. "See, it's kind of cold over here, and I'm a little lonely. So just whisper real soft, and it'll be our little secret. Did you take a shower and put on your jammies? Or what?"

"A bath," Delia said, before she could reason herself out of it. "A bubble bath. With English lavender."

"Oh, God," he whispered. "Oh, Dr. Delia, don't tease. English lavender always gets me hot."

Delia emptied her wineglass in one gulp. "And I put on a T-shirt, not jammies." She paused, staring at the dregs. "Why, what are you doing?"

He chuckled again. "Making myself go blind, sugar. Now, was that *just* a T-shirt?"

Delia giggled. "Well, no."

"What, then?"

Delia was flustered, so she grabbed what was left of the Chablis. "Well," she whispered, pouring. "You *know*."

"No, I don't have a clue, Doc," he said. "Come on, now. 'Sometimes phone sex with someone you trust can be a healthy turn-on.' That's what you told Fred from Framingham, remember? And sweetheart, you must trust me. You left your precious Volvo over here, right?"

"See, now, there's the really scary part." Delia's voice was very small. "I *do* trust you."

Nick made a strange, rough sound in the back of his throat. "So answer the question, darlin'," he softly demanded. "Whatcha got on under that T-shirt? Black leather motorcycle pants? A chastity belt? Knicker-bockers? *What?*"

"God, I don't believe I'm doing this," said Delia, cradling her forehead in one palm. *"Panties."*

"Bikini or thong?"

"Oh, God." Delia felt her face growing warm. "Why?"

" 'Cause I'm visualizing, Doc," he whispered, his voice dark and hot. *"Sensual* visualization. See, last week, I thought I was starting to lose interest in sex."

"Yeah, right."

"Oh, no, sugar, I'm serious as a heart attack," he insisted. "Then, remember last Friday? When you told

Menopausal Marge from Montreal how to use sensual visualization to—you know, to get herself fired up? Well, you were right, Doc. That shit works. I'm imagining you in your panties right now, and I'm hard enough to hammer nails."

"Nick." Delia giggled. "You are *not* menopausal."

"But it's still working real good for me. So, come on, Delia. Help me out. Describe every inch of your tight, sweet body, baby, and I swear, I'll never tell a soul. But first, let's get back to those panties."

As if to hide from herself, Delia wriggled under the covers. "Okay," she finally whispered. "They're hip huggers. Pink ones."

"Pink," groaned Nick. "God, Delia, are they the same color pink as your cheeks when you blush? The cheeks on your face now, I'm talking, because honey, I gotta confess, that's about the prettiest shade of pink I've ever laid eyes on. So far."

"Is . . . Is it really?"

"Delia, darlin', I get hot just thinking about it."

She was very quiet for a moment. "Nick, you're weird."

"Nope," he insisted. "I'm a normal, healthy male with normal, healthy appetites, burning with a whole morning's worth of thwarted lust from watchin' you in that weird skirt and those ugly shoes. Besides, remember what you told Tricia from Tallahas—"

"God, please do *not* mention my job again," interjected Delia.

"Why?"

"Because I . . . I don't find talking about my job

very . . . well, *you know.*" Suddenly Delia of the million-word vocabulary couldn't find the right one.

"Erotic?" His voice slid over her skin like silk. "Is that it, babe?"

"Yes."

"But if I talk about other things," he whispered, "you might feel otherwise?"

"Yes. Maybe. Oh, Nick, I don't know!"

"I can work with a *maybe*," he said reassuringly. "Shoot, just breathe heavily into the phone, darlin'. Given your voice, that'll probably do the trick."

"Wh-what trick?"

Nick laughed his wicked laugh again. "Oh, Delia, you just don't know what you do to me."

Despite the darkness under her bedcovers, Delia squeezed shut her eyes. "Then tell me," she whispered.

That caught him off guard. "Umm—*tell* you?"

"Go ahead, big boy," she whispered, giggling. "Tell me everything."

"Yeah, okay," he said, then hesitated. "But listen, sugar, something just occurred to me. Are you on a hard line?"

"Mmm, *hard,*" she whispered, mimicking his voice. "I like that."

Nick laughed a little nervously. "Now, be serious a minute, darlin'," he cautioned. "'Cause frequencies float, and we don't want to give old Bud Basham a coronary here."

"Oh," breathed Delia. "Okay."

"Good. Now, is that a remote phone you're using?"

"No, it's under the covers with me. Cord and all."

"Lucky phone," he rasped. "Delia, know what I'd do if I was under there with you?"

"No. What?"

Nick breathed heavily for a moment, and it didn't seem feigned. "Oh, I don't know, baby," he whispered. "It'd be so hard to choose."

"Choose."

"Okay." The springs squeaked again. "Okay, first, I think I'd slide my hands up your thighs, then just keep going, right under your T-shirt. What color did you say that was?"

"Black," she whispered wickedly. "It's vintage AC/DC, from the original *Back in Black* tour."

"Oh, baby, you rock," he choked, but she could tell he was about to laugh out loud. "I just knew you had a dark side. Okay, so, what I would do is, I would ease my hands along that pretty, pale flesh of yours, right up over your ribs, touching every one of 'em, just enough to make your skin shiver."

"Mmm." It really did sound good.

"Mmm is right, darlin'," Nick whispered. "And then, I'd brush the very tips of your nipples with my palms. Just to make sure they were nice and hard."

"Ohh," said Delia.

"Are they, Delia?"

She hesitated. "A little."

"Just a little?" Nick sounded crushed.

"A lot," said Delia. "Hard. Tingly."

"Jesus, Delia." His voice was sincere. "Touch them. Tell me for sure."

"Hard, Nick," she whispered. "They feel . . . heavy. Maybe . . . kind of lonely."

"Wait." Nick swallowed hard. "I've changed my mind."

"Nooo."

"Oh, yeah, darlin', I think I'd rather take your panties off first."

"Would you? Why?"

"Because I just can't wait, Delia," he whispered. "Because I'm about to come all over my couch. And because I'm betting you've got some other pink parts that are prettier than your cheeks, sweetheart."

Delia giggled. "Maybe."

"Maybe my white cracker ass," he rasped. "So I'd slide those silk panties down your legs, Delia—and I know they'd be silk, darlin', 'cause it'd be a sin for a woman like you to wear any other kind—and I'd slide 'em right down to your ankles. Maybe just rip 'em right off, then, and buy you new ones later."

"O-okay," said Delia. "No one ever bought me underwear before."

"Then you have not lived the life you deserve, sugar."

"I guess not."

"Delia?"

"Yes, Nick?"

His voice was dark and steady. "Slip your hand under those pink silk panties," he commanded, "and tell me what it feels like."

Delia hesitated. "Oh, *Nick.*"

Nick's breath ratcheted up sharply. "Come on, baby," he begged, his voice thick now. "Do it. Do it for me. Don't stop me now. *Please.* Just slide your palm down your belly and under the elastic, okay? And slip your fingers between your legs. Are you wet, Delia? Are you? Good God, honey, say *yes,* 'cause I'm dying here."

"Yes," she whispered, the word barely audible. "Yes. Wet. *Dripping.*"

Nick swallowed hard again. "God almighty, girl," he whispered. "I really am gonna come just listening to you."

"Are you, Nick?" Delia asked, her voice deep and foreign. "Really? Because, you know, I think you have such an incredible butt. I watched it half the afternoon, sticking out of the hood of my car, so tight and perfect. You know, I really am sorry I missed your hot tub."

"Ah, God, Delia," he groaned. "Oh, God. Keep talking, baby. Just keep talking. 'Cause, I swear—I *swear*—"

"Holy shit!" screamed Delia, leaping from beneath the covers.

"What the hell is that?" he barked. The pounding on Delia's kitchen door was so loud, Nick could hear it through the telephone. "What the hell is that? Delia? *Delia*—?"

Someone punched the bell. Six times. "Open the goddamned door, Delia!" bellowed Dr. Neville Sydney. "Open it right now. Don't you dare touch my fucking speedboat, you hear me?"

"Delia?" said Nick. "Delia? Baby, put the phone back to your ear. Put the phone back. Talk to me, sugar. Talk *now*—or I'm coming over there."

"Holy shit, Nick, it's Neville!" hissed Delia into the phone. "And for this, I *really* ought to kill him."

"Jesus Christ," said Nick. "Delia, do *not* answer that door. I'm coming over there. And I mean *now.*"

Delia's back floodlights were already on by the time Nick slid into his jeans, shoved his service pistol into his waistband, and started across the yard. He could see a big, black Lincoln Navigator idling outside her garage, its chrome trailer hitch glistening yellow beneath the lights. He could already hear the argument, too. Because Delia, of course, had not listened to him and kept her damned door shut. Instead, she was leaning half out of it, going nose-to-nose with Mr. Rhinoplasty himself.

Delia's ex-husband was waving wildly in the direction of the garage. "You vindictive bitch!" he heard Neville shout. "You've changed the remote codes! You can't hold my boat captive! How dare you?"

"Neville, have you always been such a twit?" snapped Delia. "The damned Liftmaster is broken. Didn't you hear it grinding?"

"Well, howdy, howdy folks," said Nick, sidling up to Neville.

He wasn't sure who was more taken aback, Delia or her ex-husband. She looked at him, shut her mouth, then opened it again. "Nick, Neville," she said, waving between them. "Neville, Nick. As in Woodruff. The riffraff behind your pine trees. Remember?"

Neville didn't even have the decency to look embarrassed. "Fine. Whatever. Delia, I want my boat."

"And didn't I tell you, not six hours ago, to come get it?" snapped Delia, still in her vintage T-shirt. "Believe me, Neville, I have lots more stimulating things to do with my evenings than stand here talking to you."

"Oh, I see," he said, his voice smooth and smarmy. "This is all about Alicia, isn't it?"

Nick could see Delia had got hold of a big, fancy wineglass, and she was brandishing it now. "Oh! Oh!" she screeched, balling up her empty fist. "News flash, Neville! Everything is *not* about Alicia, okay? Some of this is about you dumping me with this overblown excuse of a house, and then not moving your shit out of it."

Neville crossed his arms petulantly. "Well, now I've come for the boat."

"*Get* the boat, Neville. *Take* the boat! You think I want it? You think I want *any* of that high-end crap in the garage, Neville? I mean, what kind of self-absorbed, asinine misogynist uses engraved silver golf tees? Or a titanium racing bike? Can you tell me that, Neville? I mean, let's face it, you are so *not* Lance Armstrong."

Neville smirked. "Jealousy does not become you, Delia."

"Oh, screw you, Neville! Do you have *any* clue how glad I am to be rid of you?"

Neville seemed to find this impossible to fathom. "My God, Delia, have you been drinking?" He drew back in horror. "And—heaven forfend!—is that the antique Baccarat you're waving?"

"Nope," said Delia, crowning him with the wineglass. "Not now." The bowl of the wineglass bounced off Neville's head and hit the concrete driveway, shattering into a spray of diamonds. Delia waved the stem triumphantly.

Nick couldn't remember what a misogynist was, didn't give a shit what a Baccarat was, and was pretty certain real men didn't use the word *forfend*. But he damn sure knew when to step into a fray. "Okay, folks," he said, calmly elbowing his way between them. "This is the point in our evening's festivities when I introduce Mr. Badge and Mr. Beretta," he said, withdrawing both.

Delia and Neville turned to stare at him.

Nick smiled his best Southern-boy smile. "Now, this just got official," he said sweetly. "Y'all shut the hell up before Bud Basham calls the Durham police and this gets written up someplace official, okay? 'Cause, trust me, it won't look good on your résumés."

Neville really didn't have a clue. "Look, Woodstock, don't piss her off any further," he said high-handedly. "I've had a long day, I don't need the theatrics, and she obviously is not the nice, mild-mannered college professor she seems."

"I'd guessed that already, Dr. Snidely." Nick's drawl was even slower than usual. "In fact, I'd guess old Delia here can get pretty danged hot under the right circumstances. And she has a bad temper, too."

"It's *Sydney*," snapped Neville. "Dr. Neville Sydney."

"No shit?" said Nick, drawing back an inch. "What a coincidence. I'm *Woodruff*. As in Nick why-don't-you-take-your-friggin'-boat-and-get-the-hell-outta-here Woodruff."

"Hilarious," said Neville, turning back to his ex-wife. "Look, Delia, do you think you and Sheriff Taylor here could just put the goddamned garage door up? I'm on call."

CHAPTER FOUR

*B*y late Sunday afternoon Nick had worked his way deep into the bowels of Delia's station wagon and was fast developing an appreciation for Swedish engineering. The car looked like a piece of shit on wheels, but it was definitely built to last. Maybe her automotive taste wasn't so bad after all, he mused, cracking loose another greasy bolt near the head gasket.

Her taste in men, though, was highly suspect. Bud Basham's description of Neville Sydney had turned out to be a kind one. Sydney adored himself, and it was obvious. But Nick had been relieved to see that Delia *didn't* adore him. Not anymore, at any rate. Maybe she never had? Maybe marrying him had been a career move?

Nick shook his head and went to his tool chest to change sockets. Nope, maybe he didn't know much about Delia, but he was sure she wouldn't do that. Probably she'd just been too young to know better.

Delia still hadn't given Nick the owner's manual for the Volvo, and he was wondering when she'd dredge up the courage to come over. She'd been just a tad tipsy last night. And in the bright light of day, he knew Delia was going to be mortified by her behavior. Just picturing her conking old Neville with that wineglass last night made Nick laugh. And on the phone before that . . . *whoo boy*. Nothing funny there. The way he'd been feeling about Delia was deadly damned serious.

Scary serious. But the lust he felt—jeez, that was serious, too. And he was going to have to do something about it, or explode. One way or another, he had to get Delia Sydney into his bed. Underneath him. Around him. Inside him. Any way he could take her, he meant to have her. What he felt was worse than an ache or an itch. He didn't even know what it was. Didn't want to think about it, either.

Bedding her was doable, though, he thought. Oh, not long-term. He definitely wasn't Delia's type. He wasn't intellectual enough, or polished enough, and they had nothing at all in common. Besides, he didn't think long-term. His job asked too much of him, and once the internal investigation was finished and his administrative leave was over, work would only get worse. He'd be back on the job and working twice as hard to make up for lost time. Still, there was no reason he and Delia couldn't have a blazing hot affair. Good sex was good sex, no matter your background. And clearly, Delia needed to get laid.

Still, Delia lacked self-confidence where her sexuality was concerned. That was understandable, he supposed, after a divorce. Clinically, as Delia would say, she probably knew it, too. But a woman's psyche was a delicate thing, and it looked like old Neville had stomped all over hers. And all Nick had to do was convince her that he was just the man to bolster her spirits, so to speak.

"Nick?"

Nick jerked his hand back, almost cracking a knuckle on the engine block. He straightened up to see Delia standing by the corner of his shed, two sweaty bottles of Bud in one hand, the Volvo's manual in the other.

Nick forced a casual grin and shoved his wrench in his back pocket. "Well, hey there, Doc," he said, taking the manual. "I was wondering when you'd roll out of bed and sober up."

Delia blanched. "I wasn't drunk," she said softly. "I just . . . I don't know, had temporary insanity or something. Here, I brought you a beer. I'm sorry about last night."

Nick tossed the manual aside and took the Bud. "I'm not sorry," he said, then drank down a healthy gulp. "Best entertainment I've had in years."

Delia dropped her head. "Gosh, I was terrible to Neville, wasn't I?"

"Neville?" said Nick. "Hell, who cares about Neville? Delia, that was *not* what I was talking about."

"Oh, Nick, don't tease me!" Delia sat down in her chair—he thought of it as hers now, anyway—and rocked it back against the railing. "I feel like such a fool, acting like some horny teenager on the phone with

you, then hitting—*hitting!*—Neville like that. Just *bam!*"
She smacked herself in the forehead with her open
palm. "I can't think what got into me. I'm always so . . .
so in control."

She really did look distressed. So she'd gotten a little
tooted and whacked her ex-husband, a man who probably deserved worse. Big deal. But Nick kept forgetting
how seriously women, especially women like Delia,
took such things. Today she wore red Keds, an old University of Pennsylvania sweatshirt, and a pair of baggy
athletic shorts, all of which served to make her look
even smaller and younger than before.

He moved his work stool closer to Delia's chair and
sat down. "So, Doc, you want to talk about it?" he asked
softly.

"Talk?" Delia shook her head. "No way. I'd rather
just sit here and quietly hate myself. But I do owe you
an apology."

Nick shrugged. "Well, you're obviously holding on
to a whole heap of repressed anger in there, darlin'," he
said. "Maybe the finality of Neville's carting that boat
off bothered you more than you thought it would? Or
maybe the boat was—hell, I don't know, some sort of
symbol or something?"

Delia waved her hand dismissively. "Oh, come on,
Nick," she said. "Who's the psychologist here? Of
course I have repressed anger. But I don't miss Neville,
and I don't give a hoot about that boat."

Nick sipped his beer and shrugged. "Have it your
way, sugar," he agreed. "Sometimes a cigar is just a cigar,
right?"

"Oh, right, go Freudian on me." Her expression soured.

Nick winked at her. "So you're more of a Jungian, huh?" he teased, trying to cajole her into a good mood. "Or an Adlerian, maybe? Now, me, I'm just a good old existentialist myself."

She looked at him a little skeptically. "Why, Mr. Woodruff, what big words you have."

Her tone held just enough sarcasm to make something inside him snap. "Hey, all the better to tell you to kiss my ass with," he retorted, shoving off the stool.

Delia's eyes widened. "What—?" she demanded. "What did I say?"

Nick paced toward the Triumph. "You know, I don't know where you get off pretending like I just fell off the turnip truck, Delia," he said. "Maybe I don't have a wall full of degrees like you and Mr. Tummy-Tuck, but I don't appreciate your dismissive tone."

He heard her chair legs hit the concrete, heard her soft footsteps follow him. "Hey, come on, now," she said, touching him lightly on the arm. "I'm sorry. You surprised me, Nick. That's all."

Nick wheeled on her. "Just for the record, sweetheart, I've got a couple of master's degrees myself," he snapped. "Sometimes—say, when I run out of bad guys to randomly gun down—all those big words come in handy. After all, there's always the crossword puzzle in the *TV Guide.*"

Delia looked up at him. "Okay, maybe I deserved that," she said, holding up one hand, palm out. "But sometimes I just need—"

"The only thing you *need*, Delia, is a good fucking," he interjected, tossing his beer bottle in the trash barrel. "Maybe then you could lighten up a little."

Delia let her gaze drift over him. "Oh, and you're just the man to give it to me, huh?"

"You're goddamned right I am," he returned.

Delia put her beer down on the roof of his Triumph and was quiet for a long moment. "You know what?" she said, her voice suddenly lower. "You just might be right, Nick. Lord knows you get under my skin. I just wish I had time for a relationship right now."

Nick set his hands on her upper arms. "Darlin', I'm not offering you a relationship," he growled. "I don't want one. What I'm offering you is *sex.*"

Delia didn't pull away from him. "Sex?" she echoed. "That no-strings-attached kind, right?"

"Damn, Delia, if you don't drive me crazy," he said, jerking her closer. "Yeah, the no-strings kind. Why? You holding out for a wedding ring?"

She blushed furiously. "Don't be ridiculous," she retorted. "I just—I just—"

He was on her before Delia drew her next breath, before he realized what he was doing.

And then he felt Delia's mouth crushed beneath his, felt her struggle just for an instant in his arms. Nick had her trapped against the bumper of the Triumph, the full length of her body pressed to his. Unconsciously he gave a groan of desire and slanted his mouth over hers again.

God, she tasted of cold beer and warm woman, spicy-sweet and awfully tempting. She was a pain in the ass, but he wanted her too much to care. Delia certainly wasn't resisting. She had her hands around his waist, moving them restlessly over the muscles of his back, and when her lips softened, Nick thrust inside her mouth with his tongue and felt his blood surge hot and strong. He sensed Delia yielding to him, melting against him.

With a sound of pleasure in her throat, her arms locked around his neck, and it was like molten testosterone pulsed through the veins in his temples and his cock. Nick moved inside her mouth with firm, deep strokes, claiming her. Together, they slid deeper into the sensual abyss as he swirled his tongue around hers, sucking it and drawing it into his mouth.

It was frightening how fast he fell. Dark, mindless desire clouded his brain. Nick moved his hands over Delia, filling them with her breasts, her face, her slender waist. "God, I have to have you," he breathed against her cheek as he bent her back. "I want you so bad I'm insane from it. I want you under me, Delia. I want you in my bed, woman, open beneath me, taking me deep. Say *yes,* Delia. For God's sake, say *yes* now."

"Oh, God, Nick." The words were faint, breathless.

The *yes* wasn't there yet, but her desire was audible, urging him on. He let his hands slide beneath the elastic waist of her shorts, down and down until he'd grasped her buttocks and lifted her against the bulky length of his erection. In response, Delia's head tipped back, and she arched her body taut as a bowstring.

"Yes," she finally whispered. "All right. *Do* it. I want it. God, Nick, just—"

He surged inside her mouth again, and forced her back against the hood of the Triumph. Delia's beer bottle tipped over and hit the concrete floor. Without lifting his mouth from hers, Nick shoved up her sweatshirt, then pushed away her bra. Delia's breasts, warm and small, seemed to swell in his hands, filling them.

A little roughly he thumbed her nipples and felt her shudder beneath him. He knew he should be gentle, knew he should slow down. He couldn't. *Couldn't.* "God," he said, tearing his mouth from hers and going to her breast. "I have to taste you. Then make love to you."

Delia felt a jolt of raw lust when Nick's mouth molded over her nipple, hard, hot, and hungry. A torrent of emotions washed over her, fear and need. Doubt. Desire. *Lust.* For long dark moments he sucked, the rough stubble of his beard abrading her flesh. And then Nick drew one nipple into his teeth and bit. The pain was wildly arousing, like nothing she'd ever experienced. She screamed softly, felt her body bow up again, and felt the damp heat of desire between her thighs.

More. She wanted *more.* Her breath came fast and shallow as she tore the tails of his shirt from his jeans, and let her hands roam over him. His chest was layered in muscle, his nipples hard, too. She ached, oh, God, she ached and wanted . . . wanted him *now.* Wanted what he promised; to be open beneath him, taking him deep. The urge was so primal, Delia scarcely felt him drag her shorts and panties down. Then the metal of the car hood was cold against her back, jolting her at least partway to reality.

"Nick?" she whispered. "Here?"

"Here, Delia," he ordered, one hand going to his fly. "Now."

Expertly he loosened the button and slid the zipper down. He dragged Delia's hips down the hood and pushed her thighs wide. His penis sprang free of his briefs, hot and satiny against her belly.

Oh, God, thought Delia, *what am I doing?*

But her mouth couldn't form the word *stop.* Her clitoris had flipped the Disengage Brain switch, and the rest of her body was roaring on. Nick dragged her farther down the car hood, and Delia felt his hand touch her inner thigh, making her jump.

Unhesitatingly he slid his fingers into the folds of her flesh, into the incredible wetness. "Good God, Delia," he growled. "So hot. So pink and pretty." With his fingers, he slid back and forth until his hand brushed her clitoris. "Sweet little clit," he whispered, nipping at the flesh of her neck. "Ah, Delia, I want to taste it. Suck it. But I can't wait."

"Don't," she rasped. "Don't wait, Nick. Do it. Oh, God, *do* it before I chicken out."

Nick leaned over her, snaring one of her wrists in his big hand, and forcing her thighs wide with his body. He watched intently as his shaft probed her and slid inside, spreading her open. She needed it all. Wanted to ride down hard on his cock. Fisting her hand greedily in his hair, she said so, begged him, and began to move.

"Oh, no, baby," he rasped. "Oh, God. Hold still, Delia."

He eased inside another inch. And another. Delia

opened her eyes. Nick's face was a mask of agony. His cock was shoving into her now, slowly spreading her, pinning her to the car's hood like a butterfly, wings open and beautiful. And strangely, she felt beautiful. She almost didn't care if someone *was* watching. The incongruity of what she was doing simply did not strike her. She knew only that she wanted Nick, wanted him deep, deep inside her.

"Jesus Christ, Delia," he grunted. "Tight, baby. So tight."

"Please, Nick, please," she begged. "More. All the way."

"Go easy, darlin'," he choked. "Almost."

And then Nick pushed the rest of his shaft inside, filling her, shocking her. There was so much, so deep, it should have hurt. It didn't. With a grunt of satisfaction, Nick set his hands at her waist and urged her down against him. Then he captured both her hands, shoving them high over her head, and moved back and forth inside her.

Delia had never experienced anything so decadent in her life. This was not normal lovemaking. It was exhibitionism and hedonism and wild animal sex, just as he'd promised, and Delia knew she should be embarrassed, but she wasn't. Because Nick was pumping himself in and out of her now, rhythmically forcing her body against the cold metal of the car as he drove her down and down, holding her hands tight, forcing her thighs wide, and blotting out all reality as he plunged her into the dark, swirling desire of his making.

Over and over, he stroked her. Rode her, his hard

thighs working, his concentration absolute. The metal hood of the Triumph buckled and popped, its front suspension squeaking like old bedsprings. Nick had just the right rhythm, just the right angle, and he moved on her as if he could last forever.

Delia sensed that Nick left his mark on a woman, that tomorrow she'd still know she'd been with him. With every movement of her body, every breath she drew, Delia would know that Nick Woodruff had been inside her. Branded her. There was just so much of him, it was almost overwhelming. She had never known sex could be like this. Chaotic and wild. Wonderfully inexorable. And it was then, just as Delia felt bliss begin to edge near, that an awful truth hit her. A truth she'd denied, intellectually, a thousand times.

Size did matter.

Oh, God, it mattered *a lot*.

That was her last thought before lightning struck, and Delia screamed her release, surging and pulsing around Nick's cock.

When Delia came to—and it seemed as if she drifted for a long, long time—something felt vaguely wrong. It took her a moment to realize that inside her, Nick wasn't moving. *At all.* She opened her eyes to see his were squeezed shut. "Nick?"

Nick had let go of her hands. Still up to the hilt inside her, he now held Delia gently around the waist, his thumbs nearly touching above her belly button. "Nick?" she said again.

Nick just shook his head, and spoke one word, his voice fraught with agony. *"Condom."*

Delia's head fell back against the car hood with a metallic thud. "Oh, holy shit."

Good God, how could they have been so stupid? she wondered. Either of them? Too late now. Nick was making a low, mournful sound, like a dog whimpering to be let in from the cold, then suddenly, he lifted his body away. Delia sat up on the car hood just in time to see him hitch up his jeans and walk off. Dazed and confused, she jerked her clothes back into place, and slid off the Triumph's hood. "Wait, Nick!" she said. "You can't . . . can't just . . ."

But he could. And by God, he was. With a determined pace, Nick was striding across his backyard, his jeans still unzipped, and slithering halfway off his narrow hips.

Delia knew at once where he was headed. "No, Nick!" she cried. "No! Don't do it!"

But he did, pausing just long enough to toe off his sneakers and shuck his jeans. Delia was already running when Nick hit the water with a splash.

Delia dashed to the edge of the pool and peered over the edge. Nick was floating on his back, his chambray shirt billowing about him in the water, his cotton briefs snug, and now almost flat, across the groin.

"Well, that problem's solved," he said, wiping his plastered hair off his face. "This shit's so cold, I'll never see my dick again."

"Oh, man, I can *not* believe you just did that," said Delia, falling to her knees by the water. "Is this thing heated?"

"Barely," said Nick, rolling into a dog paddle. "That's the whole idea, sugar."

"Sorry to hear that," said Delia, standing up and dropping her shorts. She hit the water gracelessly, splashing water over Nick. The cold shocked her body and sucked the wind from her lungs. Delia came up gasping. "Oh, shit! This is f-f-freezing!"

Nick was already laughing. "What did you jump in for?"

Delia pushed the sopping hair from her eyes. "It seemed only fair," she said, paddling toward him. The water wasn't deep, thank God. Nick caught her by the waist and pulled her close. Delia was already shivering.

Nick laughed again and kissed her nose. "You're still wearing your Keds, you idiot."

"Oh, Nick," she said, setting her forehead against the top of his shoulder. "Why did you do that?"

Nick shook his head. "Had to do something," he said. Delia could hear the words rumbling in his chest. "Come on, let's get out of here and into the hot tub."

Turning, he planted his hands on the edge of the pool, hefted himself smoothly up, then hauled her out like a sopping dishcloth. They were a comical pair, thought Delia, dripping on the edge of Nick's pool. Her sweatshirt and panties clung to her body. Nick still wore his socks and briefs, and his shirt was plastered to his chest. But beneath his briefs, Delia could still make out the generous shape of his penis. No hiding that, no siree.

"Delia, darlin'," said Nick. "D'you know you're staring at my cock again?"

Delia jerked her head up and blushed.

"Gotcha," he said, grinning. "Last one in's a rotten egg."

Nick dashed toward the hot tub and shoved off the cover. Delia followed, kicking off her Keds and following him in. The scalding water surged around her knees as she went down the steps. Nick floated against the wall and pulled Delia to him, her back to his chest.

"I'm sorry, baby," he whispered, hitching his chin over her shoulder. "I'm sorry I did that. I lost my mind."

Delia turned in his arms. After the chill of Nick's pool, the hot tub was incredibly soothing. "Oh, Nick, I feel just awful," she said, unable to look him in the eyes.

Nick slid a finger under her chin and lifted her gaze to his. His eyes were sober, reluctant. "Hey, I started it," he said. "I just wasn't thinking, you know? But I could have gotten you pregnant. Or something a lot worse than that, for all you know."

But it was the pregnancy notion that had shocked him, at least in part. Delia could see the concern in his eyes. "Nick, listen to me, I won't get pregnant. It's not that time. But the other thing, God, you're right. We both lost control. But I *want* to trust you. It's naive, I know, coming from someone like me."

Stubbornly Nick shook his head. "But do you trust the woman I screwed last Wednesday? Or the guy she'd been with the week before?"

Delia stared at him, her eyes wide.

"Gotcha," said Nick again. "There wasn't anyone last Wednesday. Or last month. Hell, maybe not even last year. After making love to you, I can't remember having any other women."

"Liar," said Delia softly.

Nick chuckled and pulled her close again. "Good point, darlin'," he said. "I might be a liar. See, you don't know, do you?"

Delia smiled a little weakly. "Oh, I understand," she said softly. "A little too well, maybe. And all I can say is that this stuff is a lot easier to deal with on a radio talk show."

"Yeah, there, you're the intellectual professor," murmured Nick, his eyes drifting over her. "Here, you're a very sensual woman, driven by your needs just like the rest of us."

"You're right," she whispered, letting herself sag against him. She'd just taken one hell of a risk, and she of all people ought to know better. Next time, she swore, they would be careful. And she was already hoping there was a next time. "God, Nick, do you know how good you are?" she asked as the hot water swirled around them.

Nick touched her lightly on the cheek. "Delia, baby, that wasn't good," he whispered. "That was pathetic. I screwed you in broad daylight on the hood of a broken-down '68 Triumph, and did a damned sorry job of it."

Delia laughed. "So I should have held out for a Ferrari?"

Laughing, Nick slid one hand around to cup her behind. "Stay with me, Delia," he said, dropping his voice an octave. "Let me show you what really fine sex is. Let me teach you what a passionate creature you are. Just give in to me tonight. And I swear, I'll do a better job."

Delia closed her eyes and laid her head against his

chest. She was afraid—afraid it really might get better. "Oh, Nick," she whispered. "You scare me a little."

She felt him nuzzle the top of her head. "I won't hurt you, darlin'," he reassured her. "Look, why don't you go inside and start warming up my bed? And as soon as I get back, I'll handcuff you to the headboard and give you a proper loving."

Somehow, the handcuff remark didn't even phase her. "You're leaving?"

"Off to Kroger's," he said, giving her rump a good squeeze. "To pick up a couple of steaks, some wine, and a dozen condoms."

Delia looked up at him. "A *dozen?*" she squeaked.

Nick winked at her. "Don't fret, sugar," he said. "I can get more tomorrow."

CHAPTER FIVE

Tomorrow, he had said.

So maybe this wasn't a one-night stand? Delia pondered that possibility as she watched Nick back his black pickup out of his drive and roar off in the direction of the local strip mall. Suddenly she wasn't at all sure how she felt about continuing to have sex with him. Her heart was still tripping dangerously, and Nick Woodruff just didn't look like a long-term bet.

Well, did *she* look long-term? No, probably not. She was too career-driven. Too afraid of failure to slow down. Admittedly, that had been a part of what had ruined her marriage. But Nick had made it plain he wanted sex, not a relationship. What he offered her was pure, physical satisfaction. The chance to explore her more carnal side—with someone who was really, really good at it. The man had not been bragging.

Feeling a little lost, Delia stood in the middle of Nick's bedroom, wearing nothing but one of his chambray work shirts. He'd thrown all their clothes in the dryer and tucked Delia into his bed before heading off to Kroger. But Delia had climbed out at once, too restless to lie still. Now, in her bare feet, she roamed through the empty house. Empty save for Nick's cats, Click and Clack.

Well, at least Nick listened to plenty of public radio, she mused, bending down to scratch Click under the chin. The big gray tabbies were Tiger Lily's kittens, Nick had said proudly. After finding them in his Triumph, he'd laid claim, and Bud had been forced to concede. Click was now twirling around Delia's ankles and purring his approval, while his brother stretched out in Nick's office window, soaking up what was left of the afternoon sun. Somewhere farther down the hall, she could hear the dryer rumbling, the button on Nick's Levi's making a rhythmic *stritch-clack-scritch* as it tumbled.

Nick's house was open and spacious, the dining room, living room, and kitchen defined primarily by wide arches and thick Oriental rugs. He had furnished his home simply, in earth-toned leather and tweedy fabrics. His small, neat office opened off the kitchen, its bay window fitted with a cushion which Clack was using to good effect. A fieldstone fireplace dominated the living room. The iron grate looked well used, and the hearth was surrounded by an antique fender, at least eight inches high, its brass buffed to a mirror-like sheen.

All the floors were made of wide oak planks, stained brown and polished clean, but without any glossy finish. Delia wandered into the kitchen. Compared to the sterile steel and granite in her kitchen, Nick's kitchen looked spartan but functional. Nice, actually. And amazingly clean. In fact, everything about Nick seemed clean and simple. Uncomplicated. Straightforward. Like his approach to sex.

Click had followed her into the kitchen. He rose upon his hind legs now and rubbed his head against the side of her knee. Delia looked down to see two empty bowls on a Garfield place mat, right by the refrigerator. On top of the fridge sat a bag of cat food. Automatically Delia reached for it and filled both bowls.

How odd, she thought, watching Click began to nibble. She'd never had a cat, or any other sort of pet. Her mother had claimed to be allergic. Neville had been too fastidious. How comforting it seemed to have them there, just hanging around. Intrigued, Delia pulled out a kitchen chair and sat down to watch. When Click finished eating, he began to methodically lick his paws and wash his face. Delia found it strangely soothing to watch. And she was still watching when Nick came through the back door carrying two bulging grocery bags.

"You're back," she said, leaping out of the chair. "I fed your cat. Is that okay?"

"Hey, they rule," said Nick, bending to give her a swift, smacking kiss. Then, in what looked like one smooth motion, he dropped one bag on the kitchen island, shoved the other into the fridge, and scooped her up in his arms.

"Now it's *my* turn," he said, and carried her into the bedroom. "And darlin', when I'm done, I promise you won't be able to speak in complete sentences."

DELIA LAY IN the middle of Nick's bed, watching as he undressed. Outside, the sun was sinking in a brilliant magenta sky, the last rays of pink slanting through the window blinds, warming Nick's skin. "Delia," he said, letting his shirt drop onto the floor. "You sure do look good in my bed."

Her mouth dry, Delia watched as his clever fingers made short work of his button, then grabbed the zipper tab. Swiftly he jerked it open, then shoved both jeans and briefs down his thighs. His penis sprang free, already hard and impossibly large. Delia made a little choking sound in the back of her throat.

Nick looked up, grinning, as he kicked his brown Docksiders off with the jeans. "Don't worry, darlin'," he said. "It still fits."

He came toward the bed, sat down on the edge, and fished through his pants pockets, withdrawing a package of condoms and a small bottle of lubricant. *Whoo boy,* thought Delia, getting a really good look for the first time. Nick was tanned from his buttocks all the way up, and along the nape of his neck, his hair was razored off straight and neat, in an almost military fashion. His waist was narrow above his perfect ass, and his back looked broad and strong.

The chest was fine, too, she noticed when he turned toward her. Smoothly he rolled onto the bed, propped himself up beside her on one elbow, and began to undo the buttons on her shirt. Delia just lay there, savoring the look of him, and the feel of his heavy hand working its way down her body.

Nick tried to keep his hand from shaking as he folded back the fabric that shielded Delia's breasts. She looked so small and fragile in his shirt, which was about three times too big for her. Carefully he cupped her left breast in his hand, weighing it carefully. "So beautiful," he murmured gruffly. "So small and perfect, Delia."

He reached back to his night table and picked up the little bottle of lubricant he'd bought at the drugstore, flipping the cap open with his thumb. "I warmed it in my pocket," he said, drizzling just a little onto his fingertips. "I don't want anything cold touching your body tonight."

Then, lightly, he brushed his fingers across her left nipple, watching as it pebbled invitingly, begging him to suck and to bite. Christ, what a vision. Delia was eager, hot, and ready. But he wanted to delay. To tease. He only prayed he could hold off. She'd driven him nearly insane on top of the Triumph this afternoon, and only raw fear had kept him from pumping her full of his seed, and perhaps claiming her forever. God, what a close call. For both of them.

Shaking off the worry, Nick turned his attention to Delia's other breast, lightly rubbing the lubricant into her soft flesh. Beneath his hand, Delia moaned and closed her eyes, writhing just a little on the bed. Her hands came up, as if pleading for something, then her arms went limp, and her hands fell back into the pillows beside her head.

Surrender, he thought. *Sweet surrender.*

The sharp, exotic tang of patchouli and citrus filled his nostrils. But underlying the scent of the lubricant was the sweet smell of Delia's skin. He'd first noticed it when he'd pushed her back onto the hood of his car and shoved up her sweatshirt. It was like Dove soap, mingled with a warm, feminine fragrance that was uniquely Delia's.

Her body was so responsive, so exciting. Nick had to force himself to go slow, to savor her. How many times would Delia consent to share his bed like this? A man couldn't take such good fortune for granted. Gently he dotted the lubricant down her breastbone, then lower still. He watched, intrigued by her responsiveness as Delia writhed again, her hands tightening into fists, her back arching as if to beg for his touch.

"Nick?" Her voice was thready and uncertain.

Nick leaned into her and set his lips against her ear. "Less can be more, sweetheart," he said, lightly flicking the tip of his tongue around the perfect, pink shell of her ear.

Delia's body flexed again. "But *more* is what I want," she said thickly.

Nick chuckled softly. "Just *feel* for a bit, darlin'," he whispered. "Don't rush. Let me touch you. Let me heighten that ache."

Delia's eyes held his, ice-blue and full of need. "I want it all *now.* I want you inside me again. Please, Nick."

Impatient. He liked that. "Not now, baby," he crooned to her. "Not yet. I want to touch and taste you first. I want to make you beg just a little. And then I want to watch you touch yourself—"

"*Umm,*" moaned Delia. "And I want to touch *you,* Nick. Teach me. Show me what you like."

Nick lowered his mouth to her right breast, drew the tip between his teeth, and gently nipped her. "I want you on your knees sucking my cock, baby," he growled. "That's one thing I like. Will you do that for me?"

Delia swallowed hard, the muscles of her throat working beautifully. "Anything," she whispered, her gaze going eagerly to his penis. "Anything for you, Nick. Just make love to me again."

That hungry look in her eyes almost broke him. "Oh, I will," he rasped.

Looking mesmerized, Delia watched his hand slide over her body. Then suddenly she shuddered a little and closed her eyes again, allowing her head to fall back.

Nick studied her for a moment. It wasn't the first time she'd closed her eyes that way, almost as if she feared sensory overload. As if she had to shut out some of her senses, or explode. He was intrigued. Delia was amazingly responsive to his touch. On a whim, he got up and crossed the room to his closet.

Delia sat up a little when the door slid open. Nick reached inside and grabbed a fistful of neckties, then returned to her side. "I want to blindfold you, Delia," he rasped. "Will you let me? Will you trust me?"

Delia looked a little uncertain. "Are you going to tie me up?"

Nick smiled and slowly shook his head. "Not unless you want me to," he answered honestly. "I just want to slow down your responses, restrain you a little, and heighten your senses."

"That sounds . . . intriguing."

Nick leaned forward and drew his tongue along the

sweet curve of her jaw. "And I want you to plead for it just a little, Delia," he whispered against her throat. "Stroke the old male ego. Beg me—eventually."

Delia nodded weakly. "O-okay . . ."

Nick sat up again and drew his favorite, a dark red Ralph Lauren, from the slithering pile of silk and wool. Her eyes were round now. He flashed her a deliberately wicked grin. "Now, be a good girl for me, Delia," he said, deliberately trailing the silk over her milk-white thigh. "Be real quiet, darlin', and hold just as still as you can. That's our little game, okay?"

Delia shivered. "Yes. Okay."

Nick drew the red silk around one fist, and snapped it taut in the other hand. "Now, don't let me make you scream, Delia," he warned, reaching for her. "Make me work for it first."

Gently he positioned the tie just below the soft arch of Delia's brows and tied it just tight enough for his purposes, then followed with a second tie, just a little lower. Then he sat back on his haunches, licked one finger, and lightly brushed her nipple with it.

"Aaah," moaned Delia, arching a good three inches off the bed.

Satisfied, Nick stroked her other breast, and got the same sensual response.

"Oh, Delia, darlin', you're hot enough to melt paint," he whispered in his silkiest voice. "This is too easy, baby. Don't let old Nick make you beg for it."

Delia nodded, her soft black curls scrubbing his pillow. "I—I won't, then," she said, following his lead. "I—I'll make *you* beg for it."

Methodically, then, Nick stroked her breasts and her belly with the tip of his finger, sometimes wetting it first, sometimes trailing it lightly through the nest of curls which hid her clitoris, but never letting her guess where the next touch would occur. Soon he could feel the faint heat and dampness between her legs.

He eased his next stroke a little deeper, and Delia couldn't hold out. Soon she was punctuating the falling dusk with her little cries of pleasure and surprise, until eventually, her whole body was shivering, her pelvis tilting up invitingly.

"Now, Nick," she finally rasped. "I can't—I can't—wait. Do it *now.*"

"No, no, no," he whispered. "Be good, sugar. Be a good and patient girl."

Delia gasped for breath. "I'll try," she said faintly. "But it's *hard,* Nick."

"Oh, darlin', you don't know what hard is," he whispered. "But you keep wiggling around on that bed, and you're gonna get hard right up to the hilt."

"So *do* it, Nick," she begged. "Give it to me now. I'm bad. I can't wait. Do it now."

Then, fascinated by the raw lust in her voice, Nick picked up another tie, this one made of soft wool, and stroked just the tip of it down her belly. Restlessly she shifted on the mattress. His blue shirt was snarled underneath her now. "Nick," she groaned. "Please. *Please.*"

"God, Delia, you are such a sensual creature," he said, stroking the tie down her body again. "Your every nerve ending must be hot-wired."

Delia swallowed, and nodded. *"Do it, Nick,"* she choked. "Fuck me now. You *promised."*

Nick smiled. "I don't think so, baby," he murmured.

Then he stroked the tip of the wool tie from her belly button down into the nest of dark curls. Delia shuddered again and moved one leg, opening herself to him. Nick set one hand on her inner thigh and pushed her wider still.

Delia moaned and followed his silent command, opening herself fully. Nick felt his stomach bottom out with need. The folds of Delia's flesh were already damp and glistening. Closing his own eyes now, Nick puddled the tie between her thighs, then dragged the full length of it up her body, sliding it through her outer lips.

"Nick!" The word came out a little yelp, and Delia began to pant.

Nick pushed the other thigh open. Over and over, he teased at her wet folds, drawing the tie up, then down, and back again, the rough woolen fabric not quite capable of touching her clit, but merely hinting at the tantalizing possibility. Delia's nipples were hard as little rocks now, taut and jutting from her small, fine breasts. Nick wet his fingers, and lightly touched one, still sliding the tip of the tie through her mound. Delia gave a little scream, her shoulders coming off the mattress.

"Nick, *please—!"*

She was not going to last. Nick could sense it. He dropped the tie over one side of the bed, then drizzled more oil on his fingertips. "Okay, baby," he said. "You've earned this."

Then he set one hand above her mound and spread Delia's lips wide. The pink folds of flesh were shiny with her dew, and in the center, her delicate clit was as hard as his cock. Deliberately Nick touched her there with his lubricated fingers. Delia's breath exploded from her chest on a roar, and one hand went to her blindfold. Nick caught her wrist and pushed it firmly into the bedcovers, holding her down. At once her other hand followed, but instead of clawing at the tie which bound her eyes, Delia fisted it in the fabric of his bedspread, her knuckles white with need.

Nick stroked along her inner lip, and Delia began to shake. Greedily he bent and touched just the tip of her clitoris with his tongue. Delia shrieked, then began to sob. He stroked her again, lapping at her with long, sure strokes, ending each with his tongue teasing lightly at her nub. God, he wished he could feast on her forever. How he wanted to lick and suck every morsel of Delia's small, lithe body.

"Good Lord, Nick—!" Delia sobbed again on his next stroke. *"Oh, oh . . ."*

And he knew he'd already waited too long. One more stroke, and Delia tumbled over the edge. "Oh, my God, oh, my God," she chanted as Nick watched her explode before his eyes. She was gasping for breath, fighting to claw out for him. "Oh, God, *Nick—!*"

She was so beautiful, so lost in herself, so completely caught up in her passion. Nick stroked her with his palms, then soothed her with his crooning voice until Delia stopped shaking. Then gently he reached up and untied the blindfold. His heart lurched when he saw her eyes, wet with tears and soft with satisfaction. He gathered her up in his arms and pulled her against his chest.

"Baby, that was beautiful," he whispered thickly.

For a moment she held herself against him, saying nothing. "My God, I've never felt anything like that in my life," she finally said, her voice even huskier than usual.

Nick let her go and reached for a condom. His eyes never leaving Delia's, he tore through the wrapper with his teeth and swiftly rolled it down his cock. After all he'd been through today, he wasn't going to last, either. His erection twitching insistently, Nick slid his hands around Delia's waist.

"Get on top, darlin'," he commanded. "Climb up and take old Nick for a good hard ride."

Delia had returned to full consciousness now. At his teasing tone, she grinned and allowed herself to be dragged awkwardly over Nick's body. They ended up with his head somewhere near the footboard, and Delia half-straddling his thighs. Nick shifted his weight, and Delia rose up on her knees.

Fascinated, Nick watched as her expression shifted to one of intense focus. Then, taking his sheathed cock in her hands, Delia thrust it between her legs, tipped back her head, and sank straight down on it with a long, sweet sigh. It was the most graceful thing Nick had ever seen. Then Delia lifted herself, lightly and elegantly, and did it all over again.

Nick moaned deep in his chest and kept watching her move on top of him. It took only a stroke or two before he understood the reason for her intense focus. Each time she sank down on him, Delia clenched her vaginal walls tight around his cock, so tight she almost couldn't rise up again. With every fluid, graceful motion of her body, the woman pulled at his flesh, milking him.

It only took about ten of those tight, fluid strokes before Nick had forgotten all about grace. Two more and he was hollering loud enough to wake Bud Basham. One more, and his brain was splintering apart in about six different colors—and if he could have found the strength, he'd have begged Delia to marry him, right then and there.

But he did not have the strength. He couldn't even open his mouth. And without saying a word, Delia slid quietly off of him, tucked her body against his, and went promptly to sleep, thereby saving them both from what would undoubtedly have been a moment of grave embarrassment.

Oh, God. With an awful premonition stirring deep in his stomach, Nick just lay there, flat on his back, one arm behind his head and the other holding Delia snug against him, and feeling morally confident that he had just gotten himself into the deepest shit of his life.

THREE HOURS LATER Delia woke up with a fierce appetite. For food. Remembering the bag Nick had shoved into the refrigerator, she rolled over in his arms and prodded him awake.

Nick cooked while she sat at the kitchen island drinking his burgundy—the really good kind—and watching his delicious rear end. The food, as it turned out, was delicious, too.

"Nick, I was just wondering," she said, forking up a sliver of sautéed portobello. "You don't think there's any way Bud could have seen us, do you?"

From the opposite end of the kitchen table, Nick looked up from his steak. "What, bonking on the hood of the Triumph?" he asked with a wink. "Nope. He's gone to his granddaughter's for the weekend. Left early this morning."

"Thank God." Delia poked at her potatoes for a minute, but she was full. "Can I have some more wine?"

Nick grinned unabashedly. "Only if you'll get drunk enough to have phone sex later."

Delia felt her face color. "Nick!" She reached for the bottle, but Nick snatched it away.

"Maybe I'll make you lick it from my navel," he said, thrusting the bottle behind his back.

"Maybe I'll make you beg for it," she shot back, keeping her voice soft and low.

"Ooh, a mean woman," he said, circling the table. "I like that."

Delia smiled faintly, but she could sense that something deeper lay behind his banter. Nick bent his head and nibbled at her earlobe. "Hey, Dr. Delia," he whispered. "Remember what you told Evelyn from East Brunswick?"

"Evelyn?" Delia considered it. "The one who thought her husband was a pervert for wanting to have sex in his velour recliner?"

"That's the gal," said Nick, working his way down her throat with his teeth. "You told her that having sex in unusual places could be a turn-on."

Pushing away her plate, Delia let her head tip back against her chair. "Worked for me," she answered, feeling suddenly lethargic. "It doesn't get much more unusual than the hood of a sports car, does it?"

Nick's hands were all over her now, and his voice was thickening. "Stand up, baby," he rasped, skimming one hand down her belly to ease his fingers beneath the elastic of her panties. "Let me bend you over that table and show you just how *unusual* we can get."

AFTER DELIA AND Nick made love in the kitchen, they did it again in the living room on Nick's big leather sofa. In between they had a little foreplay in the laundry room, followed by an interesting interlude in the foyer with Delia on her knees and Nick clinging to the coatrack, begging for mercy. All of which ultimately landed them back in Nick's king-sized bed again, with him on top. The man was unstoppable.

When Delia awoke long hours later, the big red numbers on his clock radio said 3:35 and the bed was empty. Shrugging into Nick's chambray shirt, she padded through the bedroom and down the hall. She found Nick in his study, dressed in nothing but a pair of jeans. He sat at his desk, his head in his hands, staring down at a blank piece of paper. On his laptop, flying windows fluttered across his screen saver, and Delia got a distinct impression they'd been there awhile.

Delia's eyes were still adjusting to the light when she

spoke. "Hey, handsome," she said, dragging a hand through her hair. "You okay?"

Nick wheeled his desk chair around and threw his arms wide open. His smile was wan, and he looked tired around his eyes. "Well, top o' the morning, Dr. Delia," he said, pulling her into his lap so that she strad-dled him.

"I'll say." Delia stared him straight in the eyes. "It isn't even four o'clock. Couldn't you sleep?"

He kissed her nose, then lightly rested his forehead against hers. "Mmm, you smell like a sleepy, luscious woman," he whispered. "Mind if I have a bite?"

"You're avoiding my question," she pointed out.

But her shirt wasn't buttoned, and before she could draw another breath, his mouth was on her breast, nib-bling and sucking. It felt so good, Delia let her breath escape on a little sigh. But he was trying to divert her, and she knew it. She could sense the edginess inside him.

"Hey, come on, tough guy," she said softly. "What's wrong?"

He flicked a wary glance up at her. "Nothing," he said. "Except that I've got a sexy woman on my lap, and she won't hush up long enough for me to kiss her."

Delia gave him a sideways smile. "You'll kiss me. But not *talk* to me?"

Nick's eyes flashed with irritation. "Damn it, Delia, it isn't like that and you know it."

"Do I?" she answered softly.

Nick's shoulders sagged in resignation. "Okay, I've got a stressful job," he grumbled. "And a goddamned incident report I can't seem to write, even though, yes, it's keeping me awake. But look, Delia, don't nag, all right? I don't need a psychologist to chat with. I need a woman to screw. Trust me, sugar, that's the best therapy there is."

Well. Nick had just posted a NO MENTAL TRESPASSING sign, hadn't he? Delia considered it. Okay, so his interpersonal communication skills sucked. He had other talents. "Fine, point taken," she said.

"Hey," he said, gentling his tone. "Hey, Delia, look at me. That came out sounding ugly, didn't it? I'm sorry."

Delia shrugged. "Look, Nick," she said coolly. "I didn't come over here to moonlight. My day job is hard enough, remember?"

Nick seemed to take her sarcasm well. A slow, sexy, and slightly chastened smile began to curve one corner of his mouth. "Well, if you didn't come over here to psychoanalyze me, Doc," he said very quietly, "what did you come for?"

"The sex, Nick," she said flatly. "You're good at it."

The grin deepened. "Well, I do aim to please," he said, setting his hands at her waist and lifting her up just an inch.

Delia felt her eyes grow round, and Nick laughed. "Unzip my jeans, sugar, and give me some physical therapy."

Well, why not? His snap wasn't even fastened, so she lowered his zipper and pushed down his white cotton briefs. Nick's penis was already half-hard. Delia took it between her hands, closed her eyes, and felt the velvety length throb and harden beneath her touch.

Nick made a sound, a low, dark rumble in his chest, and shoved a hand into his jeans pocket, fishing out a condom. She watched hungrily as his clever hands worked the sheath down his erection, now rock-hard. It took only seconds, but it seemed like forever. Then Nick lifted her effortlessly, allowing Delia to settle herself onto his shaft with a soft, satisfied sigh. The chair's mechanics squealed in protest as she rode him. Her body was restless, needy. She pressed her lips to his throat and felt him shiver.

Good. Oh, God, it was so good. Her eyes still closed, Delia licked her lips and surrendered all her thoughts. Nick kissed her again, hot and deep, plumbing her mouth with his tongue until, by the dim glow of his desk lamp, they found satisfaction yet again. Then quietly he carried her back to bed and drifted off to sleep with her in his arms.

When next she awoke, the big red numbers said 5:07.

Monday morning. Delia felt an ache of disappointment in addition to the ache between her legs. Nick Woodruff had just about worn her out. Her extraordinary erotic encounter with him was over, and in less than three hours, she'd be back on campus, facing a roomful of bleary-eyed graduate students. Quietly she slid from the bed, stretched her sore muscles, and dressed. Nick still slept deeply, facedown with the sheets tangled about his waist. Good Lord, he looked fine. Still, Delia let herself out of the house, wondering what she'd been thinking, to spend her Sunday having sex with a stranger.

Except that Nick wasn't a stranger. In fact, Delia felt as though she'd known him for ages. And now she was left standing on his back porch, her legs dimpled with goose bumps, half afraid she was going to get her heart broken—and by a man she hadn't even liked especially well three days ago.

Well, she liked him fine now, that was for sure. Delia set a fast pace across the grass toward her house, wondering if she'd see him again. Well, of course, she would *see* him. He had her car. But at this point in the relationship—the relationship they were *not* having, she reminded herself—what should she do next? Thank him for a lovely evening? Send him flowers? Delia laughed, her breath fogging faintly in the cold air. None of her grandmother's old etiquette lectures seemed applicable here.

The street lamp from Greenway Circle cast just enough light to keep Delia from breaking a leg in the murk. Once inside her house it was a little easier to forget about Nick. After brewing a pot of coffee, she showered, dressed, then spent an hour on her lecture notes, something she should have done last night. At seven sharp she grabbed the phone and called Becky Jo for a ride to work, and soon she was back in the thick of her dull, ordinary life.

But as the day wore on, the lack of sleep caught up with Delia. Her morning dragged, and by the time her show went on the air, it was all she could do to feign interest in her guest, an epidemiologist studying the resurgence of syphilis on high school campuses. The first three calls were routine, all of them terrified teenagers who wanted to follow up on the discussion. Then Frank signaled a change of topic. The epidemiologist snapped open a copy of *Newsweek* and kicked back in his chair. Delia motioned Frank to send the next call through.

"Well, hey there, Dr. Delia," said a dark, sexy, and *very* familiar voice.

"What?" Delia's stomach lurched, and she almost knocked over her coffee cup. "I mean, good afternoon. Welcome to *Let's Talk About Sex*. Tell us who you are and where you're calling from."

"Yeah, sure, this is, um, *John,*" said the sexy voice. "From—er, from—"

Nick had obviously forgotten to plan the geography part. But Delia's shock had passed. "It's not a trick question, *John,*" she interjected in her huskiest voice.

"From Portland," he said hastily. "Portland, Oregon."

Delia adjusted her earphone. "Fabulous!" she managed. "I didn't realize this show had been picked up in Portland!"

"Not Portland," he said swiftly. *"Houston.* I mean, I'm from Portland. But I'm visiting my great-aunt in Houston. See? So I'm calling from Houston."

Frank was gesturing at his caller ID now and jerking a finger across his throat. Delia waved him off. "Well, I'm sure glad we got that straight, John," she said. "I hope you and Auntie are having a great time down in Houston."

"Yeah, sure, we're doing okay," he said, dropping his voice to a sexy whisper. "Anyway, I had a real important question. Something that's just driving me insane."

"Well, we can't have that," said Delia in her most *tut-tut* voice.

"That's what I thought," he answered. "So I wanted your advice. See, I met this girl. No, *woman*. She lives next door. And, well, last night, we had this totally mind-blowing sex."

"Okay, *John*," said Delia slowly. "Let me get this straight. You had sex with your elderly auntie's next-door neighbor?"

Nick paused for a moment. "Right."

Frank was making circles around his ear with his index finger now, so Delia shot him the bird. "And was your question about sexually transmitted disease, John?" she asked. "I mean, I'm duty-bound to remind you that having sexual relations with someone you don't know well is risky. Are you afraid you may have contracted something?"

"Oh, yeah, I contracted something, all right," said Nick. "The chronic itch to do it again. And I was thinking maybe tonight? So I was just wondering, you know, what you thought might be the fastest way to talk her into that."

Delia squeezed her eyes shut. "Well, this doesn't exactly sound like a question about healthy sex, John."

"Oh, it was healthy, Doc," said the sexy voice. "Trust me. It felt real healthy. That mentally cleansing, next-to-nirvana healthy, if you know what I mean?"

"O-*kay*," said Delia. "I'll bet Auntie was glad to hear that."

"Uh, I guess. But it's a secret, see? Which makes it even hotter, if you know what I mean."

"A hot, secret affair with the next-door neighbor?" said Delia dryly. "*Hmm*. Now, your question would be—?"

He paused for a moment. "Well, say you were in her shoes—"

"Your aunt's?"

"Who?" Nick hesitated. "No, no. The woman. Next door."

"Okay, John, I'll bite."

"Well, that's good to know, Doc," he said. "But what I wanted to ask is, if it was *you*, what would you do?"

"Well, this isn't exactly my field of expertise," Delia managed. "But I guess you could just call her up and ask."

"Hmm," he said thoughtfully. "And what do you think she'd say?"

"Well, gee, John, you sound like such a charmer," said Delia into the microphone. "How could she say anything but *yes?*"

CHAPTER SIX

*D*elia did say *yes.* In fact, she said yes with an almost startling frequency over the next two weeks. Their hot, secret affair stayed a secret, and only got hotter. Then Nick finished overhauling her engine, and late one Saturday night, Delia drove her car home.

But Nick hadn't finished with her, she soon discovered. And while he still never talked about his job or the future, he did return to SBI headquarters and began working long, irregular hours. Often he made short business trips. There was one to New York, a couple of day-hops to Charlotte. Delia traveled a lot, too. And so real life started to interject itself into their sweet, sensual idyll.

Delia, half heartbroken, kept expecting him to end their fling, or let it dwindle to nothing. But he didn't, and she couldn't find the strength to break it off, even though it was supposed to be "just an affair."

Nick continued to call two or three times a week,

inviting her over for evenings that inevitably ended in wild, crazy sex. The weather grew cool, but they did not. Sometimes Nick was a dark, dominant lover, plunging her into that murky chasm of passion and need, then leaving her gasping. Other times he was sweet, almost quaint, in his attentions. The worst of it was, no matter how she got it, the sex just kept getting better. And more satisfying. And more seductive. And Delia kept slipping and deeper into desperation, into the awful fear that soon, in the throes of one of her many multiple orgasms, she was going to fling herself at Nick's feet and beg him for some sort of commitment.

But Nick's only in this for sex, Delia kept warning herself.

Only that thought wasn't working anymore. Delia was falling in love, the head-over-heels kind, even though her head kept telling her heart that she barely knew Nick. She was beginning to feel like some desperate sorority girl, sneaking about, looking for some kind of sign that he might be serious about her. What such a sign might be, Delia did not know. A plane ticket down to Georgia to meet Daddy and the sisters? A jewelry box from Bailey, Banks, and Biddle stuck in his sock drawer? Hearts and arrows doodled on his grocery list? For a woman screwing a man who didn't want a relationship, she was pathetic and she was stupid.

Thanksgiving came, almost without Delia's realizing it. Out of duty, she flew to Pennsylvania to see her parents, who were as dour, conservative, and humorless as ever. They asked probing questions about Neville's new wife, frowning at the news of Alicia's pregnancy as if it had been Delia's fault her marriage had ended childless. She missed Nick more with each passing day, and by the time she got back to Durham, Delia was losing patience with herself.

Her house had been cleaned from top to bottom, Neville had finally hauled away all his junk, and on November first a shiny new FOR SALE sign had been staked on her front lawn. The real estate market was hot, and she'd already refused two low-ball offers for the house. Her realtor was now salivating over an almost-done deal from a retired neurosurgeon—and he was paying *cash*.

Yep, Delia was moving on, quite literally. And it was pretty obvious Nick Woodruff wasn't going with her, no matter how much she might wish otherwise. Still, it was another week before Delia steeled herself to tell him. And even then it took a coronary bypass to do it. Not Nick's, thank God—though the way he went at sex some nights made her fear he might end up with one.

No, *this* coronary belonged to her colleague, Dr. Enrique Despiza. And it came at a most inopportune time, just as Enrique had been packing for a ten-day conference in Paris, a gathering of the world's most preeminent researchers in the field of human sexual behavior. He was to have been one of the key lecturers.

Delia, one of us must go, he pleaded. A huge speaker's honorarium had already been paid, the money all but spent. Besides, the school had to be represented. And for Delia, he kept saying, it would be an unprecedented opportunity for worldwide exposure. But the only worldwide exposure Delia was worried about was the one she'd had on the hood of Nick's Triumph. Yep, *that* made career satisfaction pale, all right.

Still, the sight of her colleague struggling for breath, with one hand encircling her wrist and the other holding his oxygen tube, finally wore her down. Well, that, and the fact that she needed an excuse to leave Nick and Hidden Lakes behind, before she broke down into a blithering idiot. So, after calling her realtor, Delia beeped Becky Jo and told her to start looking for someone to sub on *Let's Talk About Sex,* then she went straight home from the hospital and dragged her suitcase from beneath the bed.

But all the while, she was really just bracing herself to go next door and do the hardest thing she'd ever done in the whole of her thirty-one years. Dump Nick Woodruff and get on with her life.

Besides, she told herself as she went `foot-dragging across her backyard, *it was just sex.* Sex was all Nick had ever asked for. She could not possibly be in love with him. Certainly, he was not in love with her. A couple of candlelit dinners, a dip in the hot tub, and a few good bounces on Nick's bed did not a grand romance make. She had been insecure after her divorce. She had fallen right out of Neville's bed and into Nick's—the dumbest, most emotionally confusing thing a woman on the rebound could do.

It was the first time she'd dropped in on Nick without calling. Through the bay window of his office, she could see him seated at his desk, intently studying something in his top drawer. She rang the bell, and

Nick's head jerked up, his eyes wide with surprise. At once he slammed shut the drawer and circled through the kitchen to let her in.

"Hey, darlin'," he said, opening his arms and dragging her hard against him. "I wasn't expecting you."

The last words were said softly, his lips pressed to her hair, but his voice sounded strained. In fact, now that she considered it, he'd been tense for the last several days. Delia looked up at him. "I'm sorry I didn't call. Should I have?"

Nick smiled. "No reason," he said, setting her away to look at her. "Hey, everything okay?"

"No, not okay." Delia shook her head, and he urged her toward the table. "Enrique had a heart attack," she began as Nick popped open a couple of beers. Then she told him about the conference, and her unexpected trip to Paris.

Nick's eyes went dark with emotion. "So just like that, you have to go? *Tomorrow?*"

Delia nodded. "It's my job."

Nick got up and began to pace the kitchen floor, one big hand set at the back of his neck. "How long?" he demanded, his voice gruff.

Delia felt her frustration spike. "Jeez, it's my *job*, Nick," she said again. "I'll be gone ten days, and it's the career opportunity of a lifetime."

Nick turned to stare at her. "Ten days?" he said. "You'll barely make it home for Christmas. Can't someone else go?"

Delia had never heard his voice so cool. "Hey, look, I'm sorry if this is putting a crimp in your sex life," she said. "So it's almost Christmas! What were you expecting? That I'd dress up like an elf and play sit-on-Saint-Nick's-lap?"

Nick's expression darkened. "Damn it, Delia, I don't appreciate your cynicism right now."

Delia stared up at him. "Hey, Nick, I'm sorry," she said, softening her tone. "I shouldn't be so sarcastic. But I came to tell you something else, too. I came to tell you . . ." She closed her eyes and shook her head. "I came to tell you that I can't keep doing this."

His tread was heavy as he approached the table. "Doing *what?*"

Delia opened her eyes. He was bent over the table now, his hands spread wide on the wooden surface. "Doing *what,* Delia?" he demanded. *"Being* with me? Is that what this is about?"

"Fucking you, Nick," she said, feeling something inside her wither and die. "Having meaningless, mindless sex with you. I mean, it's good, but I have obligations. I have to think rationally."

Nick lifted both hands, slammed them on the table, then turned his back on her. "Maybe, Delia—just maybe—if you didn't think so damned much, if you didn't have your nose shoved in so many friggin' textbooks, if you didn't pick apart and analyze every goddamn thing a man does or doesn't do—then maybe our sex wouldn't be so fucking meaningless and mindless. Did you ever think of that, Delia? Did you?"

Delia drew back an inch. "Whoa, where'd *that* come from?" she asked. "Look, Nick, we knew this had to end eventually. I mean—didn't we? So maybe eventually should be now? I have to go to Paris, and as soon as I get back, I'm moving."

"So you sold the house?" His voice was cold. Dead.

"I think so." Delia bit her lip. "My realtor says I may have to move fast, so she's arranging for the bank to give me a loan against the equity for a condo in Chapel Hill."

"In Chapel Hill," echoed Nick, as if it were the backside of the moon instead of a ten-minute drive.

"Yes." Delia tried to smile. "So I guess now I can even afford that new car," she added a little sadly.

"So while you're gone, I should just shit-can the old one along with our relationship, Delia?" he asked. "Is that what you're saying?"

"God, no, Nick! You don't know how deeply I appre—"

"Delia, just don't fucking start with that gratitude crap, okay?"

"Yes. Okay. But I appreciate *you,* Nick. I really do. This has been special. A precious, wonderful time for me. I . . . I thank you for that. Don't say I can't, Nick."

"Yeah, *special,*" he repeated. "Well, I'm glad I showed you a good time, darlin'."

Delia just sat there, watching her beer fizz. "Look, Nick, I don't know what I'm supposed to say here," she whispered. "This feels like a game with no rules. What do you want? What am I doing wrong?"

He was silent for a long moment, and when he spoke, his voice was calmer, his tone softer. "Nothing, Doc," he finally said. "You're right. And I know you've got obligations. I do, too. But it was good while it lasted, wasn't it? At least tell me that much."

"Yes, Nick," she said softly. "It was good."

Nick shrugged and turned away again. "So, have a nice trip, Doc," he said, bracing his hands on the kitchen counter. "A nice life, too. I'm sorry I'm being a jerk. And I'm sorry this is so easy for you to walk away from. But hey, I wish you well."

Delia stood a little unsteadily and braced her hand on the back of her chair. "I never said it was easy, Nick," she whispered. "I never said that."

But Nick kept his back to her. And finally, not knowing what else to do, Delia walked out of Nick's kitchen, and out of Nick's life. Then she walked on home, blinking back tears, and started packing.

A REAL CLOSE CALL.

Nick listened to Delia's departing footsteps and decided that that was what he'd just had. And it was as close as he'd ever come to making a complete fool of himself, too. Good God, he should have seen this coming.

For a long moment he simply stood with his hands clenched tight on the kitchen counter, willing himself not to do something unutterably stupid—like chase Delia down and drag her back inside the house. Instead, Nick tried to steady his breathing and focus on his brush with disaster. He had been kidding himself. He wasn't commitment material, and Delia had sense enough to know it. Besides, it was *just sex*. Not a relationship. Hadn't he once said as much to Delia?

Yes, and he'd never un-said it, either.

Okay, so maybe—just *maybe*—that was a part of the

problem? Nick felt as if his fingers were digging into the damned Formica. Maybe there had been too much sex and not enough romance? Hell, men didn't know the difference. Maybe he should have wined and dined her a bit? Or taken her to Georgia for Thanksgiving? Or told her how he felt. Yeah, that one. *Door Number Three, dumb shit.*

But the truth was, he hadn't been ready to share Delia, and it had taken him weeks to figure out how he felt. And when he had, it had scared the hell out of him. They had known each other less than two months. Everything had felt so fragile. So tenuous. So it had seemed better—*safer*—to just keep Delia to himself, to try to maintain what they had, and avoid the ravages of day-to-day life that could sometimes rip the heart out of even a strong, deep-rooted relationship.

And she was right, they both had obligations. Big ones. Demanding careers and a hard daily grind. And all they'd had together so far had been a time out of place, a fantasy. But he wasn't stupid. He'd known that was going to have to change. That eventually he'd need to brave the world and all its dangers with Delia. Still, he hadn't moved fast enough, had he?

Jesus! Nick bent down and picked up Click, who was rubbing his way around his ankles. He had to stop thinking of *ifs* and *maybes.* That way lay madness. It always did when you tried to figure women out. And it didn't matter anyhow, because Delia had been way too determined to get rid of him.

Nick pressed his cheek against Click's and considered it. Yep, she'd been calm, cool, and pretty damned collected. A woman on a mission. *Dump Nick Woodruff.* The words were probably penciled in her Day-Timer, right between *take out the trash* and *pick up the dry cleaning.* It felt like a blow coming out of nowhere. But it wasn't. A blind man could have seen it.

An idiot. He was a goddamned idiot. Still carrying the cat, Nick went back into his office, jerked open the drawer he'd just closed, dropped the plane ticket into the trash, then picked up the phone and dialed his dad.

CHAPTER SEVEN

*D*elia's ten days in the city of romance were anything but romantic. Paris in December was bleak, and her heart felt much the same. She spent her evenings alone in her room instead of networking, in the halfhearted hope that Nick would call. Which was ridiculous, since he had absolutely no way of finding her. Still, she was plagued by a gnawing sense of having made a dreadful misjudgment. Of having moved too quickly. Given up too soon. Something.

She was a psychology professor, for God's sake! But where Nick was concerned, she was acting like . . . well, like a woman. A once-bitten, twice-shy kind of woman. Making assumptions. Thinking the worst. Giving up without talking. Jeez, she was turning into the kind of female that drove family therapists insane. There was probably even a diagnostic code for her sort of neurotic behavior.

But Nick hadn't put up much of a fight, had he? Only his pride had seemed wounded. She hoped he at least missed the sex. Delia missed it; missed a lot more than just that. Nick wouldn't have much trouble finding another woman to warm his bed, and she knew it.

So one day, out of sheer boredom and sexual frustration, Delia did something she'd never done before. She played hooky. She skipped her afternoon meetings, and went strolling through the rue du Faubourg St.-Honoré, with the vague notion of buying herself some sexy lingerie. *Just in case.* And, she boldly decided, some dark chocolates. Maybe a big old pink vibrator, too, while she was at it. Yeah, *just in case* . . .

Delia found everything she wanted in one decadent little shop and returned to her hotel with two red shopping bags and a four-hundred-dollar Visa bill she couldn't afford. She only hoped they didn't search her luggage at the airport. For the rest of the conference, she tried to stay focused on her career, dragging on one of her business suits every morning and trotting downstairs to sip dark, bitter coffee and do the old grip-and-grin routine with her colleagues.

At least her lecture went well. So well that on the final day of the conference, Delia was asked to collaborate on a new research project at the University of Copenhagen. An invitation to attend the European Congress of Psychology in Vienna followed, a serious honor for both herself and the school.

So Delia should have headed for the airport that Friday feeling quite pleased with herself, but she didn't. The flight was long, the landing rough, and Delia's mood was not improved when her plane was grounded at Dulles. Her need to get home was reaching a feverish pitch. But snow and ice was pummeling its way toward the East Coast, taking a toll on the airports. Pittsburgh and Chicago had already closed. Up and down Concourse C, flight delays were flashing as frantic gate agents announced re-routings and cancellations. Hard-bitten business travelers already lined the corridors, bellowing into their cell phones like lunatics. The college kids had given up hope and lay scattered about the terminal using backpacks for pillows. Yep, it was going to be a long night.

Feeling tired and grubby, Delia scrubbed herself from head to toe in the Red Carpet Club and put on fresh clothes. Then she bought a frozen yogurt, propped her feet up on her briefcase, and started checking her office voice mail. Three hours, two yogurts, and a dead cell phone later, United performed a miracle. The club attendant announced her plane was boarding.

The flight was mercifully uneventful, and after circling Raleigh for thirty minutes while a runway was plowed, they touched down in a ferocious shudder, the last flight in before RDU shut completely down. Unfortunately, when they inched up to the gate, the plane hit a patch of ice and slid into the jetway, jamming up its hydraulics. Delia wanted to rip out her hair by the roots.

An hour later the passengers finally disembarked, made their way through baggage claim, then strolled out into a winter wonderland. Delia dragged her suitcases through the chemical slush and wished she'd had sense enough to change out of her pumps. They were Nick's favorites, she knew, because he always stared at her feet when she wore them.

In the parking garage she hefted her bags into the car, slid inside, and cranked the engine. The Volvo purred out of the garage like a tamed tiger. Delia thought of Nick, and wished she could kiss him. Traffic on westbound I-40 was nonexistent save for SUVs and snowplows. Unlike her native Pennsylvania, the Carolinas could be paralyzed by three inches of snow. Along the highway, silvery trees bowed low, beautiful but treacherous. The power lines, too, were sagging, and the precipitation was now peppering off her windshield, pure ice. The snow deepened and the sky darkened the closer she got to Durham. It was then that Delia began to notice the downed power lines.

By the time she reached Hidden Lakes, the Volvo was fishtailing. She spun her way through the security gate and skated sideways, trying to make it up her driveway. Deftly she cut into the skid, tapped the gas, and slid home, the front bumper just six inches from the garage door. Cold, starving, and glad to be alive, Delia dragged her bags into the kitchen, which felt like the inside of a meat locker. It made her remember her Parisian hotel's cramped rooms and bitter coffee with newfound affection.

After fumbling through her junk drawer, she found a stub of a candle, then felt her way toward the pitch-black dining room. There were some matches in the buffet, she hoped. But when she turned into the living room, a bright light flicked around the opposite corner, catching her squarely in the eyes. Blinded, Delia screamed, and her candle went clattering across the marble floor.

"Hey, it's just me," said a rough, deep voice. "It's okay."

"Nick?" The word was edged with hysteria.

The bobbing light, accompanied by heavy footsteps, came toward her, and a strong arm slid around her waist. "Christ, Delia, I've been worried half to death," Nick whispered, his warmth and scent surrounding her. "I was just checking upstairs before heading to the airport."

"Jeez, you s-scared me!" Delia's teeth were chattering with fright and cold. "How d-did you get in?"

Nick put the flashlight down on the buffet and pulled her close. "Resources," he said. "I kept imagining you'd wrecked your car or fallen down the stairs. United said your plane landed two hours ago."

"Yes, but we skidded into a jetway." A sense of warmth and relief was flooding through her. "How did you know my airline?"

"Resources," he repeated.

"Oh, right," said Delia. "Thank you, Sergeant Woodruff. What time is it, anyway? Why is it so cold?"

"Midnight," he said, then his tone shifted to his gruff policeman's voice. "Look, Delia, you can't stay here."

"I can't?"

In response Nick scooped her up in his arms, then somehow grabbed his flashlight. "It's twenty degrees outside," he said, sweeping her neatly through the kitchen door. "And ten in here. God only knows how long the power will be off. You're going to my house."

Delia squirmed. "Hey, put me down!"

"Why?" he asked, fumbling at the doorknob. "I have food, fire, and hot water."

"No, put me down." Delia began to push at his chest. "And don't let your knuckles drag on the way out."

"Nope. You're going next door, darlin'. And we are going to have ourselves a little talk."

"Oh, God." She wasn't sure she was ready for this. "Can I at least take my bag?"

Nick flicked the flashlight at her big rolling suitcase. "You gotta be shitting me."

"The small one," she whined. *Please?*

Somehow he snagged it off the kitchen counter.

"Okay," she said. "Now I'll go quietly, Officer."

"Yeah, I'll bet," said Nick. "Hold the flashlight."

"Just let me walk."

Nick shouldered his way through the kitchen door. "No way," he said as the wind slapped them both in the face. "Not in those shoes."

Delia didn't have much fight left in her. Nick's body was warm, his shoulders broad and protective. And she was so tired. So tired of being without him. He wore heavy boots that crunched deep into the snow as he made his way across her yard and into his. Delia pulled her coat tighter. Other than the yellow beam of his flashlight, they were surrounded by a darkness so silent and so deep it was eerie. No lights. No sound. *Anywhere.* Just the crunching rhythm of Nick's footsteps, and the certainty of his stride.

Delia really did feel as if she were being carried off by some caveman—and it didn't bother her all that much. "I'm not getting any say in this, am I?" she asked, trying to keep her tone light.

"Nope."

In his embrace she shrugged. "So I'm more or less at your mercy?"

Nick's gait faltered ever so slightly, and his breath hitched. "Yeah."

Delia thought on that for a second. "I, um, I thought we split up, Nick."

"You said."

Delia tried to look up at him, but could make out nothing but the hard angle of his jaw. "Do you want to talk about it?"

"Not now."

"I think I see," said Delia quietly. "Is this going to be strictly a monosyllabic conversation?"

"There you go again," he said. "Thinking. And using big words."

Nick went effortlessly up his steps, which had already been shoveled, and shouldered his way through the door. Delia felt instantly awash in memories. The soft candlelight, the warm earth tones, and the comforting smells of Nick's house: wood polish, dried rosemary, and his own spicy soap, all these things flooded her senses.

The place was toasty, too. In the living room a huge fire burned in the fieldstone hearth, its flames licking up behind the wide brass fender. In front of it a halfdozen quilts had been spread on the floor, and topped with a pile of pillows. To retain the heat, Nick had nailed up blankets to seal off his office and the corridor that led to the bedrooms. Delia hadn't missed the two Coleman coolers on the back porch, either. She'd have been willing to bet a month's salary they were stocked with steaks and other delicacies. In fact, she had every idea she and Nick could safely camp here for a month or better. The man was like some overgrown Boy Scout. He was *prepared*.

Mr. Boy Scout put her down next to the fire, tossed her bag on the sofa, and shucked his coat. Then he began to unfasten hers. Delia started to kick off her shoes, but something stopped her. Nick's gaze flicked up from her buttons. "Delia," he said, his voice suddenly raw. "I—"

"Yes?"

The coat slid off. Nick dropped his eyes, staring down at her breasts. Beneath her blouse and jacket, Delia could feel her nipples hard and peaked against the silk. His throat worked up and down. She touched him lightly on the face. "What, Nick?"

He tossed the coat on the sofa and set his hands at her waist. "I want you," he whispered, bowing his head until their foreheads touched. It was a tender gesture, one she'd come to love. "I still want you. Under me. On top of me. *With* me, Delia. Just for tonight, if nothing else. Please?"

Outside, the snow was still falling, soft and steady, all around them. Delia realized she was trapped here, alone with Nick. Leaving was impossible. But the impossibility had little to do with the weather, and everything to do with the hungry look in his eyes. With the swell of warmth in her heart. And the truth was, almost two weeks without him had driven her insane.

"Please?" he said again.

Delia leaned into him and set her hands against the hard wall of his chest. "Well, I am totally at your mercy," she whispered, her tone suggestive and throaty. "Aren't I?"

Nick didn't miss her suggestive tone. *At his mercy.* God, what he wouldn't give for that. But Delia had him by the balls—and worse, by his heartstrings. Surely she knew it? He watched her lick her bottom lip uncertainly, and crushed the sudden urge to jerk her body against his.

Delia's eyes had grown soft and warm. "Nick," she said, her voice husky. "The other day, you said . . . I mean, I thought we were—" She closed her eyes and shook her head. "Oh, God, Nick."

Nick just shook his head. "Don't talk, Delia," he whispered. "For once, just don't talk or think. Just *feel.* I need to make love to you, baby. God, it feels like it's been years. Like I can't breathe."

"All right."

Her words were soft. Submissive. That was her mood, too, he thought. Something inside him thrilled to that knowledge. She still wanted him. *Needed* him, at least in this one way. And somehow he'd build on that. He wouldn't screw up twice. Nick's hands went to her jacket, shaking a little as he unbuttoned it. He pushed it off and draped it over the sofa.

Delia wore a gray silk blouse with a camisole underneath. They still stood by the hearth, the glow outlining her slender waist, casting her face in shadow. Slowly he undressed her, easing the delicate garments from her body, his rough hands catching in the fabric. The camisole was just a breeze of black silk with thin, fragile straps. Underneath it, Delia's breasts swelled inside a matching demi-bra, a scrap of sexy nothing, its lace cups cut just across the tips of her hard, pink nipples. She moved to unhook it, and he caught her wrist.

"No," he rasped. "It's beautiful."

Delia smiled, dropped her gaze, and instead unhooked her skirt, and let it slide down her legs. She wore sheer black thigh-high stockings, the kind that stayed in place by themselves. Above them, she wore more black silk, and damned little of it. Just a tiny thong with a triangle of fabric. The sort of underwear a woman wore when she had plans. And she'd shaved, too, Nick noticed. Shaved real close, to reveal lots of soft, creamy skin. He wondered just how much of that creamy skin would be visible beneath her tiny triangle. Nick lifted one brow.

Delia leaned forward until her nipples touched his chest. "Do you like it?" she whispered, pressing her lips to his left ear.

Nick swallowed hard. "Oh, baby, is the Pope Catholic?"

She opened her mouth against his throat and sucked a little of his flesh between her teeth. "I'm glad you approve," she said, nibbling at him. "I paid a fortune for it in Paris."

"Why?" Nick choked out the word.

Delia pulled back, her expression suddenly shy. "I missed you," she confessed. "And, well, I was kind of hoping I might get lucky."

"Then you can stop hoping," he said, reaching down

to cup her mound. She was hot, already radiating dampness. He eased one finger beneath the silk and stroked her pubic hair, or what was left of it. "What's this about, darlin'?" he asked softly.

Delia blushed. "I wanted to . . . to do something daring," she confessed. "I'm tired of my boring old life. I want pleasure. Satisfaction. I want *you*, Nick."

"Well, that's good to know, Doc," he whispered, sliding his finger back and forth through her swollen lips, easing just a little deeper with each stroke until he lightly brushed her clitoris. Delia moaned and melted against his hand. He stroked her again, feeling the creamy heat flowing around her sex. Delia's breath came faster. With two fingers he gently parted her, then slipped his fingers inside. Her silky sheath clutched at him, inviting him deeper. Nick felt his groin tighten, and his stomach bottom out.

"Nick?" Her voice was unsteady.

"God, Delia, you are so hot," he whispered. "So beautiful. I want to lick you. And make love to you. And then I want you to walk all over me in those wicked black shoes."

She laughed weakly. Nick released her, swiftly stripping down to his jeans. Impatiently he kicked the pillows away from his makeshift bed and pulled Delia down on top of him. Her eyes soft and eager in the firelight, she shifted a little and reached greedily for his fly.

Nick watched her slender hand free the snap and ease down his zipper. She set her hand flat against his belly, skimmed her fingers underneath the elastic of his briefs, and Nick's skin shivered with want. Gently he pushed her hand away. "Not yet, darlin'," he whispered. "Let's go slow."

He rolled onto his side, his back against the couch, and dragged her against him until his erection nested snugly between the plump swell of her bottom. Delia eased her hips wickedly up and down. Nick tightened his arm around her waist and groaned. "Oh, you are going to pay for that."

Delia couldn't resist doing it again. The feel of Nick's hardness made her think naughty thoughts.

"Whoa, sugar," Nick warned, his voice unsteady. "We'd better move." He sat up and pulled her into the vee of his legs.

"Nick, you're so hard," she whispered. "You felt so wicked against my bottom." Delia let her head fall back against his shoulder.

"Yeah, and it's a loaded gun, shoved up against your cheeks like that." Nick's free hand came around, his finger easing beneath the edge of her bra.

He slid his slightly rough finger back and forth across her pouting, sensitive nipple. "God," she said breathlessly. "Oh, God, Nick."

Nick nibbled gently at her ear. "Watch us," he whispered, his voice thick. "Look how beautiful you are, Delia."

Confused, she lifted her head from his shoulder. In the polished brass fender that surrounded the hearth, she could see her reflection, or part of it. She was sprawled wantonly, her legs apart, one knee pulled up. Her thong and her black stockings looked erotic, and her black high heel contrasted sharply against the faded denim that covered Nick's calf. She watched their reflection as his right hand stroked up her inner thigh. Watched Nick ease the silk thong to one side, revealing her neatly shaved flesh, wet and swollen with need.

He rubbed between her lips again, as his other hand stroked and pinched at her left nipple. "Good Lord, Delia," he rasped. "What you can do with a Lady Shick is pure art."

Delia laughed, a little embarrassed.

"Don't laugh," he said, picking up her right hand and pressing her fingers to her damp flesh. "You are beautiful beyond words, Delia. Here, feel how pretty you are. Let me watch. Let me touch your nipples and watch you make yourself come."

Delia did as he asked, sliding her middle two fingers through her lips. It felt good. Bad. Embarrassing. "I can't," she whispered. "I can't. You do it, Nick. Make love to me."

Nick bent his head to the turn of her neck and kissed her, cupping both her breasts in his big, warm hands. "You *can* do it, baby," he whispered. "You're hot and you're beautiful."

Delia let her head fall back against his chest. She was wet. So wet. She touched herself again, and shuddered. She wanted it. Wanted it, and yet was so self-conscious. "My bag," she choked. "I have a vibrator in my bag."

Nick chuckled softly. "Well, aren't you just full of surprises tonight."

Delia gave a bark of laughter. "God, I *had* to do something. I was going insane."

"I'll take care of you now, honey," he whispered, pinching her right nipple so hard it hurt. So hard it felt *good*. "And I'll bet we put that vibrator to good use eventually. But right now I'd rather watch just you. Open your legs wide, baby. Touch yourself, and let me watch you orgasm. Then I'll give you what you really want."

He had pulled her firmly back against his chest, making her small breasts thrust out. "You promise?" Her voice was thready. Not hers.

His lips seared her neck again. "Oh, I promise."

Delia was so hot she thought she might explode. She thought of her last three nights in Paris, alone with her vibrator, missing Nick. She'd been horny then. Now she was wild with it. So she did as he instructed, rubbing herself with her fingers, massaging her flesh. And watching herself. Watching Nick nuzzle against her throat, then lift his smoldering eyes to watch her as she stroked herself. As his gaze grew hotter, he pulled and rubbed her nipples until they throbbed and tingled.

Her breasts were spilling from her cups now, the areolas dusky in the firelight. And then, as if he couldn't resist, Nick slid one hand around her thigh. The other hand followed suit on the opposite thigh. His fingers were dark against the milky whiteness of her thighs as he held her open wide. Together they watched as Delia rubbed and circled, her edge sliding nearer.

She felt so decadent. So naughty. She was *watching* herself. Good Lord, it was the wickedest thing she'd ever done. And it felt good. She listened to the sound of her own wetness. To the sharp ratcheting of her breath.

Felt her body stiffen. And then her head went back against Nick's chest, and she came undone. Wave after wave shook her, rocked her. The orgasm was so powerful she went rigid in Nick's embrace, let it flow through her body, then fell to pieces afterward, limp and sobbing.

And then he was there, hugging her. Crooning to her. Telling her how beautiful she was. How much he loved her. *How much he loved her.*

He didn't mean that, she thought. Did he? But she didn't have time to think. Nick rolled her facedown on the pile of pillows, and ripped down his zipper.

"Nick?" she asked uncertainly.

"I need to be in you, baby," he said, almost apologetically. *"Now.* And I need to watch your luscious ass while I give it to you. God, it's so pretty. So full and sweet."

Pushing up with her hands, Delia lifted her breasts off the pillows, but Nick was shoving her legs wide. With one strong arm, he encircled her waist, lifting her bottom against his rock-hard erection. Delia steadied herself on her knees, and Nick pushed himself into her dripping flesh, and thrust.

"Oh, *God!*" he cried, ramming himself deep. "Oh, God, Delia. You don't know. Oh, baby, you just do not know how good this is."

His hands on her hip bones, he steadied her for his thrusts, his thighs slapping hard against her buttocks. Eight strokes. Twelve. *Maybe.* His incredible erection pulled at her sensitive sheath, which was already open and wet. She couldn't see, really. Could only feel. It was a wild, incredible position. Facedown on her knees, she felt totally submissive. Totally at his mercy. And then Nick slid one hand around her thigh, and touched her intimately. With his every stroke, he held her, touched her, pressing and rubbing his thumb, rough and desperate, against her swollen clit.

"Oh!" she cried sharply. "Not . . . not . . ."

But it was.

Delia felt the crest of her orgasm, weaker but sweet, and rode it, pulsing and throbbing as she collapsed fully onto the pillows. Nick exploded on a guttural shout and rammed himself home, pumping her full of his warm seed. With a shuddering sigh, he fell on top of her, his damp chest hair rough against her back, his weight pressing her into the pillows.

For a long time there was no sound in the room save the crackling of the fire.

"Delia," he finally said, his drawl even slower than usual. "Delia, darlin', I have to ask you something real important."

Delia tried to lift up, but it was impossible. "The answer is *yes*, Nick," she answered weakly. "Whatever you want, yes, I'll do it. You can even spank me now. I surrender already."

Nick rested his forehead between her shoulder blades. "Be serious, baby," he said. "Listen, now, before I lose my nerve. And do *not* laugh."

He sounded deadly serious. "Absolutely, Nick. I'm listening."

"Delia," he said. "Will you marry me?"

"Will I . . . will I *what?*"

She felt Nick stiffen. "You heard me, Delia," he said gruffly. "Will you marry me? And don't think, damn it, just answer the ques—"

The sharp, twiddling sound of a cell phone cut him off.

"Shit," said Nick, dropping his head again.

The phone twiddled a second time, from somewhere on the sofa.

Delia bit her lip. "Nick, maybe you'd better answer it?"

"No," he growled. "Make that *hell, no."*

The ringing was getting louder. "Honey," she said softly, "what if it's work?"

"Shit." There was resignation in his voice.

"Go on, Nick," she said gently. "I'm not going anywhere. I can't even move."

Nick thrashed about on the sofa, snatching the phone in mid-twiddle. *"Woodruff,"* he barked, slapping it to his ear. "And somebody better fuckin' be dead."

"Nick—!" she hissed.

A long silence ensued. "Yes, sir," Nick finally said. "Sorry, Dad."

He withdrew from her body, rolled his weight halfway off her, then propped up on one elbow. "No, no, she's fine, Daddy," he said. "Real fine. Home safe and sound. Yes, sir, I'm sorry. I did forget to call."

What on earth? Delia tried to turn around and look at Nick.

"No, Dad, *not* tomorrow." Nick's voice had taken on a frantic edge. "The airport is closed. No, the roads are slick, too. Yeah, *ice."* Another pause. "Aw, come on, Dad, you're from South Georgia, for God's sake. She isn't going anywhere. Not at the moment, anyway."

Burning with curiosity now, Delia shoved Nick completely off and sat up, still clad in nothing but her high heels, her stockings, and her black silk underwear.

Nick wouldn't look her in the eye. "Yes, sir," he said. "I will, I swear."

Delia strained her ears, trying to catch the frenzied chatter emanating from the cell phone. Nick rolled onto one side. "Yes, I promise. I'll find out." Then, "Hey, Dad? I'm kinda busy right now. Can I call you back tomorrow? Okay. Okay. Yep, love you, too."

He tossed the phone back onto the couch with a soft curse and stared into the depths of the fireplace. The shifting light softened his handsome profile, and Delia felt a knot form in her throat. Oh, she loved him. She really, really did. She sat up on her knees and took Nick gently by the shoulders.

"May I ask," she said quietly, "just what that conversation was all about?"

Nick smiled at her ruefully. "My dad," he said. "He was, er, just calling to—to see if you got back from France okay. He's kind of impatient."

Delia lifted her brows lightly. "I wasn't aware he even knew I existed."

She hadn't meant to sound bitter, but she did. Nick noticed, too. "Sure he does, darlin'," he said, brushing the back of his hand over her cheek. "I told him. Weeks ago."

"*Weeks* ago?" Delia was incredulous. "And now he's coming here?"

Nick shrugged. "That was kind of the plan," he said. "But then you had to go to France, and things didn't look so good for us, so I told him . . . well, I just told him he'd better sit tight awhile."

"He was coming to meet *me?*"

Nick settled back against the couch and held open his arms. Delia dove into them. "Delia, I love you," he said, freeing one hand to fish in his pocket. "And I'm real proud of you. Now, look, darlin', I asked you a question. A real important one. Will you marry me?"

"Oh, my God!" Delia covered her eyes with her hands. "You *meant* that? I thought it was just . . . well, post-orgasmic free-association bullshit."

"Bullshit?" Nick made a choking sound. "Honey, that's a question a man *never* asks unless he means it." She felt him take her left hand in his, and with her heart still in her throat, she opened her eyes.

Nick held a simple, pear-shaped diamond engagement ring against the tip of her third finger. "So, can I put this on?" he asked softly. "It's your early Christmas present, baby, if you'll take it. Dad can't reschedule his plane reservation until you say either *yes* or *no.*"

"Oh, my God," whispered Delia. "Oh, my *God!* Where'd that come from?"

Nick looked at her strangely. "Well . . . from Tiffany's."

Delia was babbling now. "When? Where? *Oh, my God!*"

"Last month. New York. That's where Tiffany's is, darlin'." Nick looked at her and shook his head. "I mean, maybe I've never done this before, but where I come from, when a man wants to marry a woman, he asks her daddy, then he gets her a ring, then he introduces her to his family. I'm just trying to get my ducks in a row here."

Delia burst into hysterical laughter, then slapped a hand over her mouth. "Oh, Nick!" she said. "Oh, Nick, I do love you so. And I'd love to meet your dad. But for God's sake, please don't ask my father such a thing."

Nick's face colored furiously.

"What?" she said. "Nick, what? No. Oh, no. Nick. You didn't."

"Yes, I did." He glared at her defiantly.

"Oh, you never!" Her hand was over her mouth again, covering her gasp. "When?"

Nick shrugged. "Maybe three weeks ago."

"Oh, my God!" Delia couldn't get her breath. "You just . . . *called* him? And you *asked* him? And did he die laughing?"

Another shrug. "Well, he did seem surprised you'd want to marry a cop," Nick said. "And I told him that maybe you didn't, but that I wanted to ask anyway. And then he allowed as how you'd always been awfully smart, and real sure of yourself, but kind of on the willful side. And I said I'd noticed that. And he said you were also a little—let's see, what was that word?—yeah, *sassy*. And I said I'd noticed that, too. And he said, 'Well, son, you're a braver man than me.' Then he congratulated me, and hung up."

"Oh, my God, you really mean it!" Delia uncovered her mouth and waved her left hand frantically.

Still holding the ring, Nick crooked one brow. "Baby, is that a *yes?*"

Delia might have been reeling from the shock and the sex, but she'd never been so sure of anything in her life. *"Yes!"* she shrieked. "Oh, Nick, a thousand times *yes.* Put it on. *Please."*

Nick slid the ring down her finger, a perfect fit.

"Oh, Nick, I love you."

"Well, that's good to know, Doc," he said, one of his sexy smiles slowly curving his lips. "'Cause I wouldn't want you to marry me just for the sex. Besides, I'm holding two tickets to Barbados for a Valentine's Day honeymoon."

"Aah, *Barbados!"* Delia nestled close against him and held out her hand, watching the firelight wink in the diamond's facets.

Nick wrapped her tight with one arm and settled the opposite hand on her stomach. "Delia," he said quietly. "I have to ask you something else."

She looked up at him anxiously and let her hand drop.

He winced a little. "It's, um . . . well, it's kind of about that condom I forgot to use tonight."

Mentally she calculated. "It's okay, Nick. I really think it's okay."

Nick's smile went sideways. "Depends on your definition of *okay,* darlin'," he said. "See, Daddy wants R.J.N. Woodruff IV pretty damn bad. I guess I do, too. If that's not your thing, I'm man enough to live with it. I know your career is important. But I just need to know what to tell Daddy so he'll quit ringing my damned cell phone."

Delia considered it only a moment. Yes, her career

was important. And she wouldn't give it up. But Nick, and a family! Oh, there was nothing more important than that. So Delia smiled and ran a finger up his strong, square chin. "Well, I'll tell you what, Nick," she said. "You can inform dear Daddy that you're marrying a woman who just bought four hundred dollars' worth of fancy French underwear, and she just can't seem to get enough of you. Besides, I think my biological clock is about to explode off its springs."

Nick cocked one brow. "Is that right, darlin'?"

"Absolutely," she answered. "And if you do your job right, with a little luck and a nice, long honeymoon, we'll be putting little R.J.N. Woodruff IV in Grandpa's stocking next Christmas."

Nick burst into laughter and rolled onto his back, dragging Delia down with him. They landed, nose-to-nose, with Delia sprawled awkwardly over him. "Kiss me, you fool," he whispered. " 'Cause we've got a lot of lost time to make up for, and that sounded like one hell of a challenge."

THE NEKKID
TRUTH

Nicole Camden

For my mom

I couldn't have done this without my sister, who read every draft.

And I want to thank the fabulous Lauren McKenna and Amy Pierpont for being the best editors and friends a girl could have. And to everyone else at Pocket, thank you for your support and friendship.

San Diego residents, please forgive the liberties I took with police procedures and landmarks.

CHAPTER ONE

My cell phone rang just as my date for the evening leaned over to kiss me. I was tempted to ignore it (the phone, not the lips). I hadn't gotten kissed in a while and felt like grabbing the first handsome man I saw and engaging in a serious lip-lock. But since the police had an uncanny knack of calling me when it was most inconvenient, I figured it had to be them.

I was right.

"Debbie here," I answered.

"Debbie, it's Jakes. Detective Scott needs you to come down and shoot a crime scene for us."

"Oh, he does, huh? What happened to your regular guy?"

"He's at the doctor getting his ingrown toenails operated on."

"A little too much information there, Jakes." I sighed. "Okay. Where is it?"

"Over by Buena Vista Lagoon."

"Great," I muttered, and asked him where exactly. The lagoon wasn't exactly small. "Okay. I'll be there in ten," I said when he finished, and hung up.

John, my date, whom I privately call "Freckle Dick," was none too happy about calling off the party for the evening. He was a college basketball student, tall, milk-pale, gorgeous. He'd been a model for a photo shoot of mine a few weeks ago, and I'd been seeing him off and on since then. He probably thought tonight was his chance to score.

"They're front-row tickets, Debbie. Can't they get somebody else?"

I pushed his hand off my thigh. "Trust me, John, if the detective in charge could get someone else, he would have. Besides, I'm sure there are plenty of girls back at the dorm who would love to go out with you."

"Nobody like you," he murmured, leaning over to nibble my ear. *Ah, younger men.*

"Just take me to the lagoon."

He complied sullenly, as boys are wont to do. The drive from John's driveway in Oceanside to the backstreets where homes gave way to the lagoon didn't take long, though I got lost trying to find the crime scene after he dropped me off. I had no idea what kind of waterfowl refuge the smelly, muddy, bug-infested bog was supposed to be, but it pretty much proved my theory that I would've been a lousy wildlife photographer.

With my camera heavy around my neck and my three-inch heels sinking four inches deep with every step, it was little wonder I was cursing as I limped toward a group of people knotted together near the edge of the water. Most of them looked like cops, but there were a few civilians thrown in for color.

"Over here, Miss Valley," said a voice in the deep Southern drawl that always made me think of hot, sweaty sex. Detective Scott, of course. He had a habit of calling out to me when I showed up so that I'd know who he was right away. I appreciated the courtesy. I know it's tough to believe, but even though I had been working with him for four years, and lusting after him almost as long, I was rarely able to pick him out of a crowd.

It had nothing to do with him. He was six three, wide across the chest, with thick brown hair and arms that looked strong enough to lift small cars. Most women met him once and made a point of seeking him out in bars, at the station, in the men's room at the station. I'd seen it happen. Not on purpose, mind you, I was just walking by.

I, on the other hand, would always have trouble recognizing him. Him and everyone else.

I suppose I was lucky. Five years ago, when his previous partner, Bruce Johnson, lost control of their patrol car and knocked me headfirst into the pavement on Coast Highway, the doctors said that by rights I should've been dead or at least brain damaged. Instead, I just lost the ability to recognize faces.

No one ever really understands what I mean by that, even most of my doctors, but after several months of tests they finally came to the conclusion that whatever spark or synapse that allows humans to recognize other humans was busted in me. It's not like I look at someone and see those fuzzy blotches they put in front of people on TV. It's more complex than that. The way they explain it in psychology books is to show someone two upside-down pictures. One is of someone famous like Madonna, the other is a hugely distorted picture of someone with similar coloring. Nine times out of ten a normal person can't distinguish one from the other while the photo is upside down. Well, I'm like that all the time. I can see someone's features and even mark them if they have a really beaky nose or a strange birthmark, but it's like I'm looking out into a sea of strangers. Not even people I've known my whole life stand out in any way. Cops understand better than most people. They see something similar whenever they ask a white witness to ID a nonwhite suspect.

It's a stupid disability and for a while it really fucked me up, but all it takes is one look at something like the crime scene laid out before me to realize that while I may not have been handed the best deal on the planet, it could've been a helluva lot worse.

The man's naked body was lying half in, half out of the algae-covered water. I lifted my camera and took a shot automatically, using a low flash and high-speed film since the haze had never quite managed to burn off that day. He lay on his back, skin marble pale, face missing from what I guessed was a gunshot. I didn't even blink.

A field evidence technician was standing near the body. He pointed glove-covered fingers at a couple things he wanted me to shoot: the position of the body relative to the water, grooves in the soft muck where the body had been dragged. Then he left me alone to photograph the body as I'd been trained.

I'd been taking photographs of crime scenes for the police since I'd recovered from my little accident. Detective Scott had gotten me the job (out of guilt, I think); Lord knew I wasn't a great photographer back then. I am now. My current photography is celebrated, some might say worshiped, though if you ask me, it's the subject matter and not the pictures that inspire devotion.

I keep working for the police, partly because I like them, partly because I feel strangely that my surviving the accident means that I should repay the cosmos in some way, and taking pictures of crime scenes is one way to do that.

"Miss Valley, you might want to watch that skirt. You're giving the boys a show," Detective Scott said from somewhere above me.

"Let her be, Marshall. This is the better than *Playboy!*" one of the men shouted. *Have I mentioned that I love cops?*

I had just squatted down—awkwardly, I admit (a crime scene is not the place for a miniskirt and high heels)—to place a quarter next to a strangely familiar tattoo high on the victim's inner thigh. I didn't have my ruler and I needed a scale comparison. "Then tell the boys not to look. I have to squat if I'm going to get this shot, and there's no ladylike way to do that." I hadn't looked away from the viewfinder to reply, but at his muttered curse I turned my head. I was eye-level with the crotch of his jeans, and wonder of all wonders, the little detective looked happy about something.

Since he wasn't gay or a necrophiliac (as far as I knew) and the only things for him to look at were (a) a dead body, (b) a bunch of birds and water, (c) other cops, and (d) my Lycra-covered ass, I naturally assumed that the good detective liked me more than he let on. Of course, I was probably wrong. I mean, if the man wanted me, he could've had me anytime in the past five years, and don't doubt that caused me more than a little irritation.

Just to annoy him, I made sure to plant my feet and bend from the waist on the next shot. A wolf whistle came from somewhere behind me, and I sensed Scott moving around to block the view of my butt from the rest of the men. A chorus of boos erupted from my fans, and Scott conceded defeat, walking off to interrogate the old woman who'd found the body. I went back to shooting the scene. If they won't be seduced, they can be annoyed. That's my motto.

He was still talking to the woman when I finally finished up. It was going to take forever to develop and print the film, and I wanted to get home and get started. I usually used my digital camera for the police photos, but I'd been shooting with my old Nikon FE2 earlier that day and had taken the digital out to make room in my bag.

I rooted around in said bag for more film, pulling out a canister of black-and-white. I loaded it quickly, wondering what the hell was taking Scott so long; he was usually Mr. Efficient, which I mocked but secretly admired. I had noticed over the years that when he set out to do something, it got done, no whining, no hemming and hawing, no "what do you think we should do?" I've dated enough since the accident to say unequivocally that if a man isn't willing to say what he wants for dinner, then he's not the man for me. I'd rather argue about it than second-guess him all night long.

It didn't take long to figure out what the delay was all about. Scott's back was to me, so I didn't notice what he was doing, but it turned out that the woman was deaf, and Scott was speaking to her in sign language. I was shocked. I mean, who would've guessed the man knew sign language?

I found myself staring at his hands as he moved them in the graceful, almost magical gestures that communicated thought without sound. Not consciously thinking about it, I began taking pictures, zooming in on his hands. They were long fingered, wide palmed, callused, and scarred. If the Lady of the Swamp had suddenly appeared and offered to grant me one wish, it would've been to have that man's hands on my body.

I got my wish a few minutes later, when those fingers clamped onto my elbow and steered me in the direction of his shiny gray truck. "I'll take you home now," he said loudly, for the benefit of our audience.

"Why, thank you, Detective," I said in my best breathy Marilyn Monroe imitation, which made the guys laugh, but only garnered a frown from the repressive detective. He hustled me to his truck, holding my door open while I climbed inside.

Now, I'm not the best at reading faces (for obvious reasons), but I can watch the direction of a man's eyes, and his ran the length of my legs before he closed the door.

We didn't say much on the way to my house. I asked him where Stevens, his partner, was, and he muttered that he'd had a dentist appointment. He refused to talk about the case, and only grunted in response to small talk, but I was still very cheerful as I waved goodbye to him from the steps of my house. You see, having seen the earlier evidence of his desire, I took the liberty of inspecting his lap as he got into the truck.

A leg and ass man. Not what I expected, but then, he's never failed to surprise me.

CHAPTER TWO

I usually get one of three reactions when people see my studio for the first time: shock, disgust, or rapture. I converted two bedrooms and a bathroom on one side of my house into a work area, darkroom, and studio less than a year ago. Before that I worked out of the darkroom at the local high school, but my rise in fame allowed me to purchase a three-bedroom house a couple blocks from the beach in Encinitas.

It wasn't fancy; a one-story white stucco with a wrought-iron gate and plenty of bougainvillea. There were tons of gracefully arching windows, high ceilings, and hardwood floors. I'd loved it on sight and had decorated most of the house with antiques that I found at flea markets and thrift stores as well as in the high-end shops. I went with simple and comfortable rather than flashy, and the result was a restful, charming space that exhibited my love of life and beauty.

The studio, on the other hand, could be seen as a

reflection of my dark side. There wasn't a lot of furniture: a few stools, lighting equipment, some backdrops. What really stood out were the photographs. There were hundreds of them hung on the walls, some framed, some matted, but most were just held up by pushpins. Color and black-and-white prints vied for attention against the stark white paint, and more than one person had commented that they didn't know where to look. Half the time they played it safe and just looked at their shoes. I didn't really blame them. Some people had a problem with nudity, and my walls were covered with lots and lots of naked people.

The first thing everyone asks is: "Why do you always take pictures of naked people?" To which I usually say that I just happened upon it, and it turned out I was good at it. I rarely mention the accident, or my subsequent fascination with bodies rather than faces. I think that for a while I thought that if I couldn't recognize people by their faces, then I would recognize them by something else.

In the case of men, it was dicks. Some of my first subjects were the men I dated. And since I had lost about thirty pounds after the accident, I dated a lot. Most of them were all too willing to pose for me. I kept pictures of their dicks in the file folder in my office, all neatly labeled on the back with their real name, height, weight, relevant birthmarks, tattoos, etc. Their nickname was written in the white space below the image. Some of my favorites were: Pencil Dick, Sumu Wrestler, Little Turtle Head, Knob Job, EWF (Every Woman's Fantasy), EGMF (Every Gay Man's Fantasy),

Corn Pone, Listing Aft (he was a sailor), and Vienna Sausage.

I got so good at it that I was approached by the friend of one of my subjects to shoot some photos for their gay porn magazine. I was barely scraping by at the time, so I took the job. Needless to say, it was only the beginning, though now my work is considered "art" rather than porn.

My grandmother was horrified when she found out what I do. I think my mom was, too, but since I freaked out a little every time she came over and I didn't recognize her, she refrained from lecturing. But at twenty-seven, I'm the only one of my brothers and sisters who owns her own home, and I'm often the only one with a job.

I wouldn't know what else to do now anyway. I love photographing the body, the lines and curves, shadows and planes. I can't help but feel that if it's my destiny to live life without ever again knowing the relief and joy of seeing a familiar face, then at the very least I can enjoy what I do without shame and sometimes with a great deal of pleasure.

THE NEXT MORNING I started work developing the black-and-white prints from the crime scene. The color film I took to a friend of mine who owned a photo-processing and framing shop next to the old theater in Oceanside. He was a lean black man named Burtis Ewell, and one of my most enthusiastic supporters.

"Hey, there, Miss Debbie."

I always identified him right away. It was easy: he had a distinct voice, a sort of wobbly tenor, and he always smiled at me like I was sunshine after weeks of rain. "Hey, Burtis."

"Whatcha got for me today?"

"Nothing fun," I said, setting the two canisters neatly on his countertop. He swiped them up with one big hand and deposited them in the special envelopes he kept on hand for my work. "Just crime-scene photos. You know the rules." Burtis had been cleared through the department as well, and knew most of the cops better than I did.

"Yes, ma'am."

"You going to The Man's birthday party tonight?" I asked, deliberately casual.

"Why, you need a date?"

I smiled at him. "Oh, yeah. Jason would like that. Besides, I'm not bringing a date. It'd be like tossing a puppy into a tank of piranhas."

He chuckled, knowing I was right. The last time I brought a date to a cop party, they'd teased him unmercifully, asking if I'd brought pictures of his important bits and what nickname I'd given him (I had told them about my little hobby one drunken night at a bar several years ago, and they'd never let me live it down).

I shifted my feet. "I was just wondering what you'd gotten the detective. I can't think of anything good."

He winked at me. "Jason and I got Stevens to steal his signed photo of Alyssa Milano so we could frame it."

I burst out laughing. It was perfect. Detective Scott had an obsession with Alyssa Milano that had started in his teens. Everyone knew about it thanks to Stevens. Jason Markham was Burtis's much-younger lover, and Stevens's half brother. There had been some tension over the match a while back, but most everyone at the station was over that now. How could they not be when the two of them were so entertaining? They cooked up more pranks to play on the indomitable detective than any man, arrogant know-it-all or not, should have to endure.

"Didn't he notice it was missing?" I gasped out between giggles, my eyes watering.

"Oh, yeah, he noticed, and threatened to have Stevens's car stolen if he didn't get it back."

That set me off again. Stevens owned a cherry-red 1965 Mustang convertible that he worshiped even more than his new wife. She'd told me at their wedding that he'd asked her to marry him on their first date, when she'd genuflected at the sight of the red beast and proceeded to ask him a million questions about the engine, the condition, and assorted other car questions that I would never understand. She looked like a schoolteacher, worked as a mechanic, and had the vocabulary of a truck driver. I'd liked her instantly.

It didn't help me with my dilemma, though. I had absolutely no idea what Detective Scott would want, other than naked photos of Alyssa Milano, and I was pretty sure that if he wanted some of those he could look on the Internet.

I sighed and wiped my eyes. "Maybe I'll get him a camera. One of those really small digital ones."

Burtis shook his head, "This is the detective we're

talkin' about. Get him a big one. Big, with lots of buttons and an instruction manual thicker than a phone book."

"I don't know him well enough to spend that kind of money."

"Mebee not. But you want to."

He had me there. "He'll think I'm nuts," I argued.

"Honey, you are nuts, that's why he wants you so bad." He leaned over the counter and motioned me closer. "You see, the detective, he's a man that just loves figuring things out. And you," he said, tapping me on the forehead, "are some kind of puzzle."

CHAPTER THREE

The brightly wrapped box sat next to me in the passenger seat like a bomb. I kept chewing on my bottom lip and giving it nervous glances. *What if he doesn't like it? This was a dumb idea. Really. Really. Dumb.*

I'd dressed up in one of my favorite outfits, tight jeans with flared legs and colorful beaded embroidery on the back pockets, a fitted white dress shirt, and high-heeled Western boots. I'd rolled my hair and let the thick mass fall down my back in dark waves that would undoubtedly fall straight again by the end of the night.

I'd brought my camera—okay, two cameras—and my little flipbook of photos so that I could match faces to names if I got stuck. I'd stopped carrying it around all the time years ago. It didn't always work anyway. It sometimes gave me a general idea, but if two people had similar coloring, I was usually out of luck.

A wave of smoke hit me as I pulled open the heavy wooden door to Dave's, the guys' favorite hangout and probably one of the few bars in California that paid absolutely no attention to that pesky antismoking law. I stepped inside and immediately felt my heart speed up.

AC/DC was blasting my eardrums and there were people everywhere. Some said hi to me and smiled, a couple waved, but I couldn't get out my book to see who they were while I was holding the detective's present. I smiled vaguely at everyone and looked for somewhere to set the box before my sweating hands made me drop the thing.

"Hey, Debbie, let me take that for you," said a voice to my right. *Stevens, thank God.*

I handed him the box with a grateful smile and took the hand that he held out to me. He led me over to a table near the end of the bar that was already covered with presents, then waved for a couple guys to clear a stool for me at the bar. They did, hugging me and ruffling my hair like I was the team mascot or something. I thought they might be Harris and Carlyle, but I wasn't sure.

Stevens ordered my usual, Vanilla Stoli and ginger ale, and leaned down to whisper in my ear, "Did you hear what we did?" he said gleefully.

"I heard," I said, smiling. "Where's Darla?"

"She's on her way with Burtis and Jason in *my* car."

I laughed. "Nobody stole it, huh?"

"I kept it at Jason's house."

I grinned and leaned into him for a hug. "So how was the honeymoon?"

"It was wonderful." He nodded, and one lock of curly brown hair fell across his forehead. He was adorable, built like an Italian god, and sweet as apple pie. I'd felt nothing but affection for him from the beginning.

"Did Darla like the pictures?"

"Are you kidding? The first thing she did when we got back was open the package from you. I might as well have fallen off the face of the earth."

"Tell her to call me. There's another set of photos that I still need to give her."

"I'll do that."

"Cool," I said, and took the icy glass the bartender handed me. I smiled at him, knowing he was either Simon or Hank, but not wanting to guess wrong.

"And the man himself, where's he at?" I was starting to calm down, though if I had to move off this stool I was going to lose it again.

"He's over at the other end of the bar," he said gently, pointing, and I jerked to attention.

A dark-haired man with a stubbled jaw and a dress shirt opened to reveal a tanned throat sat almost directly across from me, surrounded by men and women vying for his attention. He would say something occasionally, but mostly he just stared at me, and I supposed it must be Detective Scott. God, he was hot.

I saluted him with my drink and he lifted an eyebrow in return. The man had arrogance down to a science.

Another large crowd of cops and their wives spilled into the bar, and the noise level increased exponentially. Stevens leaned down to shout in my ear. "You should go talk to him."

I took a long sip of my drink. "I don't think so."

"I've never met two people more stubborn than you guys. He wants you. You want him. So go get him."

I looked at him, frowning. "I tried that once, he wasn't interested, remember?"

"You offered sex, nothing more. And that was four years ago. Neither of you was in any shape to get into a relationship, especially with each other."

Stevens knew all about the accident and my history with Detective Scott. He'd been a rookie when it happened, and when Johnson resigned, Stevens became Scott's partner, and my friend.

"What?" I shouted, pretending I couldn't hear him.

"Fine, be an idiot," he muttered with his pretty poet's mouth and stalked off.

I grinned to myself and looked up to see that Scott had gotten off his stool and was heading in my direction. He wasn't making much progress. He kept getting stopped for a pat on the back and a birthday greeting. One of the female cops kissed him on the cheek, and I narrowed my eyes.

I waved to Simon/Hank to get his attention. I ordered another drink, silently vowing that it would be my last. I had to drive home, and it was never a good idea to get wasted around a bunch of cops. They remembered everything.

"Hey, Debbie!" shouted a young, curly-haired man as he rushed toward me. I steadied him, taking the beer bottle out of his hand and setting it on the bar. He hugged me enthusiastically and I laughed. It had to be Curly. The mop of hair and the smell of Old Spice aftershave was always a dead giveaway.

"The party only started an hour ago, Curly, what have you been drinking?"

"Beer. Shots. You're pretty."

"Thank you," I said, laughing, and noticed that Detective Scott had finally managed to traverse the crowd and was standing behind the young cop with his arms crossed.

"Debbie," Curly whispered loud enough to be heard across the bar, "remember the time we did lemon drops and you took your top off?"

I know I'd remember if *that* had ever happened. "In your dreams, cute stuff."

"Curly," Scott barked, and my drunken admirer snapped to attention. "Your friends are looking for you." At that, two other men, Larry and Moe respectively, hurried over to take the arms of their inebriated companion.

I glanced at Scott warily, but he was busy giving the cop on the stool next to me a dirty look. The man picked up his drink and stood, smiling, and wished Scott a happy birthday.

Scott sat down and I could feel the heat of his big body through the thin fabric of his shirt. My stomach quivered. I don't know what it was about the man, but the minute he got near me I always felt like a teenager again, aching and unsure. So I reacted the way I always did: I turned on the charm.

"Happy birthday, Detective," I said, smiling with only a corner of my mouth and looking up at him through lowered lashes.

"Debbie," he said flatly, but there was a twinkle of amusement in his eyes.

I blinked and forgot all about being charming. "Since when am I Debbie? For five years it's been nothing but Miss Valley this and Miss Valley that."

He just shrugged. I nearly slugged him.

I frowned at my glass, then drained the sweet drink with a few deep pulls on my straw. Scott waved for the bartender to get me another before I could stop him. It arrived immediately, and I could tell from the smiling glances that were floating around the bar that everyone and their mother had noticed the attention he was paying me.

"What's with you?" I wanted to know.

"You look nice tonight. Cute."

I stared at him. *Cute? Did he actually say I looked cute?* "Are you on drugs?"

He laughed, white teeth flashing, and I wanted to kiss him silly. He never laughed around me.

I don't know what he would've said next. Burtis and Jason came through the door then, carrying the framed Alyssa like a prize of battle. They were singing the theme song for *Who's the Boss?* at the top of their lungs. I was guessing they were already drunk.

A young woman with curly brown hair pulled back in a bun followed behind them, shaking her head and laughing: Darla.

Stevens scooped her up with a roar and planted a deep kiss on her waiting lips. Everyone cheered, me included, though the twinge of envy went deep. Since I'd gotten hurt, I had doubted, often, whether I was capable of loving anyone anymore. How could I? I wouldn't recognize

Mel Gibson if he walked through the door, much less someone I loved.

The crowd cleared a path to Scott for Alyssa and her bearers. Scott had turned his back on me to watch the procession. I admired his broad shoulders, which were shaking with the force of his laughter.

They reached him just as they finished off another rousing chorus, and Scott stood to receive his gift.

"Kiss! Kiss! Kiss!" the audience shouted, wanting Scott to kiss the photo of Alyssa's smiling lips. The thought annoyed me and made me want to laugh at the same time.

He bent as if to kiss her, holding the frame in one hand, then grabbed Jason in a headlock and yanked him down to deposit a smacking kiss on the boy's lips. Everyone roared with laughter again and began singing "For he's a jolly good fellow."

After that the night just got plain crazy. Scott never managed to open the rest of his presents. People kept buying him drinks and calling him over for games of pool. I talked to Darla for a while about her wedding pictures, drank from what seemed like an endless supply of Vanilla Stoli and ginger ales, and somehow or another managed to end up sitting in the detective's lap and singing Marilyn Monroe's rendition of "Happy Birthday" with a group of four cops backing me up like a demented barbershop quartet.

I don't remember what happened next. I woke up on my bed the next morning with a raging hangover and a note stuck to my forehead:

Keys & cam bag on the kitchen counter. Car in the drive. Darla says get it detailed (esp. backseat).

Love,

Stevens

I groaned and rolled over, memories of the previous evening flashing against my closed eyelids. My stomach cramped up, and I wanted nothing more than to pull the covers over my head and die. I might have done just that, if the need to pee hadn't been considerably urgent.

I shuffled into the bathroom still wearing everything except the boots from the night before. I gave myself a cursory glance in the mirror, wincing at the tangled mass of my hair and the sallow tint to my skin.

A microwave pizza, two Cokes, and a hot shower later, I felt almost human, though I didn't manage to throw on anything more than stretchy pants and a white tank bra. I watched TV for a while, but I kept thinking about Scott, and the way he'd been the night before. It was a little fuzzy, but I could've sworn that when I was snuggled up in his lap and singing my little off-key tribute, he'd been smiling at me and squeezing my waist to hold me close to him. That was ridiculous, of course; Scott was more likely to frown in disapproval and tell someone to take me home.

I shook my head, not wanting to think about it anymore. If I'd embarrassed myself, I'd embarrassed myself. There was no going back. I clicked off the TV and went into my studio, staring blankly at the nudity-covered walls for a moment before grabbing my apron off a stool in the corner and heading into the dark-room.

The negatives with the photos of the detective's hands were dry. I cut the long strip into pieces and slid them into negative sleeves before uncovering the enlarger and preparing the chemicals to make the prints. I immediately felt calmer. My mind was an unsullied sea. When all else fails, work will see you through. Or make you rich. Either way, you're better off.

CHAPTER FOUR

There was a knock on my door that evening. I had finished drying all the prints and had laid out the black-and-white shots of the crime scene on my kitchen table. They were well done, clear and even in color and tone. I'd taken the black-and-white photos because they often showed details that were overlooked in color, and I preferred them anyway.

I still hadn't figured out why the tattoo on the man's inner thigh seemed familiar. It was unusual, a clown face, divided down the center, half smiling, half frowning. I supposed I might have seen something like it during one of my trips to New York. I'd been in plenty of tattoo parlors looking for models for an assignment.

I went to answer the door wearing the clothes I'd had on earlier, apron and all. "Who is it?" I called out.

"Detective Scott," a gravelly voice replied, though it was muted by the thickness of the heavy oak.

Oh, my.

I opened the door quickly, putting one hand to my hair in an automatic gesture. He was standing in the entryway at the top of the steps to my house, big. How is it that some men just seemed like men, and others, oh, others, could just seem so much more? My front porch was covered in plants, all blooming with color and life at this time of the summer. He stood in the middle of them like a lion in a jungle. I stood back to let him in, but deliberately brushed my breasts against his arm as he passed me.

I felt him stiffen, and thought I had my answer about last night. He definitely wasn't pleased with me.

"Well, this is a surprise," I said mildly, and led the way into the kitchen. I felt him behind me down the short hallway, and I deliberately swayed my hips, hoping he was watching, the jerk.

"How'd you make out on presents?" I asked casually, wondering what he'd thought of the camera. I hadn't bought a huge mechanical camera, but I had gotten him a really expensive digital, a card reader, and extra memory. I had blown maybe a thousand dollars. Maybe he was here to tell me that it was an inappropriate gift or something. I knew it had been a dumb idea. I don't know what I was thinking; I had just wanted to please him. Stupid, I know, wanting to please a man.

"I don't know. They're still in Stevens's car, I think."

"Oh," I said, relieved and disappointed, pushing open the batwing doors that led into my kitchen.

I went immediately to the refrigerator. "Did you want something to drink?"

"A beer, if you have it."

"I've got Guinness or Amstel Light." Frankly I was shocked that he wanted to drink at all, though perhaps he hadn't been quite as inebriated as I had been. He didn't look as if he had a hangover.

"Guinness is fine," he said distractedly, and ran a hand through his hair. He had taken one of the pictures in his hand and was looking at it carefully.

I got two heavy glass mugs out of my freezer and poured his Guinness into one with the expertise I had learned from a bartender in Ireland. He'd been eighteen, ruddy-cheeked, and convinced that American girls were easy. I'm afraid I didn't discourage that belief in any significant way.

I took a two-liter of Vanilla Coke out of the fridge for myself while the thick Guinness settled. I was trying to quit drinking soda, but hadn't quite managed it. Before the accident I had always struggled with my weight, and called myself an idiot for my addiction. I didn't worry so much about my weight anymore, now that I exercised daily, though I supposed that was a compulsion all its own.

"You surf?" Scott said to my back. I turned around and he gestured to the surfboard I had propped up in the corner of the kitchen.

"Yeah," I said sullenly, sounding for all the world like one of those white-trash girls in movies with ripped cutoffs and see-through shirts. I glanced down at myself automatically, feeling my nipples peak against the front of my tank and apron. He watched me do it, and for the first time I saw in his eyes the lust that I had seen demonstrated by his lower organs two days earlier.

"Do you surf?" I asked, suggestively, I admit.

He turned away, and picked up the photo again. I sighed and poured the rest of the Guinness into his glass, watching the foamy whitish brown head rise like bread dough. The man was driving me crazy. If he was anyone else, I would've just taken off my clothes and pushed him down into one of my kitchen chairs, but I had tried that once and he'd rejected me. I wasn't interested in a repeat of that little scene.

I handed him his drink, which he sipped absently, licking the foam off his lips. I sat quickly in one of the chairs and pretended a keen interest in one of the photos. It just happened to be a picture of the tattoo.

I turned the photo and heard him curse. "Do you do it on purpose?" His voice was harsh. I looked up quickly, blinking.

"Do I do what on purpose?" I had no idea what he was talking about.

"Nothing," he muttered, and took the picture out of my hand.

"So who is this guy?"

"I can't tell you that."

I rolled my eyes. "Jesus, I've been working with you guys long enough."

"No, I mean we don't know who he is." He didn't sound happy about it.

"No shit," I asked, raising my eyebrows. He smiled a little at that and I felt my breath go. The man was truly beautiful when he smiled.

"No identification, clothing, or any other possessions that might belong to the victim were found at the scene. Preliminary forensics indicates that the body was probably dumped."

I could've told him that. I worked with forensics a lot, shooting what they told me to shoot, touching only what they told me I could touch. I'd picked up a few things over the years, and one of them was that a bullet through the head left an awfully big mess, and the ground that would've been in the shot's trajectory had been clean, or at least free of blood and brain matter.

"You got nothing on his prints?" I asked, surprised. Just about everybody was listed somewhere. The DMV required a thumbprint scan in order to issue driver's licenses, and prints were required on gun permits. I'd had to have a complete set of my prints made before I could even work for the department.

"*Nada.* And no one has called to claim him, though the news ran some gruesome shots on the eleven o'clock news that night."

"Buzzards," I muttered, and he shot me a wry look.

"Hey, I work for you. There's a big difference," I argued defensively. He conceded that with another of those little smiles and sipped his Guinness again. I felt myself melting again watching him. He seemed massive sitting at my dainty little kitchen table, and dark somehow, as if I had let in a brewing storm.

"So," he continued, flicking the photo onto the table. "It seems like this tattoo is the best we have to go on right now."

I glanced at the picture again. "You know," I muttered, picking it up again, "there is something familiar about it."

"Really?" he asked, sounding interested, and a bit reluctant. I had gotten good at reading voices, since looking at the strange faces of those near and dear to me often left me feeling unsettled. His face was a pleasure to look at, though, and his handsomeness was always a surprise. I didn't know why he would be reluctant, but I imagined it had something to do with the thought that if I recognized the tattoo, then I had probably seen it in person. I wasn't discounting the idea. I'd seen too many dicks to remember them all; although I thought the tattoo was unusual enough that I would recall it.

"I don't think I've seen this particular tattoo," I said, studying it intently, absently noting that the hair on the fuzzy ball sack in the frame was dark, and that the man had been extremely long, well over ten inches. *No, I wouldn't have forgotten seeing that.* "But I've seen one like it," I finished, and handed it back to him.

He was looking at me. "Do you know that your eyes squint and your forehead wrinkles when you concentrate?"

"Yes," I said shortly, and got up from the table.

"What did I say?" he drawled out, and the warmth in his tone had me half expecting him to add "honey" or "baby" to the end of his sentence.

"Nothing," I said, flustered, and trying to hide it by opening the fridge and getting out some more Coke. An interesting side effect to my little disability was that in addition to not being able to recognize the faces of others, I could no longer recognize my own face. For a long time I refused to have a mirror anywhere near me, but once I started losing weight I surrounded myself with them. Floor-to-ceiling mirrors had covered the walls of the apartment I'd lived in before I'd gotten the house. My therapist said that my obsession with improving my body undoubtedly grew from a fear of losing my identity.

Well, duh.

It still bothered me a little when people commented on my face. I couldn't imagine what the detective had seen while watching me examine the photo, and that thought had me a **little** unnerved. I was reminded of a fantasy book I'd read **once**, where a present-day heroine was transported to a world where no one used mirrors, and was told all she needed to know about her presence and beauty could be read in the eyes of the men and women who looked back at her.

It didn't help me, though. There was only so much a person could understand by looking into a stranger's eyes, and in my little world, everyone was a stranger. Blanche Dubois, I was not.

"Where have you seen it?" he asked me then, and it took me a moment to recall what we were talking about.

"Oh . . ." I said, thinking of the tattoo. "I'm not sure. I'll have a look in my files. Maybe I've got it in there somewhere."

"Can you let me know by tomorrow?" His voice was gruff.

I thought about the massive files in my office. There was no way. "I don't think so, Detective, not without help. You willing?"

I let just enough heat roll off with the words so that there was no mistaking my meaning. I watched his face as I said it, fascinated that behind that stranger's mask was someone I knew. I understood how mob wives felt when their husbands got plastic surgery.

I watched his eyes narrow. He stood and slowly stalked me back against my kitchen counter. Heat came off him in waves, and I put my hands against his chest in reflex. His muscles were hard and resilient against my fingers. I spread my palms wide, and ran them up and down his chest. Just once, but we both shuddered.

I felt a strange joy welling up in me, and I had trouble believing that he was actually there, touching me. I had imagined this for so long, imagined him, and now his gorgeous hands were reaching for my hips, pulling me against him.

The bulge beneath his jeans pressed into my belly and I pushed my hips forward.

"Oh, yes," I said eagerly, rubbing my hips in circles against him.

He leaned forward and nipped my ear, his big body blocking most of the light and making me feel small and fragile.

"Do you want me?" he growled in my ear, sounding like deep-fried sin. He slid his hand across my hip and under the apron and the waistband of my stretchy pants, pausing when he realized I wasn't wearing underwear.

I held still, breathless with anticipation, as those large hands combed through the springy curls of my bush. I imagined those hands, the long fingers that I had seen developing only hours before.

"I want to come into this kitchen someday," he said in my ear, still not touching me the way I wanted to be touched. "And I want to see you wearing nothing but this apron." Both hands slid to my ass, one hot against my skin. He squeezed my cheeks, his fingers sinking deep into the crease where the curve of my bottom met my thighs. "I want this ass to be the first thing I see."

I whimpered, my head falling back. He slid his hand up my back and caught it in the tangled mess of my hair. He kissed me then, his lips brushing gently before his tongue came out to taste my bottom lip. "You taste just like I remember," he said, and kissed me again, his tongue probing deep. I kissed him back, sucking on his tongue, nipping his bottom lip when he withdrew.

He set me away from him and adjusted himself carefully while I watched. "I can't stay tonight, but I'll come by before work tomorrow and help you look."

I heard the words, but I was still thinking that at any moment he would strip off his jeans and take me against the cabinets. He didn't do that. He went to the table while I stared at him incredulously. He took one of the 8-by-10 photos of the tattoo.

"I'm going to have Stevens check with the local tattoo parlors to see if any of them claim this particular design, or remember someone requesting it. What time do you surf in the morning?"

"Six A.M.," I said numbly.

"I'll be here," he said, gripping my chin and placing a quick kiss on my mouth. I leaned toward him eagerly, parting my lips, but he turned away like he didn't notice.

I was still standing shell-shocked in my kitchen when I heard the front door open and close. I ran after him, spilling down the porch steps just in time to see his truck driving away.

"Prick!" I shouted.

There was a couple sitting in a porch swing across the street staring at me. I imagined I looked like a wild woman, barefoot, wearing an apron and shouting obscenities. I waved and went back in the house quickly.

I leaned back against my front door and closed my eyes. *Why now? Was he just fucking with me?* I couldn't imagine he disliked me that much. I know he disapproved of me a lot. He'd already turned me down once. I didn't understand him, but whatever had changed, I was looking forward to seeing him in the morning.

I shook my head at my idiocy and headed for the shower. I knew there was a reason I'd bought that removable showerhead.

CHAPTER FIVE

On a summer day in San Diego, sometimes there's no sunshine in the mornings. The marine layer hangs on all morning, turning from a dark gray to a pearly gray that doesn't burn off until about noon, if it burns off at all. Neither that nor the chilly water temperature deterred me or the other surfers.

I left the house at six on the dot, but when I stepped outside with my board under my arm, Detective Scott (I didn't know if I'd ever be able to call him Marshall) was waiting for me.

At first all I saw was a strange man wearing a blue half-suit and holding a yellow surfboard, and I tensed, because while Encinitas was a pretty safe little town, I'd seen the evidence of too much violent death to believe the world was a safe place.

"Good morning," he said thickly, and suddenly I was filled with a different kind of tension. *Scott*. All my nerve endings tingled at the sight of his powerful body encased in neoprene. I noticed his muscled calves, and strong brown feet covered in flip-flops. He was all strength and size and I had an insane urge to kneel down and lick his toes.

I turned my back on him and locked my door instead, still miffed at him for leaving me wanting the night before and for not telling me that he could surf. I'd thought he'd meet me after I got back from surfing. The thought of seeing that big, muscled body riding the waves was enough to make me feel all tight and itchy.

I stomped toward him, hoping that my budding excitement didn't show on my face, and wondering what it looked like if it did.

We walked the two blocks to the beach in silence. I had my house key in a little Velcro pocket in my suit, but wasn't carrying anything else. He wasn't, either, so I assumed he had them stashed on his body somewhere. I ran my eyes over him to see if there were any suspicious bulges. I found one, and it was suspicious all right.

I don't know what I expected him to do, kiss me? Hold my hand? I wasn't sure I was comfortable with either idea. I wanted him, no doubt about it, but I wasn't sure I wanted a relationship. I hadn't been good at them before the accident. Now I downright sucked.

He didn't touch me at all. The sand was cool beneath my feet when we hit the beach. We kicked off our flip-flops onto the sand, and I wriggled my toes in pleasure. The air smelled of brine, and the sea birds yawked and chased around the beach like wild dogs.

We walked companionably to the water's edge, and I

smiled at him. All the animosity, tension, and even lust sort of floated away. There were few things I loved more than playing in the ocean. When surrounded by its endless depths and unceasing rhythm, everything crazy in my life seemed insignificant and a little silly. The endless blue didn't recognize me, no matter how many times I came back.

The water was shockingly cold on my bare toes, and I looked down to see Scott's feet covered by the white foam of a running wave. He smiled at me and led the way out into the water. I thought that maybe the ocean eased him, too. He certainly seemed less tense, more human than I'd ever known him to be.

I followed him out into the water, where we floated for a while, watching for the good waves. He caught one before I did, balancing effortlessly on the long board.

I barely remembered leaving the water a couple hours later. I felt dreamy and disconnected, but I took the hand he held out to me. It was rough and callused, but warm, and for once in my life I didn't feel disgusted at the sappiness and intimacy of the gesture. It felt right, almost a pleasure in itself. I found myself hoping that it would last, that this time, I would let myself go, and in the morning I'd still want him there to catch me.

WHEN WE GOT back to the house, he stood behind me as I fumbled for my key. We had propped the boards against the wall in the entryway, and now the only thought in my head was that I would finally, finally get to have him.

I pushed open the door and faced him as he stalked in after me. I put one hand to the zipper at the top of my suit and slid it down slowly. His zipper was in the back. He caught the pull-tab and drew it down behind him, the thick material bunching around his shoulders and armpits. His eyes were fastened on my chest as I peeled the suit away from my arms and pushed downward, the tops of my breasts squeezed together by my bikini top. He pushed his arms free quickly and came to me, his suit hanging down in front of him.

His cold fingers stroked my collarbone, and then he bent his head and kissed me there, his lips warm against my cool flesh. I gasped, and my hands fell away from my hips and went around his shoulders. His tongue flicked out, burning me, and I twisted closer to him. The rubbery suits kept us from feeling each other, and we both broke away to shove at them impatiently. I was careless in my efforts, and my bikini bottoms came off as well.

His suit dropped to the ground, shorts and all, and I got my first view of his dick, thick and long, pointing at his stomach while his balls swung heavily between his legs. I stared, riveted, wanting to touch and lick and nuzzle my face against that hardness. He grabbed my hands before I could move and began to nip and suck on my fingers, sliding them into his mouth and circling them with his tongue.

I moaned and fell to my knees, my arms stretched high. My head fell forward automatically, my wet hair sliding in front of my face, curtaining my face and his flesh in a cocoon of musky salt-and-sex-scented air. I breathed in deeply, and nuzzled my cold cheeks against his dick, exhaling my hot breath against him. His hands tightened on my wrists and drew my arms higher, so my shoulders lifted, and my mouth was poised at the rounded head. I flicked my tongue out, catching a couple pearly drops of pre-cum that had collected in the tiny slit. His hips jerked, and I caught him in my open mouth, taking him as deeply as I could, which was only about halfway down. He was thick and pulsing against my tongue as I ran it along the underside. I pulled upward, tracing the raised veins with the tip of my tongue.

He dropped my hands and pushed my shoulders back until I rested on the cool tile looking up at him. He stayed there for a moment, looking at me, and I let my legs fall open, just a little. He groaned and fell to his knees, straddling me. He put his hands on my chest, pulling the skimpy top down so that my breasts popped out, nipples eraser hard and pointing at him. He hummed his appreciation and leaned down to take one pink tip between his lips. I gasped, arching up to him. It was probably the first time I'd ever managed a back bend with outright enthusiasm.

I could feel him pressed against me, and I reached down and parted my lips, so that the velvety smooth length of him slid against the wet slickness of my flesh. We both gasped at the sensation, and I felt his teeth clamp teasingly on the point of my nipple. I struggled then, trying to free my legs from the prison of his thighs and spread them wide.

He controlled me, scooting me forward and catching

the backs of my knees in his hard hands. He pushed them upward, still not spread wide, until my knees were hugged to my chest, and my pouting flesh was fully visible to him, the red nubbin of my clitoris undoubtedly swollen and protruding. He crouched down, pushing my knees even farther so that my hips rose off the ground. I felt his tongue lick from the base to the top of my sex, and everything in me clenched in pleasure.

"You like that," he murmured, tasting me again, lapping at the dewy wetness.

"Yes. Please," I begged shamelessly. He feasted on me then, lips and tongue swirling and sucking until I screamed, undulating my hips against his mouth. He rose up abruptly and sank his dick into my hot, willing flesh.

I gasped at the feel of him probing deep, working his thick length into me. The walls of my passage tightened convulsively around him as he inexorably pushed his way in. I lifted my head and looked past my knees to the place where we were joined. My pink flesh was stretched tight around him and I gasped even as I watched him slide slowly out until only his thick head was inside me, rubbing gently, spreading my juices on my sensitive entrance. He stuffed inside me again, more easily this time, and began thrusting with slow, even strokes.

"Keep your knees there," he ordered, and slid one hand down to cover my clitoris, rubbing me even as his dick thrust in and out. He did me hard, his rough fingers stimulating me even as his dick moved in and out with increasing force and pressure.

I circled my hips in counterpoint, wanting him deeper, harder, just a little faster. I gave myself up to the feel of him pounding inside me, to the slide and the heat and the scent of sex and salt water. I felt it first in the base of my skull, that tingling awareness that ran down the center of me like a blade, a painfully sweet ache that was growing, growing, and then I was coming, trembling and crying out as my inner walls convulsed around the hard intruder. He stayed deep inside me, rubbing gently to extend my pleasure, then when I had calmed, he took me with deep driving thrusts, chest heaving, hips plunging desperately. He came with a shout and I felt his warm seed flowing inside me.

He collapsed on top of me then, and I put my heavy arms around his shoulders and hugged him to me. We stayed like that for several minutes, breathing into each other, sinking heavily onto the floor and each other.

He got up, pushing himself up with his arms, sending his now softened flesh deeper into me for a moment. I closed my eyes to savor the feeling and heard him chuckle softly above me.

"Come on, baby," he said, and lifted me to my feet. My legs felt like wet noodles, so I collapsed against him. He laughed again and swung me up into a fireman's carry, one hand running appreciatively over my bare bottom. I smiled against his back and let myself go limp.

He carried me into my bathroom, though how he knew where to go is a mystery to me, and set me inside the tub. He looked at the showerhead hanging down forlornly and laughed wickedly. I felt my face heat, which only made him chuckle more as he stepped inside the tub. I wrapped my arms around him and clung like a limpet as he turned the knobs and grabbed the hanging showerhead before it began whipping about with the force of the water.

I felt the forceful jet of water on my back first, and then at the top of my skull, moving down in slow strokes to wet the length of it. He rubbed his thumb over the scar that started at my hairline, massaging gently. I arched my head back and purred at the sensation, loving the feel of him wet and hard against me. He sprayed my back, butt, between my legs. He took more time there, letting the hard stream of water jet into me until I moaned. Then he turned me around so that he could wet down my front, holding me with one arm across my chest, his palm cupping my left breast. He let the water beat into my belly button, making me ache, before positioning it between my legs again.

"I should have protected you," he murmured against my neck.

I shook my head. "I'm on the pill."

"I still should've used a condom."

I laughed shakily, too caught up in what he was doing to me now.

"But all I could think about was getting inside you. It's all I've thought about since I met you, taking this sweet little ass."

"Why?" I gasped as the stream of water moved to beat directly on my clitoris, making me tighten and shiver again, arching against him.

He spread his legs a little wider apart, and I could feel him growing against the globes of my butt.

"Why what?" he asked, rubbing himself against the crease between my ass cheeks.

"Why now?" I asked desperately, the "now" turning into a plea.

The arm holding me up pressed me back against his chest so that I was leaning into his body, then released me and stretched to grab the lavender-scented soap in the little tray next to me. I watched him roll the bar easily in his large hand, lathering it with white suds, while the one holding the showerhead kept the pulsing water hard between my legs. I knew where this was going, and already my buttocks were tightening in anticipation.

He set the bar back down, and that soapy hand went behind me, going directly between my cheeks and rubbing the soap over my tight, puckered flesh. I felt close to climax already; just the thought of having him take me that way had me shivering on the brink. I felt one of his long fingers probing, working its way inside me. It felt so good and bad and it was Detective Scott with his finger inside me. Oh, my God, I was coming again, my muscles clamping on his finger as I shivered and shook against him.

He withdrew from me gently and took up the bar of soap again. I thought he was going to lather himself and take me as he'd said he wanted to, but he washed me tenderly instead, holding my head in the crook of his arm and shampooing my hair as gently as he would a baby's.

I looked at him as he rinsed out my hair, silently asking him why now? Why me? I studied him, trying to make his features come together in my mind as something I recognized. It was no use: I was broken. The switch that allowed all humans to differentiate one face from another just wouldn't flip inside me, not for friends, family, or lovers. I often doubted that anyone could really love someone who couldn't recognize their face, or if, indeed, I was even capable of loving anymore.

I felt tears burn my eyes, and I turned my face against his chest, absently licking water off the tense muscles. He hummed in pleasure again, and I thought I could grow to love that little inquisitive, interested sound that came from his throat. I straightened, taking the soap from his hands, and began washing him as tenderly as he had me, sliding hands over the hard broad plain of his chest, the washboard stomach, the tight hips and heavy thighs, making him lift his feet one by one so that I could wash them thoroughly. He really seemed to like that, and I thought I would have to make a point of investigating them later, but right then I was more interested in the hard flesh that had risen to attention between his legs. I captured him, one slick hand at his base, the other holding the heavy sac of his balls. He smiled in bliss and lifted his arms to brace them on the wall opposite me.

I worked him up and down, squeezing and rubbing, gripping the base of his staff hard when I thought he was about to come. I held him off until his hips began moving in short involuntary thrusts, then I worked him fast and hard with both hands, rising to kiss him fiercely even as he shook and spurted his seed onto my stomach.

He washed me again, turned off the water, then reached outside for the towels that hung on the bar next to the shower. He knotted one expertly at his hips and used the other to dry my hair a little. He wrapped it around me then, effectively trapping me, and lifted me high into his arms.

I spared a momentary thought for how much it would hurt if he slipped and dropped me, then gave myself up to his strength and dexterity. He carried me into my bedroom, depositing me on the far side of the bed, then climbed in after me. I was sleepy, and drifted off into a doze before he'd finished arranging the quilt at the end of the bed over my damp body.

CHAPTER SIX

"**D**on't you have to work?" I asked hours later as I sat at my kitchen table. The clock on the stove said it was a quarter to eleven. I had a photo shoot in Point Loma at four, but I thought Marshall (I figured that I should call him by his first name now) would've had to go into the office by now.

"I took today off. I went in last night and took care of some paperwork. Besides, I will be working. We're going through your files, remember?" He cast a smile at me over his shoulder.

"Yes," I said to his back. He was making omelets, and the smells filling my kitchen were heavenly. "So, you never answered my question."

"I know," he said, cracking an egg against a glass mixing bowl.

"You're not going to tell me?" I asked in disbelief.

"No, I'm just thinking."

I shut up then, and sipped my coffee. He finished the

omelets, sliding mine expertly onto a plate and setting it down on the table in front of me. I'd gathered up the photos in a file folder the night before and would have brought them to the station already if Marshall hadn't come over.

I picked up my fork and dug in, moaning ecstatically at the taste of cheddar cheese, ham, green pepper, and tomatoes. He paused on his way back to the table to sit down, his plate held in one hand, his coffee in the other.

"That's the noise you make when I'm inside you," he said gruffly.

It took me a minute, but I managed a calm rejoinder. I was going to get a couple answers from this man before I fucked him on my kitchen table. "You should hear me when I eat cheesecake."

"I'll bear that in mind," he said, and sat down across from me, hard knees bumping mine beneath the small round table. I didn't pull away.

I laughed shakily, knowing he was serious, and that I might very well find myself eating cheesecake off various parts of his anatomy. I couldn't say I found the idea unpleasant.

"You asked, why now?" he began.

"Yeah, I thought you didn't like me very much."

"It wasn't that exactly, honey," he drawled out, and I was tempted to say fuck the conversation, take me now, but I didn't because I desperately wanted to hear what he had to say.

"After you recovered, and you came to thank me for saving your life, I'd already been to see you in the hospital a couple times. Always while you were sleeping. I felt like it was my fault you were there; I should've known Johnson was drinking."

"It wasn't your fault," I began, but he waved me to silence. I got the feeling he didn't talk about his emotions much. Well, that made two of us.

"I know that now. It's taken me a while, but I don't feel guilty about you anymore, or about Johnson's death." Johnson had killed himself shortly after his resignation. I'd been in the hospital still, awake, but not fully recovered. He continued with a little half-smile in my direction, and I felt my heart stutter. "I was mad at you, though. There I was trying to be noble, and not take advantage of you, but you didn't seem to want anything more from me or anybody else. You were so angry." He shook his head self-deprecatingly. "I thought I was just someone you wanted to use to prove that you were alive. I had these awful dreams that I would finally give in and take you, and then I would see a double-page spread of my dick taped to my locker at work."

"It would take a double-page spread," I said, deadpan, and he laughed.

"And then you'd come to a crime scene and look gorgeous and make cracks like that and it was all I could do not to haul you to my car and take you like a madman."

"I wouldn't have minded."

"I know, you made that abundantly clear, but I knew from Stevens that you were pretty messed up. What is it about that guy? You women are always telling him everything."

"He's got a sweet face."

"Humph," he snorted. "And you were always flirting with the guys at work. I was sure you were sleeping with most of them as well. The ones you dated always came in to work with happy smiles on their faces. It wasn't until Stevens's wedding that I found out you never slept with any of them."

"Who told you that?"

"Adams. After I punched him out in the bathroom."

"That was what that was all about? You punched him over me?"

He shrugged. "You were dancing with him most of the night. And laughing."

"And you frowned at me from the head table every time I came by to take a picture."

"You kept calling me 'The Repressive Detective' and sticking your tongue out at me when no one was look-ing. Feel free to try that now by the way."

It took me a second to get it, but when I did, I stuck my tongue out and crossed my eyes for good measure. He kissed me heatedly, pulling my tongue deep in his mouth and sucking on it. He released me a minute later with a smile and a parting nibble on my lower lip.

I sighed.

He took my hand. "You'll have to tell me about those years after the accident sometime. I know it wasn't easy for you."

"Okay," I said, but inside I was trembling. I didn't want to explain myself, and the thought that he wanted to be with me, that he was already planning on having other deep conversations, made me want to jump with joy and run away at the same time. "So that's why you changed your mind? You found out I hadn't slept with your friends?" I asked, mildly insulted.

He poked at his eggs, "Well, that made it easier, but no, not exactly."

"I want details," I said, pointing my omelet-laden fork at him.

He leaned forward and took the fork in his mouth, sliding the food off slowly. I inhaled sharply and he raised an eyebrow at me while he chewed.

"You're not always going to have the upper hand, you know," I muttered, and stabbed at the omelet again, bringing my fork to my lips with the inner knowledge that I was tasting him as well, and it made that bite all the better.

"I overheard your conversation with Burtis after Darla and Stevens took off that night."

"Oh," I muttered, and took a big gulp of my coffee. I had been in rare form during the reception. A little tipsy from champagne, delighted for my friends, and desperately lonely. All I'd done the entire evening was take pictures of the happy couple and the love shining from their faces. I recognized love even when I didn't really recognize them, and the sight of it, the power of it, had made my heart ache.

I danced like a loon to make the feeling go away, but the sight of all those unfamiliar faces swirling past had made me dizzy with nausea and fear. I was lost, lost, and surrounded by strangers.

Burtis found me hyperventilating in a corner, and I'd

sobbed into the familiar curve of his shoulder as I hadn't done in years.

I got up, not wanting to think about this anymore, but Marshall tightened his grip and I sat back down. He put one hand under my chin and lifted my face. "I didn't bring this up to make you hurt, baby, it's just that when I heard you crying, I realized that I felt the same way, lonely and kind of empty, and I'd just punched out one of my friends in a jealous rage for suggesting that he could score with you that night. It seemed kind of ridiculous to stay away in the face of the evidence."

I blinked back tears and smiled at him. "But that was a month ago. What else happened?"

"I went to the gallery showing down in the Gaslamp a week ago that had some of your work on display. It was beautiful. I wanted the one you'd taken of yourself, standing with your back to the camera and looking over your shoulder, with your face kind of in shadow."

"You would like that one." I smiled. My ass was a prominent feature, if I recalled correctly.

"And then you showed up yesterday wearing that hot skirt and those ridiculous shoes, and you were such a smart-ass, bending over just to aggravate me. I wanted to push you down on your hands and knees and take you."

"With a naked dead man right there? That's romantic."

"You know by now that death makes a lot of us horny. Why do you think you got harassed by the guys so often after you finished with your photos?"

"I just thought you were all pervs."

"Well, we're that, too," he said, and grinned.

"Thank God."

I ALREADY WANTED him again by the time we finished breakfast, but I thought we should get started going through my files if we were going to make any progress before I had to leave. I thought about canceling the shoot, but it had taken me months to get permission to use the old lighthouse on Point Loma, and I wasn't sure I'd be able to get it again.

Marshall told me to go ahead and start looking; he wanted to call Stevens and ask him if he'd made any progress with the tattoo parlors. I doubted it, since I didn't know of any tattoo parlors that opened before noon, but I shrugged and went cheerfully enough, feeling a deep inner excitement that had nothing to do with solving the case and everything to do with the thought of having him again. I knew he'd take me again before I had to leave. It was only a matter of when, and how. I shivered and opened the door to my studio wondering what his reaction to it would be. With my luck he would get irritated rather than horny.

I'd moved the pictures of his hands to an easel in the center of the room in preparation for matting. I smiled at them dreamily, thinking of the places they had been just hours earlier. I shook myself and went to a nearby closet where I kept cardboard file boxes of my work. There were at least twenty, all filled with photos, journals, contact sheets, and carefully labeled negatives in three-ring binders.

I thought the contact sheets might be the best place

to start. They were a print of all the negatives on a roll of film without enlargement. A lot of commercial photo developers added them now when a customer requested photos on CD. It prevented a photographer from wasting a lot of photo paper on a shot that didn't turn out so great. It was also a handy record of what photos had been taken. Unfortunately, there were probably hundreds of contact sheets in the boxes, and even more prints of the negatives from my medium- and large-format cameras, which were larger than 35mm film.

I was dragging out a box dated six months ago when I heard footsteps coming toward the room. I turned around.

"Jesus Christ," he said, stopping dead, and I bit my lip to keep from laughing.

He looked at me and shook his head. "A little warning would have been nice."

"What's the fun in that?" I said cheekily.

"I'll show you fun," he said, and grabbed me and tickled, making me squirm and buck as I shouted with laughter.

"No, stop, please. I can't breathe." Tears were streaming down my hot face as I giggled and sputtered. He smacked my ass and let me go, wandering around the room and looking at the pictures on the wall. He looked delicious in the black silk boxers I'd loaned him. They had bright red lips on them and were too tight, being mediums. I hoped he had clothes in his car; otherwise the neighbors were going to get a show when he left.

"I don't mind the women," he said after a minute, "but all those dicks make me feel like I'm being watched. Look at this guy," he said, pointing to a dick as big around as a beer can. "I got nothing on that."

I had collapsed on the floor after he let me go, but managed to drag myself to a sitting position while he looked around. I smirked at his comment and flipped the lid off the box. "Don't be an idiot, I like what you've got just fine."

"Well, I like it, too," he said, rubbing himself absently.

I smiled and shook my head. *I love men, I truly do.*

"Are you going to help or compare yourself to all of them?" I asked waspishly, when he still hadn't bothered to come and help. So far I'd gone through half the box and didn't see anything remotely similar to the design we were looking for. I thought I would dig out the 2000 box next. That was the year I'd done the shoot with the tattooed models for an out-there gay mag in the East Village.

"What's this?" he asked, and I looked up. He was standing in front of the easel and looking at the photos of his hands.

I waited, wondering what he would say.

"I like these," was his comment, and I stared at him wonderingly. *Can't he see that they are his hands?*

"You did someone else's hands, too. I saw them in the showing. An old woman's."

"She's not old," I said, and he looked over at me inquiringly. "They were my mother's hands. I gave them to her for her birthday."

"They were beautiful. You really love her, huh?"

"Yes, I do," I said simply, and went back to sorting through the files. I didn't know if I could explain what that picture had meant to me. When I woke from the coma they'd kept me in to keep the swelling in my brain under control, the first thing I'd seen was a tiny blond woman with blue eyes looking down at me. She was crying and laughing at the same time and calling me her baby. It took me a minute to recognize her voice, and when I did I became even more frightened than before. I didn't recognize her. This stranger had my mother's voice. I panicked and jerked away, screaming, and the doctors came in and sedated me. It took days to sort out what was wrong with me, and I cried every time I looked at my mother and didn't see the woman I loved more than my own heart.

I remembered learning in college that when a baby first looks into its mother's face, there is an instant connection. Something about the mother being a mirror of that child's self, and that mirror in some way defines what it means to exist. I would argue that it also first defines what it means to love. I think that was the hardest part for me, losing that connection, and it wasn't till I looked down at her hand clasped in mine weeks later that I found a measure of peace. They were my mother's hands, wrinkled and tiny, filled with love.

"You okay?" Marshall asked, jerking my attention back to him.

"Yeah," I said. "Why don't you get the box marked 2000. I took a picture of a bunch of tattooed freaks that year."

"Should be interestin'," was his only comment. He didn't know the half of it.

THREE O'CLOCK ROLLED around before either of us had found anything, though we'd spent a good part of the time fucking rather than working. The first bout had started innocently enough. He'd pulled a 3x5-inch print out of the box he was looking through and told me he wanted to keep it.

It was a black-and-white shot of a woman sitting cross-legged on a mat, stark naked and smiling brightly. She looked familiar, but I didn't recognize her.

"Why?" I asked.

He looked at me kinda funny and took the picture back. "Because I want a nekkid picture of you and I like your smile in this one."

"Okay," I said quickly, but he caught on.

"You don't recognize yourself, either, do you?"

"Nope," I said offhandedly, but he wasn't buying my nonchalance. He caught me by the back of the neck and pulled me to him, kissing me roughly.

"My poor baby," he murmured. "Sweet girl." And then he began kissing my face. My eyelids, cheeks, the tips of my nose, my chin, all got the same reverent attention. He pushed me down on my back and slid his hands under the man's button-down shirt I wore, catching the top of my panties and pulling them down my legs. I tried to help, unbuttoning the top button of my shirt before he pushed my hands under my head and told me to keep them there.

He shoved the boxers down, spread my legs, and

took me. I was already wet. Wet just from sitting near him while he was half-naked, wet from the sound of his voice, and the tenderness of his touch.

He rode me gently, abrading my back on the hard-wood floor as his thrusts moved me back and forth. I trembled, lifting my chest toward him. He obliged, sliding his hands under my shoulder blades and lifting me up. I let my head drop back, my fingers laced tightly behind my neck as he suckled me through the fabric of my shirt.

It felt as if he did me for hours, so tirelessly, so carefully did he work me. My orgasm caught me by surprise. One minute I was just enjoying the feel of him inside me, running himself over all my secret places, and then I was biting my lip and whimpering in pleasure as my body convulsed and shuddered around him. My climax brought his own, jerking his hips into me spasmodically.

"Damn woman, you're going to kill me," he said into my neck.

I stretched under him, lifting one knee and hooking it on his hip. Rubbing against him, I murmured, "You'll die a happy man," and he groaned and proceeded to take me again, at some point lifting one of my legs over his shoulder while the other rode high on his hip. I'd never been so grateful to the yoga classes that kept me flexible and strong. I wasn't sure I'd be able to walk otherwise.

He helped me load up my car with camera equipment. I would have to hurry to get everything set up when I got there, though I wouldn't even begin shooting until sunset, which didn't start until about eight P.M. this time of year. I'd been allowed to take light readings about the same time the week before, so I had some idea of what to set my equipment for.

He'd made me get his clothes out of his truck, a pair of old jeans and a white T-shirt that I'd lifted to my face and sniffed as I brought them back to the house. It smelled like laundry soap and the warm, musky scent of his body.

He called Stevens again, but his partner still hadn't found anything, so he asked me if I would mind if he stayed and kept looking through my files while I was gone. I said no, I wouldn't mind, and it was the truth, though I was surprised that I was so comfortable letting him invade my space. God knows he'd invaded my body.

I gave him my spare key in case he needed to leave and left him standing in the doorway wearing nothing but his jeans, waving my white undies at me like a flag before going back in the house. *Dirty man,* I thought happily, and drove away with my body tingling and a smile on my face.

CHAPTER SEVEN

I've always loved driving on the freeway in
San Diego. Everyone goes like ninety
miles an hour and the weather is usually nice enough
to roll down the windows. The traffic could suck,
though, especially on the I-5. It was even worse than
usual that day and it took me a while to figure out
why: the Del Mar fair. I'd forgotten about it. The traffic always caused a backup that hung around for
hours. I twitched impatiently, wanting to get the
photos done and get back home so I could screw my
detective's brains out.

A half hour later I was passing the fairgrounds, looking at the brightly lit rides. *I could take him there*, I
thought, remembering that I had free tickets. I used to
enter my photographs in the competitions there in
high school, and now gave a lot of money in scholar-
ships to the winners. As one of the contributors, I got
complimentary passes every season.

I hadn't gone in a long time. Almost two years, not

since my friend Sara had been stationed in San Diego. I smiled, remembering that night. I loved Sara, but even I had to admit that she was a slut. A beloved one, but a slut nonetheless.

We'd been drinking quite a bit beforehand. My little sister had driven us with a bunch of her high school friends, making us promise to leave when she called us. We'd agreed, though I think both of us secretly intended to find other accommodations for the evening.

I have to give Sara credit. She found them in record time: twins, tall, gorgeous, and from the look in their eyes, more than willing to give her a go. I had doubts at first; they were carnies after all, though they seemed reasonably clean, but when Sara pulled me aside and whispered that they were hung like horses, I laughed and told her to take her time.

I waited in a lawn chair outside their brightly painted trailer in the staff parking lot while she entertained the boys. I thought about asking if I could photograph them after the sex marathon was finished. I'd never shot twins before, but I didn't have my tripod and the ick factor was a little too high since they would have just taken a dip in my best friend.

She fucked them until the park closed. I had to bang on the door like a madwoman to get their attention. One of the guys opened it, stark naked, and asked if I wanted a go.

I declined politely and shouted for Sara to get her butt outside. She came out ten minutes later, kissing and petting each of the boys, a Cheshire-cat grin stretching her face. We hurried to meet my irate sister in the parking lot. She'd been waiting for an hour, calling frantically on my cell phone, which I'd forgotten to charge. I apologized, and Sara gave her the giant pink panther George (or was it Willie?) had given her as a farewell token. She took it, but made me promise to tell our mother it was my fault she was late getting back. I promised and we got in the backseat. Two of my sister's friends were in there, staring at us like we were insane.

I laughed at the memory, coming back to myself, and thought wickedly that maybe it was my turn to get laid at the Del Mar fair.

I was fifteen minutes late getting to the lighthouse. It was gorgeous, white, and shining. I'd read up a little on its history. It'd been built in either the late eighteenth or early nineteenth century (I couldn't remember), but was shut down shortly after. The designers hadn't considered its position very well, and its guiding light was more often than not blocked by low fog.

It was privately owned, though there were public tours in and out during the day. The best part of the interior was the great full-length windows looking out over the ocean. The models I'd chosen for the photographs were four women: a great-grandmother, grandmother, mother, and daughter. All gorgeous, stately, green-eyed brunettes. I'd met them while having dinner at a nearby Italian restaurant, which they owned and ran together.

I didn't expect them for another hour, but I still hurried to set up my equipment. I thought maybe I would try to get some shots of them on the beach as well, just for shits and giggles.

They arrived in a blue Ford Escort, laughing and singing as they got out of the car. The youngest, Lena, spotted me first, giving me a hug and a water bottle full of sangria, which explained the rosy glow to their cheeks and the bright smiles on their faces.

I smiled in return, enjoying them as I did so few people. They were such a happy, laughing family, but I think I liked them mostly because their features were so similar. Only their ages marked the gaps between them, and I felt strangely that when I spoke with one, I spoke with them all. It took the pressure off me to separate them as individuals, and something in me sighed and relaxed.

I photographed two of them hugging each other and smiling while the others lounged naked nearby. They were my priestesses, my goddesses of love and beauty. I took several rolls of photographs in different poses while the sun sank slowly in the sky. I asked the women if they wanted some shots on the beach as well, which I'd made sure was private property, so we wouldn't get in trouble.

The two youngest women squealed in delight at the idea and ran for the stairs. I took my Nikon, loaded with color film this time, and walked more sedately down the steps with Rosa and her daughter, Isabel, following behind me.

The two younger women were already splashing in the shallow water, naked and frolicking like nymphs. I snapped a picture quickly, at a high enough shutter speed to freeze the droplets of water sparkling gold against the orange and red sky.

When the light got too low, I stopped and let the camera hang around my neck. I breathed in deeply, enjoying the feel of the wind in my hair.

Rosa spoke next to me, her eyes on her children. "You bring your man, eat dinner with us."

I nodded, smiling at her, not asking how she knew I was with someone. It probably showed on my face.

She turned to me then, reaching up with her gnarled hands to cup my cheeks. "This hurt in you," she said, and waited for me to nod my understanding, "this hurt is not everything. Is not so deep that it touched your heart. Understand, *cara?*"

"Yes, ma'am," I whispered, and wanted to cry.

"Good," she said briskly, and dropped her arms. "Come, children," she called out, loudly for such an old woman, "we go now."

I stayed on the beach for a while after they left, letting the sound of the surf roll in my ears and wash away all my worries, then I got up and went to collect my stuff before the lighthouse keeper arrived to lock up.

CHAPTER EIGHT

The drive home seemed to take forever. I didn't relax until I turned down my street and saw that Marshall's truck was still in my driveway, though he had moved it in front of my garage door for some reason. I parked my car beside it and jumped out with only my purse and my camera bag. I figured I'd get him to move the car with all the camera equipment into the garage later.

It was about eight-thirty. Too late to go out on a weeknight, but I didn't care. I wanted food and his body, and I didn't particularly care what order I got them in. I thought he should've been able to look through everything by now, which meant that either he'd found something, or I was probably wrong about seeing the tattoo before. At any rate, he was all mine, and I was looking forward to enjoying him.

The first thing I noticed was the heavenly smells emanating from the back of the house. He was grilling. I could see him through the French doors that opened out onto my back porch. He was still barefoot and shirtless, wearing only the holey jeans he'd had on before.

He'd put on my Elvis's greatest hits CD, and I could've sworn from the motion of his head that he was singing along to "All Shook Up." I bit my lip to keep from laughing and walked quietly through the living room and the French door he'd left wide open.

I slid my arms around his back, and he stilled, craning his neck around to look back at me.

"Hello, gorgeous," he said, twisting to drop a kiss on my lips. I kissed him back, gripping the belt loops on the back of his jeans.

We broke away and I smiled at him. "Hello, handsome. Don't you know better than to let people sneak up on you?"

"You can sneak up on me anytime."

"You heard my car, didn't you?" I said suspiciously.

He grinned and turned back to the grill, humming again.

"Uh-huh," I said. "Well, I can't be too annoyed with you. You might not feed me."

"Are you hungry, then?"

"Starved."

"Good, you can start the greens."

"I have to cook?" I pouted, and he looked at me again.

"God, I love it when you do that," he said, yanking me into him and nipping my lower lip. I squealed and tried to nip him in return.

"The greens, woman, or no meat for you," he ordered,

pushing me away, and went back to expertly flipping sauce-covered chicken pieces with a pair of tongs.

"Okay," I said with a heavy sigh, "but can you move my car into the garage later? It's got all my equipment inside it."

"Sure," he said. "How was the shoot?"

Was it me, or did he sound deliberately casual? "It was great," I said, a little confused. "I'll tell you about it while we eat."

"Okay," he replied with what I thought was a decided lack of enthusiasm.

I didn't know what his problem was. I thought he would've loved to see those four naked women set against a panoramic backdrop of the ocean. I know they would've enjoyed his attention.

"How long till they're ready?" I wanted to know.

" 'Bout fifteen minutes, I think."

"Cool," I replied, and went back in the house.

I pulled a box of butter beans out of the freezer, hoping that was the kind of "greens" my Southern boy meant. I certainly didn't have collard greens or okra handy; there just wasn't much of a market for it in Southern California. *What a shocker.*

I thought corn bread would be good, too, so I got out the cast-iron pans my grandmother had given me and pulled out a box of instant corn bread mix.

I put on a white chef's apron that my sister had painted a dragon on and given to me on my birthday last year. I didn't take her choice of beasts as a comment on my character, but I probably should have.

It was as I was wrapping the ties around my middle

that I remembered Marshall's comment to me the other night. His fantasy was to come into the kitchen and find me wearing nothing but an apron. I thought about that for a second, flushing a little at the idea of it, and carefully turned off the stove.

I set the apron aside and quickly undressed, folding my clothes and setting them aside on a far counter. I put the apron back on, tying it around my waist. I could feel my cheeks heating. I felt exposed, vulnerable, almost silly, but I was wet, too, and my thighs trembled where I held them pressed together.

I took a couple deep breaths, wanting to appear nonchalant, and got the milk out so I could start mixing the corn bread batter. I was pouring the thick yellow liquid into the pan when I heard him closing the French doors.

I finished pouring, counting his footsteps as he walked through the living room. I set the bowl in the sink and turned on the water, taking a long time to do it, watching as the bowl slowly filled, knowing that he was going to come through the kitchen door any second and see the perky round cheeks of my ass. I hoped he didn't drop the chickens.

He did, but they mostly stayed on the baking sheet that he'd used to carry them. I heard the clatter as the pan hit the floor, and I took a quick peek over my shoulder.

"Holy shit," he said, and I turned back to the sink, biting my tongue.

There was a heavy silence, broken only by the sound of the running water and the remix of "A Little Less

Conversation" playing in the living room. The next thing I knew, two hard, hot hands were on me, and I gripped the edge of the counter in anticipation.

"Spread your legs."

I whimpered and did as he asked, widening my stance. He gripped my hips and tilted me toward him.

"Witch," he said gruffly, and I pressed backward, into the hard hot strength of him.

I heard the sound of a zipper and then a shuffle as the heavy denim of his jeans fell to the floor. I felt him moving behind me, the heat of his body replacing the coolness of the air against my feverish flesh.

There was a gentle rubbing and then the hard pressure of him against the entrance to my body. He rubbed himself against the wet slickness, making me gasp with pleasure, then he pushed inside, spreading me, filling me as I clenched around him. I whimpered, and he pressed deeper, gripping my left hip while his right hand slid around to my front to touch me there. His chest heaved like a bellows and the motion moved him gently inside me.

"You okay, baby, can you take me harder?" he asked, rubbing circles on my clit with a callused fingertip to convince me.

"Yes," I gasped, and he slid out, then in again, harder, working me with his fingers from the front.

He hunched over me, letting go of my hip and bracing himself with a hand on the counter next to mine, and I knew he was about to fuck me in earnest. I could feel his legs shaking behind me and guessed he was on the edge of his control.

He thrust faster, pounding inside me and making me gasp and bend my elbows forward till I was almost kissing the countertop. He did it again. And again. Ramming his hard flesh into me with merciless intensity, the hand between my legs rubbing faster and faster.

"I can't last much longer, Deborah, take it," he growled in my ear.

He didn't have to. I thrust my hips back against him and came so hard that I was afraid the clamp of my muscles had bruised him.

He groaned and jerked against me, and I felt the individual pulses of his climax as he came inside me.

We were both sweaty and breathing heavily, his body still braced over mine. I felt as if I'd just run a marathon; my knees were shaking and I felt light-headed. He pulled out of me gently, and I gasped as the feeling made my body clench in pleasure again.

He noticed, hugging me from behind, one hard arm curving just over my collarbone. I laid a kiss on the hairy, muscled expanse, feeling safe and protected, though I'm sure we looked ridiculous, him with his pants around his ankles and me in nothing but an apron.

He let me go, running his hands over me like he couldn't get used to the feel of me. I looked over my shoulder at him, wanting to smile, but feeling strangely unsettled. I told him I wanted to change and escaped into my room to change into one of my yoga outfits, hemp pants and a cotton tank.

He was stirring the butter beans on the stove when I came in. He'd put his jeans back on and rescued the tray with the chickens.

"I was going to bring it to you in bed," he said, and kissed me when I tilted my face up to him.

"That's okay, I wanted to talk to you."

"You can make the iced tea."

"Okay," I said, and opened the drawer with my collection of tea. I had a lot of herbal, green, and European teas, but I kept a stash of good old Lipton handy for barbeques.

I took out the basket on my Mr. Coffee and began washing it while he watched me curiously. Once it was clean, I put the tea bags in and put it back in the machine.

"What in Sam Hill are you doing?"

I blinked at him, then laughed, forgetting that not everyone used their coffee machine to make tea. "My mom always made it this way. She said it tastes better."

"Doesn't it taste like coffee?"

"Not that I've ever noticed."

"I'm not gonna hold my breath."

"You'll like it," I promised, pouring in a carafe of cool water and listening to the hiss and spit as it brewed. "So, did you find anything?"

"Nope. And Stevens turned up zilch on the tattoo parlors he called and visited, but he pretty much stayed in the North County and that tattoo could have been done in Hong Kong for all we know."

Since my best friend had gotten a tattoo of a giant bullfrog on her ass while visiting Hong Kong, I could pretty much attest to the truth of that statement.

"So I guess it's pretty much on hold until I remember why it's familiar or something else turns up."

"Yep. Nobody's gonna get in a dither over a John Doe unless someone claims him, or other bodies with the same MO start showing up."

"Do you think that's likely?" I asked, interested in learning the way he thought. All the other cops respected him; some of them looked at him with something akin to awe.

"No, something about it felt personal, you know, and sloppy. Like a fight that got out of hand."

"Why strip him naked, then?"

"I considered that. Blood gets everywhere. It could be the killer was just trying to clean up the mess, but honestly, I think he was naked when he got shot."

"But there would have been blood all over him," I argued.

"Not if the killer washed it off. Did you smell the body when you were taking pictures?"

I wrinkled my nose at him. "Gross, we're going to eat soon, you know."

He laughed. "Not that smell. It was faint, but the man had been washed with perfumed soap, like that purple stuff you have in your tub. The guys will never let me live it down if I go in there tomorrow reeking of flowers."

"So go home and shower first," I said, not at all surprised to learn that he intended to spend the night with me.

"So . . ." I extemporized, hopping up on the counter and picking up a drumstick from the tray next to me, "he and someone else, probably a woman, got into an argument, and that person shot him in fury. He or she panicked, washed off all the blood, and carted the body off to the lagoon to dump it."

"Something like that. The simplest explanation is usually the right one. The only problem is, that guy was pretty tall, and dead weight is the heaviest kind. Most women wouldn't be able to haul him anywhere."

"So, it was probably either a man, or a woman who had some help," I guessed. "That's creepy."

"What is?"

"The idea that there might be people willing to help someone haul off a dead body. And why dump it there? That's a pretty public place. Those weird guys are always fishing off the highway."

"I don't have any idea why they chose that spot, but any number of people will help a murderer cover up a crime, mostly family, friends, or lovers. Some do it out of loyalty, others perversion, but I think most people usually help because they think in some weird way that if they get rid of the evidence, then the crime never happened."

"I can understand that," I said, thinking of some of the rape victims I'd seen down at the station.

"Fortunately for us, those same people usually crack under the strain and tell everything they know."

I toasted him with my half-eaten drumstick. "Here's to mental breakdowns and the secrets they reveal."

He grunted and opened the oven to check on the corn bread. A hot rush of sweet corn-scented air hit me and I breathed in deep.

"It's done. Where are your pot holders?"

"In the drawer next to the stove."

He pulled out the heavy pan and cut the corn bread into even, pie-shaped slices. I watched him over his shoulder until he told me to sit down before I drove him batshit.

I did, and presently he laid a plate in front of me with a full chicken breast, a slice of corn bread, and a small mountain of beans. It was nothing compared to his plate.

"Are you going to eat all that?" I asked incredulously.

"I had a lot of exercise today," he said, and I rolled my eyes at him.

We munched companionably in silence, my smooth legs entwined with his hard hairy ones under the table.

"So, who was the guy you took pictures of today?" he asked between bites.

"It wasn't a guy. It was four women."

"Is that right," he said with what sounded like surprised relief.

"That's right," I said, suddenly understanding that he'd thought I was shooting a male model, and he hadn't been happy with the idea.

I set my fork down on my beans, not terribly hungry anymore. "Is my work going to be a problem?" I asked carefully.

He tilted up my chin to meet my eyes and I blinked; I'd been watching his hands.

"Not the photography part of it, but the dick-collecting, that bothers me some, yes."

I rolled my eyes. "That's just a game I played. I wouldn't sleep with anyone else, not if we're together."

"I guess that's what I want clear, then. Do you want to be with me and will you stay faithful?"

"Will you?" I countered.

"Yes," he said steadily, not looking away. "You're the sexiest, funniest, most interesting person I've ever known, but I'm not like those guys in *Penthouse* letters; I won't share you with anyone."

I wanted to shout that of course I'd be faithful, but something stopped me. I wasn't sure he really understood what it meant that I couldn't recognize him. Would he get tired of having to identify himself in a crowd? Would he get annoyed if I got confused and put my arms around some strange guy? He'd never said he loved me, just that he wanted to be with me. Did that mean marriage? Kids? *My God, kids.* I'd never be able to pick mine up from school without making them wear some stupid hat or something.

I could feel myself kind of panicking. This was all way too fast for me. I mean, I hadn't known him that long. Well, I'd known him, but I hadn't *known* him. And just because he was funny and smart and sexy didn't mean that I should promise him everything I had. What if I couldn't deliver? What if I wasn't capable of loving him or anyone else?

He put his hand over mine, and I must have looked a little wild-eyed because he used his most soothing voice to calm me down.

"Debbie, honey, I'm just telling you what I want. You think about it. But be sure, because once I have you I'm not letting you go, understand?"

I nodded, wanting to ask if he loved me, but a little

afraid of the answer. I thought he might. I was almost sure of it, and my heart felt tight in my chest.

He took both our plates then, and started doing the dishes. I sat there and watched him, aware that he wasn't completely happy with me and wanting to cry because if I fucked this up, where else would I find a guy who would do the dishes without being asked?

CHAPTER NINE

$\mathcal{S}$ara called late the next morning. It was strange. So often I would think of her, and she would call, or I'd get an e-mail. She was stationed over in Virginia Beach this time, and I hadn't seen her in the better part of a year.

"Hi, baby, it's Sara. What's up?"

"Sleeping with my detective. Think I love him. Help," I said without preamble.

Understand that Sara has been engaged about five times. She is one of those women who truly love and appreciate men. She has an amazing capacity to give, though it's slightly tainted by the fact that she has trouble saying no to just about anything.

I, on the other hand, have never told any guy that I loved him, and I hated it when they fell in love with me. A one-sided relationship just isn't fun for anyone.

I switched to the cordless for this conversation and went into my studio to work on matting the photos of Marshall's hands. He still hadn't realized they were his, and that struck me as oddly significant, though I couldn't have said why.

"Ohmigod. When did this happen? Is he any good?"

That's the thing with best friends—there's no need to mess around with preliminaries.

"A few days ago. And amazing."

"How did you do it?"

"The deciding factors seemed to be a short skirt and a smart mouth."

"I'm so jealous."

"You're surrounded by men."

"Yeah, but I can't sleep with half of them."

"Since when has that stopped you?" I said, laughing.

"So, what's the problem?" she wanted to know. "He loves you back, right?"

"I think so."

"So go for it."

"But—"

"You're not going to go on about that face thing again?"

I pouted. "Maybe."

"Listen, pet. What happened to you is fucked up. God knows I think it's weird when you come to get me at the airport and you pick me out of the crowd by the 'big boobs, tight jeans' elimination method, but it doesn't change the fact that you're my best friend and I love you."

"I know," I muttered.

"So, why does it matter with him?"

"Sometimes, when he's making love to me, I look up at his face, and it's like a stranger's inside me."

There was a pause after that which could've held a four-course dinner.

"Wow," she said. "Sounds like a lot of women's fantasies."

I laughed, and drew my knees up until I was curled up in a little ball on the stool. "I've done a lot of strangers. Being with someone forever means that you know his face as well as your own. It means that you can meet his eyes across a crowded room and know exactly what he's thinking."

Sara sighed. "I'm sure you're right, but if you ask me, that's only one part of loving someone. Why get stuck on that? If he's worth it, then you'll find your own way of loving each other."

"How?"

"Sex?"

"Got that covered."

"Lucky bitch." She laughed. "Why don't you ask him?"

"Just tell him what's bothering me and ask him how we can fix it?"

"Why not?"

Why not, indeed. "Okay," I said.

"Well, now that you've gotten me all horny, I'm gonna go see if I can find a stranger of my own."

"Wait, when are you going to come to visit me again?"

"I'm not partying with you anymore. I have three words for you: tequila, twins, tattoos. Never again."

"Are you talking about that night at the fair?"

"Of course. You think I do that all the time?"

"What tattoos?" I asked, dropping the mat board I was holding and coming to attention on my stool.

"The clown tattoos."

"What are you talking about?"

"They had clowns on their dicks, or near their dicks. Those suckers were long."

"Are you sure?" I said, dropping my legs and straightening on the stool.

"Yeah, you didn't notice?"

"No, it was dark. I was drunk."

"That's right. You weren't with me when I checked them out in their booth thing."

"What kind of booth was it, do you remember?"

"Why?"

"It's important, just tell me."

"I think it was one of those dart-throwing things, or maybe a ring toss. I wasn't paying much attention. The clown face was painted on the outside of it, too."

"Sara, I've gotta go. I'll call you later."

"Don't forget that I get to be maid of honor. Your sister will understand. Love you, pet," she finished, and hung up before I'd stopped sputtering.

I CALLED MARSHALL at work, but he wasn't there, so I changed into jeans, a tank top, and my lime-green flip-flops, grabbed one of the photos of the body, and headed down to the station to see if I could find him. I brought my digital camera and a framed picture of me for his desk. And no, I wasn't naked. It was a shot from his partner's wedding. I hesitated to do it, but some little imp inside me wanted to aggravate him, just a little. A girl couldn't change her spots all at once.

I went into the garage, not too distracted to notice that he'd moved my car into it at some point last night. I wondered if he'd always take care of me, or whether he was sucking up until he'd convinced me to take him on.

I thought that maybe he was just the kind of guy who took care of things, his woman included. Besides, he was already getting lots of enthusiastic sex, and I was pretty sure that most men only sucked up to women when they wanted to get laid.

It was about noon, so the trip down the 5 wasn't too bad. I was starving and the fairgrounds weren't going anywhere, so I picked up *carne asada* burritos for me and whoever was on duty when I got there.

The guard at the gate waved me inside when I showed him my pass, and I parked next to two cruisers near the front of the building. I walked into the office, which was your basic institutional building. Formica desks, folding chairs, and dirty white walls.

A resounding cheer went up, as it always did when I walked in the door. Most of the women even liked me; I'd gone out for drinks with them a couple times. I starting pulling out the extra burritos I'd brought, handing them out on a first-come, first-serve basis. The taco shop had included chips and salsa as well, so I set that out and watched the vultures feed.

I wandered over to Marshall's desk, carrying my burrito. I set the package with the framed picture of me on his desk and then wandered back over to the crowd. "Anybody seen Scott or Stevens?" I asked around a mouthful of heavenly seasoned meat and onions. I wandered back over and perched on someone's desk. Someone I knew, I hoped.

"They left an hour ago," a young blond cop said next to me, bending to take a bite of my burrito. I figured it must be Alex Barnes, a cute young thing who had asked me out a couple times. "What do you want with those old guys when you can have me?"

"You're just too easy, Boston, a girl likes a challenge."

He put a hand to his heart in mock agony, and I laughed.

That's the picture that greeted Marshall and Stevens as they came into the room. Me sitting on the desk surrounded by cops munching burritos. I suppose it could've looked worse.

"Don't y'all have work to do?" the deep voice that I loved commented from the doorway. I looked up, eager to tell him what I'd found out.

I hopped down, handing the last half of my burrito to Barnes, and hurried over to him. "Hey," I said cheerfully, and started to move in for a hug. Something in the stiffness of his body stopped me, so I turned to Stevens and hugged him instead.

"Did you need something?" my lover asked, interrupting, and I narrowed my eyes at him.

"Actually, I found out where I've seen that tattoo."

They snapped to attention like hound dogs. "Where?" Marshall asked, taking my elbow and leading me toward his desk.

I shook him off. He didn't get to touch me right now.

"At the fair two years ago."

"Two years?" they said in unison. "That's gonna be—"

"It was on a carnie. Actually two carnies. But I think the design was painted on the outside of their booth as well."

"And carnies, while not always predictable, generally follow established travel patterns. . . ." Stevens began.

"And since they usually go out of their way to avoid government agencies . . ." I continued.

"What do you mean you saw this tattoo on two carnies?" Marshall asked, and while I suspected part of him wanted to know for the sake of the case, another part of him was remembering the location of the tattoo.

"Sara hooked up with them. They were twins," I said defiantly, and noticed that Stevens shifted his weight uneasily beside me.

"Twins."

"Yep."

"So they might have other family there," he ventured.

"I think so," I said thoughtfully. My memories of that night were vague at best, but I thought I remembered them saying to Sara that their sisters would be out for the evening.

"But why dump the body near the lagoon?" Stevens asked. "They would've done better to chop it into little pieces and bury it or feed it to one of the animals. They have animals, don't they?"

Did I ever call him sweet? "I don't think they have lions or anything," I said. "It's not the circus."

"We won't know unless we find out more. We'd better check it out," Marshall said to Stevens, ignoring me completely.

"What about me?" I asked archly. The man was so in for it.

"What about you? The twin is our most likely suspect at the moment. What we really need is a sketch of the man's face, and you can't give us that."

I don't know if he said it deliberately to hurt me, but it worked like a charm anyway. I think my mouth might have fallen open, but it didn't take me long to recover. "Well, you can forget about what I can give you," I said coldly, and stalked off.

As an exit line, it lacked something, but he followed me anyway, catching me just before I reached the sliding-glass door to the parking lot.

"I want to talk to you," he growled at me through clenched teeth.

"Too bad."

"Damn it, Deborah, I didn't mean that."

"I don't care."

"Yes, you do," he said, shaking me. "Come on," he ordered, pulling me roughly back down the hall and into some kind of utility closet.

He shut the door and we were enclosed in the musty, ammonia-scented darkness. The only light came from the crack under the door. I held myself stiffly away from him, trembling, but there wasn't so much room in the little closet that I wasn't completely aware of his every breath.

"You'd better watch out, someone might get the

wrong idea and think you're screwing me or something." Sarcasm has always been my defense against tears.

"Stop it. I'm sorry, okay?" His hands cupped my face. I turned it away from him. "Honey, I didn't mean to make you cry." I felt him lean forward and his lips touched my forehead, my hot cheeks.

"I always cry when I'm mad. It doesn't mean anything." I felt him smile against my skin.

"I was jealous. I saw you laughing and flirting like you always do. Looking gorgeous, and for a second I was back where I was weeks ago, wanting you and hating you at the same time."

"Are you ashamed of being with me?"

"No." He sounded appalled. "Is that what you thought?"

"It's kind of hard not to."

"No," he said, kissing me. "Not ever."

"Uh-huh."

"You want me to prove it?" he demanded. "I'll go right now. I'll walk in there and tell all of them that I love you. I love Deborah Valley."

I put a hand over his mouth. "Shut up." I was crying again, on the verge of hiccupping sobs, and once that happens I'm completely out of control. So I took my hand away and kissed him instead, and that felt so nice and he tasted so good that I put my arms around his neck and sank into him.

He kissed me back at first, but when my lower belly rubbed against his erection, he tried to pull away. "Honey," he said, catching my arms, "we can't here." I ignored him. "Baby, I have to work. Stevens—"

"Stevens will understand," I said wickedly, and nipped him on the chin.

"But . . ." he started to say, and I slid my hand down the front of his slacks and gripped him.

"I want you," I said, low in my throat, massaging him with my hand. "And if you try and stop me again, I'll make sure everyone in this station thinks you fucked me in here anyway, so what have you got to lose?"

He shoved me back against the wall and put his hand on the crotch of my jeans. "When you put it that way . . ."

I could feel myself getting wet as he rubbed me, and for a few seconds we just groped each other over our clothes. Then I undid the clasp on his pants and slid the zipper down. His erection had already worked free of his boxers, and I gave him one good long stroke to show him how much he pleased me. His hand paused in its endeavors.

"God, I love you."

I gasped and pulled my hand away.

He just laughed and shoved down his pants and boxers. Then he rubbed up against me. "Don't worry. You don't have to say anything."

He put his hands on my shoulders and pressed downward. I went willingly, even eagerly, sliding my hands down on his chest as I went to my knees, curving them around to grip his tight buttocks as I leaned forward.

I sucked his balls first, rolling them in my mouth, and his hands tightened on my hair. Next I probed the tip of my tongue into the little triangle of skin on the underside of his rod, right above his ball sack. I took it gently between my teeth and nibbled, making him hiss.

"Take it in your mouth," he said hoarsely, and I moved to do as he asked, sliding my tongue along his undercarriage, and sucking briefly on the tip before sliding my lips down and taking him deep. I pulled on him once, opening the back of my throat, and waited, teasing. His hips moved forward, begging wordlessly, and I began sucking in earnest, pressing my tongue hard against him. His grip on my neck changed, moving my mouth up and down on his shaft.

I relaxed, breathing through my nose and sliding the wet, hot sheath of my mouth over him again and again. I could feel him getting close; several pearly drops escaped his control. I cupped his balls in my hand and lifted my mouth off him, rubbing one finger along the slick length of him, swirling it gently around the tip.

"Don't stop."

"Spread your legs a little."

He did as I asked, spreading them as far as he could with his pants around his ankles. I licked his pulsing staff as a reward, running the edge of my teeth over the sensitive tip before taking him full in my mouth again. I sucked once, hard, and slid my wet finger over the ridge of flesh behind his balls. I held it there, pressing, while he gasped and panted, then I rose higher on my knees and blew him in earnest, working him, feeling him strain on the knife edge of pleasure.

He came with a loud grunt of surprised pleasure, jerking into me. I swallowed quickly, drinking the evidence of his fulfillment, prolonging his pleasure. When the silky pulses ended, I licked him clean, kissing his softened penis farewell.

I grabbed the waistband of his pants and boxers and pulled up as I stood, tucking him away gently and zipping his fly. He kissed me, sending his tongue deep, telling me without words what he intended to do to me.

"Your turn," he said, and slid his hands over my breasts.

I stopped him. "No."

"No?"

I put one hand against his chest to hold him still. I unbuttoned the top button of my jeans and slid two fingers under my panties and between my legs. He couldn't see me very well in the dark, so when I drew my fingers out, wet from my body, and touched them to his lips, he drew in a deep breath.

"Taste me," I ordered, and put my lips to his so that I could feel his tongue sampling the sap from my body. I whispered against his lips, "I want to go home wet from wanting you. I want to think about you all afternoon, coming home and taking me no matter where I am. I want you to think about me waiting for you, so hot that when you get to me, you'll do anything to have me."

"Good sweet Jesus," he groaned. I stepped away from him, buttoning my jeans.

"Come on, Detective, Stevens is waiting." I laughed and opened the door a crack, slipping through when I saw the hall was clear. I walked toward the entrance, taking my sunglasses from where I'd hung them in the neck of my shirt and sliding them on.

I heard him close the door to the closet and knew he was watching me walk away. I lifted a hand over my shoulder and waved, deliberately swaying my hips.

I didn't glance back until after I stepped through the glass doors, and saw him leaning back against the wall like a man who'd just gotten punched in the gut. But the smile on his face, oh, that smile. In that moment I knew I was a lucky woman. That smile would surprise me every time, and I would never fail to appreciate the beauty of it.

CHAPTER TEN

Thirteen hours later I opened my eyes to an infomercial for some miracle cream. I was lying on my bed, decked out in a black satin nightie and smelling like a harem dancer. I'd gone shopping for the nightgown after I'd left that afternoon and had spent the rest of the time getting ready. I must've fallen asleep.

I looked around. There was no sign of Marshall.

Pulling on my robe, I padded into the kitchen to pour myself a glass of water. I drank deeply, spilled some down my front. I grimaced, brushing the droplets from the black satin.

I wandered into the living room to check my machine. Zero messages. I dug my cell phone out of my bag. Same thing. The man was gonna get an earful when I saw him again.

There was no way I could go back to sleep. Nine hours was more than enough.

I tried to work, but I kept getting distracted by

thoughts that something terrible had happened and Marshall was lying in an alley bleeding to death. When I ruined the third print of my four Italian ladies frolicking naked in the ocean, I knew I had to do something.

I called Marshall's cell phone and got a message. I called the station and got some newbie I didn't know who refused to tell me anything. I finally said to hell with politeness and called Darla. She answered on the first ring.

"Hello?"

"Darla, it's Debbie. Sorry to call so early."

"That's okay. I wasn't asleep."

"Do you know where Stevens and Scott are?"

"They didn't call you?" she asked, surprise in her voice.

"No, *they* didn't," I muttered ominously.

"Oh," she said very carefully.

"Yes, oh. Are they all right?"

"They're fine," she rushed to assure me. "They got a call. Someone found a body down by the Oceanside pier about five o'clock. It turned out to be the mayor's youngest daughter."

"Shit."

"Yeah, I don't think we'll see them until sometime tomorrow."

"He still should've called me."

"I know."

"Men suck."

She laughed and said she'd call me if she heard anything more. I said okay and hung up.

I tried making some more prints of my ladies, but

couldn't really concentrate. I knew that the tattoo investigation was probably tabled because of the mayor's daughter's death, but I thought checking the Internet was worth a try.

I wanted to scan one of the photos and send it to some friends of mine who did nothing but play on the Internet and surf all day, but knew I'd need Marshall's permission to release that bit of information. I ran a Google search for images with similar descriptors and read what I could about the Del Mar fair vendor application process and history before a pounding headache forced me to give up. I changed into my bikini and wet suit and went out in the hazy dawn light to catch some waves.

I only stayed in for about an hour, and even then I mostly just sat on my board and drifted in the deeper water. My heart just wasn't in it. Peace eluded me today. So I dragged myself back home.

I looked up when I got to the corner of my house, and there he was, my handsome stranger, still wearing the clothes he'd had on the day before and sitting on the steps to my house with his head bent and his keys dangling from his hands. He seemed exhausted.

I sighed and went to him, leaning the surfboard against the wrought-iron railing. His head jerked up like someone who'd caught himself nodding off. His eyes met mine. I concentrated on the dark brown depths of them and let the rest of his features sort of fade out.

"Are you sorry?" I asked.

"Yes."

"Okay, then," I said wearily, and tried to move past him to unlock the door. He caught my legs and hugged me to him. I sank my hands into his hair and held him in return.

"I'm getting you all wet," I said after a second or two.

He laughed and released me, moving out of the way so I could get past. I held my hand out to him as I went through the door.

He took it, smiling sleepily, and I felt a rush of affection for the big idiot. I led him into the bedroom and pushed him down. He kissed me. A long deep kiss that seemed to have no other purpose but to connect us for a time, to ground us both in the realm of the pleasant and familiar.

I pulled away and went into the bathroom to peel off my wet suit and take a quick shower. When I came out, he was sound asleep.

I ran my fingers through his hair again and bent down to kiss his forehead, then changed into my favorite pair of boxers and a T-shirt and wandered into the kitchen to find something to eat. I was starving, but nothing looked appetizing. I ate half a bowl of Cheerios and poured the rest into the sink, then unrolled my yoga mat and tried to meditate for a while. When that didn't work I gave up and went back to the bedroom.

I crawled in front of him on the bed so that he was spooning me and pulled the covers over both of us. I didn't think I'd be able to sleep, but I wanted to be held for a while. He was a cop, and if the gods were kind, then I was going to be with him for a while. There would probably be many nights like the one that just passed, and I thought that would be okay, as long as there were moments like this afterward, moments where I could feel the warmth of his body against me and the strong grip of his arms holding me tight.

A WARM KISS was dropped on my lips and I smiled in my sleep, stretching my arms like a cat. They were caught and pulled deliciously upward while a deep voice whispered in my ear.

The click of cold metal around my wrists woke me. I opened my eyes and saw him above me, covering me like a mountain lion does much smaller prey. I was handcuffed to the headboard. Excitement tightened my body in a rush that was its own kind of pleasure. I hadn't expected this when I'd crawled in beside him.

"Surprise, honey," he drawled from somewhere in front of me.

"What time is it?" I asked him, writhing a little impatiently against the cuffs, watching his eyes follow the motion.

"Lunchtime," he said slowly, giving each consonant and vowel due consideration and meaning, "and I missed breakfast."

"Oh," was all I could think to say. I was bombarded by a mental picture of him pulling down the stretchy waist of my boxers and feasting on me.

"What are you thinking about?" he asked.

"Nothing," I mumbled, blushing.

"That's what I'm thinking about. What I did think about. All day yesterday. I damn near killed Stevens and me trying to get back to you. And then that call came in."

He pushed away from me and I lifted my head, straining my neck, to follow him. "What're you doing?"

"Using my new camera. I love it, by the way. I meant to tell you sooner."

Oh, God.

"Well, well," he said, standing on the edge of the bed and looking at the viewfinder on the back, "I think I'll use the portrait setting, or maybe the landscape," he teased, reaching out to pinch the soft skin where my ass met my thigh.

"Come on. Quit teasing," I ordered.

He laughed. "You're going to wait, beautiful. Wait until I'm ready to take you."

"Please."

"Begging already? This is going to be a long day."

"Marshall, touch me."

He didn't answer, but he climbed back on the bed, tossing the camera down next to me. I arched my body with a relieved sigh. I felt his hot hands on my waist under the shirt, and I let my head fall back, sinking into the pleasure. He slid down my boxers, drawing them over my feet and tossing them away. I held my legs closed, wanting him to open them, to take me.

"Open your legs," he demanded, mimicking my words from the closet earlier.

I closed my eyes and did as he asked, spreading my legs, making myself vulnerable to his touch. His fingers drew circles on the insides of my knees before tracing a path down the inside of my thigh. I arched up, wanting him to touch me where I already ached for him. He stopped, and I held my breath.

I knew I was already wet. The air was perfumed with the scent of my desire. He smelled of soap and man. A hungry man. The need radiated off him in waves that I could feel even with my eyes closed.

Then suddenly there was no more teasing. The hard length of his cock entered me, and I cried out in shocked pleasure. His hands lifted my hips with each thrust, and I whimpered at the hot glide of his staff in my body.

I could feel it already, the sweet ache and tingling awareness that said I was almost there, almost ready, and then on the next thrust he pulled wetly out of my body, leaving me empty.

"No!" I shouted, and received a gentle slap on my thigh in punishment.

I gave a frustrated shriek and he chuckled. I felt the brush of his hair from his forehead before his tongue touched the quivering warmth of my belly. "Mmmm. Soft. Sweet."

He licked up my stomach, riding up the bottom of my T-shirt, nuzzling my breasts through the soft white fabric, then smoothing his hands up my body and cuddling them around his face. His beard pricked against me, lightly abrading my nipples now. I lifted my hips against him, wanting him back.

"I'm ready. Please, Marshall."

"Call me Detective, like you used to do. I've heard that snotty voice of yours in my dreams."

"Detective Scott," I said, with all the haughtiness I could muster while handcuffed to a bed.

"Yes, just like that," he said meanly, and gently pinched my nipple, which was undoubtedly tenting the soft white fabric of my T-shirt.

I felt him moving again and tried to lift my head. "Keep your head back and your eyes closed," he said. "This is better than a wet T-shirt contest."

I couldn't laugh; I wanted him too much.

He bent down and took one nipple in his mouth, sucking hard for several seconds, until it felt like a line of heat was running from my nipple to where I was wet and throbbing for him. "I've wanted you like this," he murmured, his breath blowing over the wet fabric and making my nipples even harder. "I've wanted you bound for me. I bet you knew that. I bet you know that I hate the thought that I care for you more than you do for me. It makes me feel weak."

"Is that why you didn't call me?" I challenged, lifting my head to glare at him. "You didn't think I'd care?" It felt good to fight, like we were both part of a furious, lusting tangle that would come undone in an explosion that would rock us both.

"Maybe I wanted to know if you cared. Were you worried about me?"

"No," I lied, and held my breath, head falling back again.

Suddenly his hands were at the neck of my T-shirt. It ripped with a shredding sound that masked my gasps of anticipation and fear. The halves of the shirt fell to my sides.

"Tell me you were worried," he ordered.

I whimpered in response and felt the sharp sting of teeth in the bend of my arm.

"Tell me," he said again, rubbing the swollen head of his penis against the knot at the top of my flesh.

"No," I argued, and lifted up abruptly, wrapping my legs around him and holding on fiercely. He reared back on his arms surprised, and I took advantage of his motion, lifting my hips up and onto him, forcing him inside me with the strength of my legs.

He speared me. Hot and hard, stretching me and making me shout out a triumphant, "Yes," and the painful tightness burst, releasing me in waves of shuddering pleasure.

He plunged inside me, helpless, drawn in by the rhythmic clamping of my muscles, his head falling between his arms as he shuddered and let himself go.

I lay there limply as he pulled himself out of me. I felt him reach for the keys to the cuffs, managing to rub his whole body against me in the process.

He kissed me and I smiled, content now. "Do you have to go back to work?" I asked, drawing a finger over his lips, trying to memorize the feel and shape of them.

"In a little while," he murmured into my neck. I breathed in the smell of his hair and held him against me.

"Again," I queried softly, and he nodded, rolling over so that I was straddling him.

"Only now it's your turn to do all the work," he ordered, petting my thighs.

I laughed and rose up to take his newly aroused body into mine. Work was, after all, one of my favorite things.

CHAPTER ELEVEN

*H*e got a call that afternoon. Someone meeting the general description of the victim had been spotted at the fair. He wouldn't let me come, but he came over as soon as he got back, walking in the door and scowling before plopping down on my couch.

I let him relax before I started pestering him, snuggling against him on the couch while he watched cartoons. The man really was a lunatic.

"Was it him?" I asked, unsure why I was so interested. Maybe it was just because this case marked the turning point in my relationship with him.

"Nope. And no one admitted to recognizing the tattoo."

"Any of the carts look freshly painted?"

"Quite a few, actually," he said, glancing away from the Road Runner long enough to give me a pleased look. It was nice to be appreciated for my brain as well as my other talents.

"I don't suppose you'd like to go back tonight?"

"Why?" he wanted to know.

"Well, I have free tickets, and there's a chance, a small chance, that I might recognize the twin."

He made a noncommittal noise in his throat.

"We could go to dinner at the restaurant of the pretty Italian women beforehand. I'll let you ogle them and not say a word."

That got his attention. "Promise?"

"Uh-huh. But if their husbands beat you up, I'm not lifting a hand to help you."

"Okay. But you're not leaving my side at the fair, and if you do see someone, you tell me quietly, don't shout and point."

As if I would. "Anything else?" I asked with only a touch of sarcasm.

"Yeah, make out with me in the Tunnel of Luv," he said, drawing out *luv* into a ridiculous exaggeration of a country hick's drawl.

I shouted with laughter, bashing him with a throw pillow, until he tossed me down and tickled me mercilessly. *What did I do for fun before this crazy man?*

STEVENS CALLED LATER that afternoon to say that the coroner had said that the mayor's daughter had apparently committed suicide, taking a large dose of sleeping pills and jumping off the pier. Marshall relaxed completely for the first time in days.

I put on my makeup, coming out of the bathroom twenty minutes later with pouty red lips the same color as one of the swirls in my dress, acres of dark brown tresses, and (thanks to mascara) eyes that would make a doe cry with envy.

"Damn," he breathed when he saw me, and I smiled. This was the reaction I'd been hoping for. "Are you sure you don't just want to stay here?" he asked hopefully.

"Yes, I'm sure," but I smiled at him and patted his shoulder as if he were a particularly good puppy dog. He had such nice shoulders, all strong and corded with those yummy muscles.

"We'd better head out then, the traffic probably sucks."

"So, who was the guy who drove you to the crime scene?" he asked after we'd gotten on the freeway. We were in his truck. The sun was still pretty high and the air smelled like the ocean and flowering plants. The windows were down, messing up my hair, but I liked the fresh air too much to complain.

I had to think. "Freckle Dick?" I asked, surprised.

"You *actually* call him Freckle Dick?" he wanted to know, sending me a doubtful look across the front seat.

"Not in public."

"Why?"

"Does it really matter?"

"No." Then, "Do you have one for me?"

"I haven't thought about it," I said honestly.

"Liar."

I laughed. "I'm not lying."

"Then you have to tell me what the deal is with all the men."

I fiddled with the strap on my purse. "Okay. I need to talk to you about it anyway."

"So . . . tell."

"Well, you know when you and Johnson ran into me?"

"Yes," he said shortly, and I knew he was still horrified by the thought that they almost killed me. I caught his quick glance at the scar that ran in a curved line from the top of my forehead to behind my left ear.

I sometimes wonder if I'd seen Marshall's face in the instant before the car struck me. I imagined I did. I wanted to believe that I had seen him at least once knowing that I would remember his face if I saw it again.

The funny thing was, if not for the accident, I don't think I ever would have met him, much less fallen in love with him.

I looked at his hands on the steering wheel, aware that he was waiting for me to elaborate. He still hadn't recognized his own hands in the photos I had taken. It was amazing to me, just as my little problem was amazing to everyone else.

"Well, you know some of what I went through to get better. You were there for a lot of it."

"Yes."

"You wanna know what I was doing right before Johnson hit me?"

"What?"

"Breaking up with my boyfriend."

He didn't say anything, so I just kept talking, thinking if I just got it all out in one go it wouldn't be so difficult. "I did that a lot. I would date a guy a couple times and somehow end up as his girlfriend without really thinking about it or intending to get in a relationship, and then after a few weeks or if they mentioned the word *love,* I would call it off."

He looked at me, probably thinking about his declaration in the closet and the fact that I still hadn't replied in kind.

"Anyway," I said, looking out the window, "when it became clear that I would never recognize anyone again, I got a little squirrely. There were lots of things going on in my mind. Things like, I can never go into a party again and see a familiar face. Watch my favorite actors and see a face I've watched a hundred times. If I have kids, I will never look into their faces and see myself or their father."

"You mean like, 'he has my nose' kind of thing."

"No, not exactly. That's what's weird. I can take a picture of myself and a picture of my father and see that we have the same nose. Sometimes, if I look for a specific feature on someone, I can always identify them by it."

"Like a birthmark?"

"Yes, the problem is that if someone has a similar-looking feature, I can't tell them apart. When my dad is around my uncle Ron, I am constantly confused. That's the best I can explain it really."

"Okay, so you had all this stuff going on in your head, and your solution was to sleep with as many men as you could?"

I frowned at him. "I was, am, pretty messed up. I

can't even look in the mirror and see myself, the girl I feel like I am inside. It's like I woke up from that coma and she was gone. I was missing somehow, and I tried to get her back by grabbing and holding to whatever I could. I exercised like a maniac, so that I could have a perfect body. That, at least, I could recognize and call my own."

"And you took photographs of bodies . . ."

"Because that's what I'd felt like I'd become, a body without a soul . . . or a heart. I just took pictures of dicks because at least that was one way of telling you all apart, but I became fascinated by the process of it. The search for meaning in the physical. Eventually, in my later work, the stuff you saw in the museum, it became my way of looking for the soul in the body."

"You've managed it."

"Thanks," I said, and felt my eyes sting, and then I told him something that I'd never told anyone else, not even my therapist. "I thought that this was a punishment. The way I am now."

He sent me a surprised glance, but was too much of a cop to glance away from the road. I was glad we had done this in the car. I wasn't sure I would've been able to get it out while he looked at me. "For what?" he asked, sounding faintly outraged, as if I could never do anything to deserve such a horrible fate.

"For never loving any of those men, for never wanting their mind or their heart."

"Honey, if that was a crime worthy of divine punishment, don't you think half the people in the world would be struck with it, too?"

"At least the male half."

He gave me an impatient smile and took my hand. "You have a soul and a heart; you just got lost for a while."

I lifted his hand and kissed it, wanting to tell him about my conversation with Sara, wanting to ask if he really thought this was going to work. I still wasn't sure what other ways we could find of loving each other, but to keep him, I was willing to try, and keep trying.

I would tell him later. If I started crying now, I'd mess up my eye makeup. I couldn't bring a picture of my face to mind, but I was certain that I didn't want to have raccoon eyes the first time I ever told a man I loved him.

ROSA GREETED US at the door, her gnarled fingers taking mine as I bent down to kiss her cheek.

"Welcome, *cara*. You look lovely."

"So do you, ma'am."

"Call me Nonna," she said imperiously, and winked at me. "Is this your man?" she asked with a great deal of appreciation.

"Yes," I said, turning so that I could eye him as well, and I could've sworn that a blush tinged his cheeks.

She laughed and ordered him to bend down so that she could kiss his cheeks, first one and then the other, and I found myself pulling out my camera and taking a shot before I'd completely realized what I was doing.

Marshall looked up at me, and I thought that if I had seen a total stranger look at a woman that way, I would've said that he loved her like a crazy man. I stared back at him, wondering if he saw the same thing in my eyes.

Nonna led us to our table, and all the women crowded around us, giggling and asking when the photos would be ready.

"Soon," I told them, and nodded at Marshall. "I've been a little distracted," which sent them into gales of laughter again. Isabel's husband, a strapping older man with a barrel chest and a twinkle in his eye, winked at me from the kitchen door.

They opened a bottle of the house red for us and left us to ourselves in our dark little corner of the restaurant.

"How did you find this place?" he asked around a mouthful of garlic bread.

"I thought you wanted to make out with me later," I said, staring pointedly as he pulled off another piece.

"So you eat some, too, and you won't know the difference," he said, feeding me.

I chewed, looking around at the other diners. "I was just wandering around mostly. I had an idea for taking some photos using the old lighthouse as backdrop, so I came by one evening and found this place."

"And the rest is history."

"It will be. I did a couple prints. They're amazing. And there are some even better ones if the contact sheets are anything to go by."

"That's the one with all the negatives printed on it."

"What a man."

"I can't wait to see the ones from last night. As long as I'm the only one seeing them."

"What, you're not willing to give it up for posterity?"

"Not on your life. Those are going in my private collection."

"Along with your *Playboys* from 1978 to 1986 and your signed photo of Alyssa Milano?"

"How'd you know about the *Playboys*?"

"Stevens."

"Is nothing sacred?"

"He's probably told the whole station about us by now," I said, and waited uneasily for his reaction.

"He didn't have to. Everyone was sitting around innocently when I got in yesterday. Never mind that the mayor's daughter had turned up dead, the package on my desk still looked as rumpled as my date the morning after prom."

"They saw the photo," I guessed, already picturing the scene.

"'What's the photo for, Scott?'" he mimicked, wiggling his eyebrows. "'I never got a photo, Scott,'" he said, doing Barnes's high-pitched Boston accent so perfectly that I snorted with laughter. "And then they began a rousing rendition of 'Scott and Debbie sitting in a tree, K-I-S-S-I-N-G.'"

"Cops are so juvenile."

"That's why they like you so much."

"Ha ha. Did you always want to be one?"

"A cop?"

"No, a juvenile. Yes, a cop."

He looked down at his plate, then back up at me. There was something in his eyes that made me think of a five-year-old who just shoved his sister's Barbie down the toilet. "Actually, you wanna know a secret?"

"Oh, yeah," I crooned, leaning over my half-eaten salad. Unfortunately, one of the many DeTavola men showed up bearing a heavy tray with steaming plates of pasta and vegetables.

I smiled at him, he was gorgeous after all, but I really just wanted to hear Marshall's secret. I had a feeling he didn't make that offer lightly.

Our plates were set in front of us. Chicken cacciatore for me, mussels in clam sauce over a bed of linguini for him. It looked delicious, but I had another kind of sustenance in mind.

"So, don't leave me hanging here. What?"

He wasn't paying me any attention. He'd just wrapped his fork in his pasta and taken a bite. Even I couldn't mistake the look of divine bliss that passed over his face. DeTavola's restaurant had that effect on everyone.

I smiled and shook my head at him.

"This is . . . this is . . ."

"I know," I said, taking pity on him.

We ate in silence for a while—Marshall letting out an occasional moan of pleasure while I laughed at him.

When we were finished, a different handsome Italian boy came over and took our dishes. Isabel followed shortly after him, smiling at our empty plates as they passed her in the strong arms of her grandson.

"Nonna said you were to have tiramisu and coffee. Is that all right with you?"

"We'd love it," I said immediately. I'd had their tiramisu before.

The gorgeous, multilayered dessert was brought out to us on china plates while the coffee was poured from a silver urn. I wouldn't let Marshall touch it until he'd told me his secret.

"No, don't take a bite until you tell me."

"Can I sip my coffee at least?"

"Fine, but I have to warn you, it doesn't taste like the coffee down at the station."

"You mean it doesn't taste like it was run through someone's dirty socks? What a disappointment."

"So—the secret. I'm dying here."

"Well," he began, sipping his coffee, "my first look at the inside of a police station actually happened the first time I was arrested."

I'm sure my jaw dropped. I couldn't have been more shocked if he'd smacked me one. He snickered at the look on my face.

"I was a bad, bad kid. Stole, did drugs, ran wild. My mom and I lived in a trailer just outside a small Georgia town. We were dirt poor and I had no idea who my father was. I got teased by all the other kids. My mom did the best she could for me, but I was always bored in school. Thought I knew everything. When I was about thirteen, I got hauled into the local station by a big, burly cop named Ted Fields. He called my mom to pick me up, and when she came tearing into the station, it was love at first sight. My little sister was born eight months and one wedding later."

I smiled, hearing the affection in his voice.

"She was beautiful. A little moppet with big green eyes and a silly smile. It took us a while to figure out that she was deaf."

I nodded, remembering what I'd learned at the crime scene that day. "That's why you know sign language."

"Yeah, the sergeant and I learned together, and I figured out that I wanted to be like him more than I wanted to be a badass."

"So you became a cop," I said quietly.

"Yeah. I started going to school, skipped a couple grades, and eventually went on to Georgia State."

"Did you play football?" I'd always been a sucker for football.

"Yeah, only second string. The girls liked me anyway, though."

"I'll bet."

He laughed and reached across the table to take my hand. "So, now you know why I like you so much. At heart, I'm a man who likes his women hot and just a little wild."

"Isn't that a song lyric?"

"No, that's 'I like my women on the trashy side,' or something like that." He winked and let go of my hand, picking up his fork. "Can I eat my dessert now?" he asked.

"Sure," I replied, still reeling a little from the tale. I couldn't get over the idea that my detective had been a bad boy. Maybe we really did belong together.

CHAPTER TWELVE

The fair was in full swing when we arrived about nine P.M. We went by the photography displays first, and I showed him my name on the list of contributors. He bought me cotton candy, and kissed me on the Ferris wheel.

The air smelled like popcorn, peanuts, and sea air. Trash cans were overflowing with wrappers and paper cups. There were stands for fried sausages, crepes, pretzels, smoothies, deep-fried Oreos (which I refused to let Marshall try), and other disgustingly fattening treats.

I looked for the twin, but didn't see anyone whose body even remotely resembled the one we'd found. Marshall told me to stop staring before some strange guy thought I liked him.

We went into the fun house, one of those ones with a maze of full-length mirrors on the walls. It reminded me of my old apartment.

Marshall was following behind me and would occasionally squeeze my butt or drop a kiss on the side of my neck. I was giggling as much as the teenage girls ahead of us.

I walked up to a mirror that had a spot in its center where my face was in perfect focus while the rest of me stretched outward crazily, like the reflection you get when you look in the drain stop on a bathtub. I touched my lips, my nose, my eyes.

"Hey, baby," Marshall murmured, putting his face next to mine, so that we were both strangers in that little spot of perfection.

"Hey," I said, and he wrapped his arms around me.

"What are you thinking?" he asked, rocking me a little.

"I'm thinking about a question I asked my best friend, the morning after you told me you wanted to be with me."

"What was that?"

"I asked her how it could really be love, when I'll never recognize your face. I'll never be able to look at you across a crowded room and know your thoughts just by the look on your face. You'll never look in my eyes and see that recognition, that joyous connection that says I belong to you."

"You're wrong about that. You might not recognize it, but I want you to know that the look you see on my face right now—that's love." He gave me a squeeze. "And the look on your face, that's love, too. It's there, even if you can't ever see it."

"She said we could find other ways of loving each other," I whispered, covering his hands with my own.

"She was right."

"Are you sure?" I asked, knowing that I was making a huge commitment.

"Uh-huh. I've had a lot of time to study you. And you don't look at anyone the way you look at me. It's a great start. We'll just take it one step at a time."

I bit my lip and twisted around, hugging him tight. "Promise you'll tell me all the time."

"That I love you?"

"No. Well, yes, that, too. I want you to tell me how I look at you. Every day."

"I will," he murmured, placing a kiss on my forehead and then my lips. Suddenly the little fun house was a little too public, even for my taste.

"Let's go home," I said, tugging on his lower lip with my teeth.

"We're gone," he agreed, setting me away from him and taking my hand.

We hurried outside. I was so focused on him that I almost missed seeing her. I froze suddenly, and Marshall's grip practically yanked my arm out of its socket.

"What is it?" he asked, suddenly tense and looking around like a wolf scouting its territory.

"That clown, look at the face."

"I'll be damned."

She was short and skinny, dressed in hot-pink tights, a tutu, and a red curly wig, and her makeup matched the tattoo on the body exactly. She was walking fast, not looking particularly jovial, and I motioned to Marshall that we should follow her.

He frowned, but nodded his assent, and took my arm again. He hustled me along, and I did my best to make it look as if we were hurrying off to have sex rather than stalking a demented clown.

She went past the line for the Ferris wheel, waving to the man running the controls, then down past the corridor of food vendors, and we had to dodge a family carrying baskets of butterfly chips.

We thought we'd lost her then, but Marshall spotted her wig going into a rickety shack painted like the night sky, with astrology symbols in a rainbow of colors. MADAM CARLA'S TAROT READINGS was written in gold letters over the top of the door.

He whispered for me to stay put, and I did, though it chafed. I took my camera out of my purse, something I hadn't been able to do while Marshall was tugging me along like a rag doll. It was my tank, my heavy Nikon FE2, complete with flash.

Marshall entered the shack, and I waited, jittery and tense, wondering how cops did this all the time. I felt as if I was going to pee my pants.

When several minutes went by and there was no sign of my detective, I started to get nervous. My palms were sweating, but I managed to dig in my bag for the cell phone and keep my camera focused on the shack at the same time.

I dialed Stevens's number from memory.

He picked up. "Stevens."

"Stevens, it's Debbie."

"What's going on?" he said quickly, and I thanked God for smart cops who knew when something was up.

"Marshall and I are at the fair. We saw a clown, a woman, with her face painted exactly like the tattoo on the body. We followed her until she went into a shack, a psychic's booth. Marshall went in to check it out. It's been five minutes and nothing."

"I'll be there as soon as I can, but it'll be about twenty minutes. See if you can find a cop. And stay put," he ordered, and hung up.

"Stay put. Stay put," I muttered. *What am I? A Labrador?*

I could get closer. I was standing across the dirt path from the shack, right next to a bunch of tables covered in tacky silver jewelry. I made my way over, making like I was just browsing.

I still don't know what possessed me, but one moment I was pausing indecisively next to a stand of wooden African masks, and the next I was heading for the door to Madam Carla's.

It was dim inside and smelled like patchouli and sage. I blinked, trying to focus out of the bright lights.

An old woman sat behind a card table covered in purple velvet. A curtain of the same fabric covered the wall behind her. She had sagging jowls and beady black eyes. She looked at me inquiringly.

"Hello, my dear," she said in a voice like tearing paper, and I shivered, suddenly even more afraid for Marshall than I'd been before.

"Hello," I murmured shortly.

"Come closer and I'll tell you your future."

I didn't want to, but I did it, figuring it would seem odd if I just glared at her for a while.

I took a seat on the low stool she'd set up in front of

her table. She began turning over tarot cards from a stack in front of her. I was barely paying attention, looking around the room, noting that there was a dim light showing underneath the purple curtain directly behind Madam Carla. There was probably a room in the back. If Marshall was still here, he was probably in that room. If he wasn't, then he still must've left through the back, because I was fairly certain he would've come straight to me otherwise.

"Very strange. Very strange," the old woman muttered, and I jerked my gaze back to her.

"What?" I asked, looking at the cards she'd laid out in front of me. There were three cards running along in a row: Death, the Devil, and the King of Spades.

"I've never seen anything quite like this before. These three cards represent your past, the strongest forces of change. The Death card signifies a change in consciousness, but I think, also, in this case, you actually came close to death. The card tells the means of the change as well as the effect of it."

I felt the hairs on my arms stand on end. This was a little too close for comfort. Was there a chance this woman knew me? My face and story had been in several newspapers and magazines as well as art journals. *The Union Tribune* had done a story on me a couple weeks ago at the same time as the gallery showing downtown.

"The Devil card appears directly afterward. Blindness and misconception. Strange, very strange. And then this King of Pentacles indicates a struggle, the battle you fought to attain your desires."

"Uh-huh. Is that it?" I asked her, impatient now. The light underneath the curtain had gone out.

"Not quite," she murmured, and turned over another card on top: the Hanged Man. I watched her hands as she laid it down, noting for the first time that something about them bothered me.

"The Hanged Man means that something is not as it seems."

I heard her as if from a distance. Her hands . . . they were trembling. I looked up, studying her, feeling the strange tingle of an idea tightening the back of my neck.

She was looking down at her cards, turning over another. "The Tower," she called out in surprise, jolting me, and placed the card next to the Hanged Man. "The moment of understanding."

I blinked, hardly breathing, staring at the folds of flesh hanging from her jaw. There was makeup, white makeup, caked in the creases of her flesh.

I knew my eyes widened, knew my fear and anxiety were probably written all over my face. She fixed me in her beady black gaze, and in her eyes I saw both hatred and a strange sort of acceptance.

She turned over another card. "Justice," she muttered, and placed it carefully above the other two, snapping the corner as she released it.

"Where is he?" I asked harshly, hands tightening on my camera.

The old woman sighed and slumped in her stool. "In the room. Back there."

I jumped off my stool and rushed for the curtain,

realizing as I reached for it that I really didn't know if I could trust her, or what I could expect when I crossed through the veil.

I turned back just in time to see the old woman swinging her stool at my head. I fell on the floor, instinctively cradling my camera, and she missed, her swing carrying her away from me. I scooted backward away from her, but couldn't seem to find my feet.

She was like a cat, twisting and leaping toward me with the stool raised. I kicked out at her, catching her hip and sending her to the side, but the stool grazed my shoulder, stunning me.

I hurried to my feet. I was twice her size and weight, but I was terrified, terrified, of the look she was giving me, of her eerie strength. I started to run for the exit, but she reached into her robe and pulled out a gun.

"Stay the fuck away from me!" I shouted, but my voice broke.

"It's girls like you that take them away," she hissed, pointing the gun at my face. "Pretty young things."

"Debbie, get down!" Marshall roared, rushing through the front entrance. The old woman turned the gun toward him, and before I thought, before I even knew what I was doing, I launched my camera at her head.

The heavy metal body hit her in the head, and she went down like a collapsed tent, robe flaring outward and showing the pink tights that still encased her legs.

Marshall was there in a second, taking her gun and putting it in the waistband of his pants before bending down to check her pulse.

"She's alive, just unconscious," he murmured to me and hurried over to yank me into his arms. He held me, so tight I couldn't breathe. Not that I cared.

A man with a gun ran in a few seconds later with a light of battle in his eyes. I tensed, but Marshall held me still. The man looked at the body, then at Marshall. "She okay?" he asked, and I recognized Stevens's voice. Marshall's chest moved as he nodded above me.

Stevens put his gun away and nodded toward the exit. "We got the guy we think is the twin trying to drive off in the trailer."

"Good," Marshall said shortly, and pulled out of our embrace. "What the hell were you thinking? I told you to stay put."

"I told her, too," Stevens chimed in.

I gave him a dirty look, then petted Marshall's chest. "When you didn't come out, I got scared and thought something happened to you."

"I only went in for a second. I heard the clown talking to a man behind the curtain. I came back out, hoping that he would leave and I would get a glimpse of him. Didn't you see me?"

I shook my head. "I must have been looking down, or I missed you in the crowd of people."

"Jesus," he muttered, and grabbed me again. "You could've been killed," he said against my temple, and I hugged him tighter, whispering, "So could you."

He pulled away again, and a look that I couldn't interpret passed over his face. He looked at the old woman and then at the camera lying forlornly next to her.

"That was some throw," he said finally, and a giggle escaped me.

"Is it broken?" I asked, feeling strangely disconnected and light-headed, as if I'd just drunk a two-liter of Coke after not eating in days.

He bent down to get a closer look, but didn't touch anything. "The flash definitely is. I don't know about the rest."

"I really must be crazy in love with you," I said, shaking my head and struggling not to start laughing like a lunatic.

"What?" he said, sounding surprised.

"Well," I began, "that was my favorite camera," and completely lost it, giggling until I fell on the floor, doubled over.

The two of them loomed over me, shaking their heads.

"Don't look at me," I heard Stevens say. "You're the one that's in love with her."

"God help me" was the drawled reply before I was unceremoniously picked up and hauled over a hard shoulder. My clearest memory of the entire event was hanging upside down and admiring Marshall's ass in his jeans while laughing until I cried. All in all, not a bad way to end an evening.

EPILOGUE

*O*nce upon a time there was a beautiful girl. She had a tall, willowy body, a bright smile, and the belief, strong and frighteningly certain, that she was the most beautiful woman in the world. As she got older, and time marched over her like an invading army, raping and pillaging the fresh skin and pouting lips, the girl lost many things: her husband, her career on the stage, and her ever-loving mind, but never her belief.

When her grandchildren, twin boys, were born, she had them marked with the symbol of her new life—the mask, the divided face—and vowed that no other woman would ever have their hearts. They were hers, body and soul.

This was true, for a time, but then one of the boys fell in love.

"You're shitting me. The mayor's daughter?"

"Yep."

"She killed him over that?"

"Apparently he wanted to leave the carnie life behind and get a real job."

"Yeah, right," I snorted, "like her daddy would go for that: the princess and the carnie."

"Don't be cynical," Marshall ordered, tapping my nose with a finger dripping champagne.

I sucked it, smiling as his eyes heated.

"So when he told her," I continued, smiling at him and shrugging out of the straps of my top, "she shot him."

He nodded and leaned over to place a wet kiss on my collarbone. I shivered.

"And then bathed him, washed the blood from his body, and ordered her other grandson to get rid of the evidence," I said breathlessly as his kisses moved lower.

"Umm-hmm"—he nuzzled the slope of my breast—"but not before telling him to visit his brother's girl. Visit her and convince her that the man she loved was really a complete bastard."

"I guess he managed it," I choked out. He was suckling one nipple through the pink silk of my camisole while rolling the other between his fingers.

He lifted his head, staring at the dark rose spot his mouth had left on the fabric. "Okay, I've told you the details. Now answer the question."

"Could you run it by me one more time?"

"I'll run something by you one more time," he growled, and pounced on me.

"No!" I shouted, convulsing with laughter. "No tickling!"

"Then tell me," he ordered, pinning my hands above my head, "or I'll have to get the cuffs."

I wiggled my hips under him and smiled my lazy half-smile.

"Promise?"

THE NIGHT AT the fair had taken on a stunning unreality in my mind—almost as if it happened to somebody else (maybe that strange girl I see in the mirror every morning), but it was nothing compared to the dreamworld I was floating in now.

"Are you sure I look okay?" I asked Sara, turning to face her.

"You know you look beautiful, stop asking."

"But do I look like me? Like the Debbie you used to know?"

"No, actually."

"No?" I said, turning back to the mirror.

She hugged me from behind, careful not to wrinkle my gown. "You look like beauty itself."

"Oh," I said, tearing up, "that's sweet."

"That's me, sweet as honey. Now let's get your ass down that aisle so we can get on to the reception. I want first pick of the groomsmen."

I linked arms with her and headed slowly for the door and the long hallway where my sister and the rest of the bridesmaids were waiting for Sara to lead them down the aisle. My mother was there, too, undoubtedly wringing her hands and crying and smiling all at the same time.

I stopped Sara in the doorway and smoothed her nametag. I'd had them printed up for everyone in the wedding and most of the guests. Tacky, but effective.

"Just so you know," I said casually, "all the names of the single cops are printed in blue foil, the married ones are in black. I'll let you decide which ones you go after."

She smiled. "So I have my pick of them all, huh?"

I nodded and started walking again, knowing that at any minute I would take the hand of my detective and promise to love, honor, and cherish.

"Just don't touch the one in the gold. He's all mine."

FINALLY
A WEBSITE
YOU CAN GET
PASSIONATE
ABOUT...

Visit
www.SimonSaysLove.com
for the latest information
about Romance from Pocket Books!

READING SUGGESTIONS

LATEST RELEASES

AUTHOR APPEARANCES

ONLINE CHATS WITH YOUR
FAVORITE WRITERS

SPECIAL OFFERS

AND MUCH, MUCH MORE!

A love like you've never known
is closer than you think...

Bestselling Romances from
Pocket Books

The Nosy Neighbor
Fern Michaels
Sometimes love is right
next door...

Run No More
Catherine Mulvany
How do you outrun your
past when your future is just
as deadly?

Never Look Back
Linda Lael Miller
When someone wants you
to pay for the past, you can
never look back...

The Dangerous Protector
Janet Chapman
The desires he ignites in
her make him the most
dangerous man in
the world...

Blaze
JoAnn Ross
They're out to stop a deadly
arsonist...and find that
passion burns even hotter
than revenge.

The Next Mrs. Blackthorne
Joan Johnston
Texas rancher Clay
Blackthorne is about to
wed his new wife. The only
question is...who will she be?

Born to be BAD
Sherrilyn Kenyon
Being bad has never felt
so right.

Have Glass Slippers,
Will Travel
Lisa Cach
Single twenty-something
seeks Prince Charming.
(Those without royal castles
need not apply.)

Love a good romance?
So do we...